His Cocky Valet

UNDUE ARROGANCE #1

COLE MCCADE

Print Edition

Cole McCade
blackmagic@blackmagicblues.com

Cover Artist: Cole McCade

Table of Contents

Content Warning

This story contains content that may be difficult for some readers to consume. That content includes:

- Penetrative cis male/cis male sexual intercourse.
- Sexual interactions between an employer and employee.
- Alcohol consumption.
- Brief non-graphic on-page description of a character vomiting.
- Mild, non-kink-related humiliation.
- Situations of consenting codependency and control as part of kink play similar to Daddy/little dynamics.
- Unprotected penetrative sex.
- Terminal illness of a parent, specifically bone cancer. **(Please take heed to this. Many scenes are graphic.)**
- A very fucking large, very fucking hurty needle.
- An instance of…I don’t know how to describe this. Sexual interaction with consent, only for that consent to be revoked because one character doesn’t feel right. There’s no non-consent or shaming or force or assault, but the feelings the character has as they realize they don’t want to have sex right now may be evocative of

feelings associated with those things.

- Discussion of implied sexual assault.
- Depiction of a car crash.

Some of these warnings may seem undue to some, but please keep in mind that it is impossible to know what is or is not hurtful for some to read. While this is not meant to criminalize consenting sex acts between two adults or turn queer sex into some sort of taboo, this warning is included out of respect to those who are sex-averse and do not enjoy reading sexual content, as well as to those who may be triggered by workplace sexual interactions and power dynamics.

Even if something isn't a trigger for you, respect that it may be for someone else.

And for those of you who may need to heed these warnings, I understand if you need to walk away.

As I always say…be good to yourselves.

-C

Chapter One

Ashton Harrington truly needed better friends.

Or at least, friends who gave better references. Friends who weren't trying to ruin his reputation. Friends who weren't half the reason for his rapidly escalating stress levels. Friends who, at the very least, gave a damn about his ability to function as a human being.

Friends who *gave a damn*, period.

Perhaps, in this hypothetical universe where he had such friends, he wouldn't be staring at this flinty-eyed, utterly cold behemoth of a man who stood stiffly before his desk—and apparently thought Ashton was going to give him a *job*.

Ashton offered a thin, formal smile and lifted a finger. "If you'll hold a moment, please," he said, fetched his cellphone from his inside breast pocket, and pushed the third number on his speed dial.

Vic picked up on the second ring; Ashton didn't have to see his face to know he was grinning from the sound of his voice. "I was waiting for this. Hullo there, Ash."

Ashton narrowed his eyes. "You ass," he hissed, then

flicked another glance at the motionless man.

His stone-set expression hadn't changed, lips thinned as if he already disapproved, eyes narrowed behind rimless, reflective glasses. It was like being raked over by one of his old professors, that *I don't know what it is yet, but I know you've done something wrong* stare that could cut down to the bone, and it made Ashton's stomach flip.

He flashed a frozen smile, then dropped his voice and spun his desk chair around to face out over the broad glassed-in wall and the glimmering New York City skyline. "I ask you for a PA and you send me—" *Conan the Barbarian* "*—this?*"

"I'm telling you. He's worked for my family for years. Brand's amazing." Vic's cultured British accent made everything he said sound utterly polite and reserved, even when he continued, "Maybe he'll help you get your shit together, Ash. Something's got to stop your downward trajectory into pure fuckery."

"I'm well aware," Ashton grit out through his teeth. "Hence why I asked you to find me someone. If he's so amazing, why isn't he still working for your family?"

"Mum and Dad went back to the old country. Brand wanted to stay. And me, I prefer my personal assistants a little…leggier." Vic snickered. "Not that Brand couldn't be absolutely fetching in a short skirt, but I do believe that's more to your taste than mine."

“Oh my God, fuck you.”

“Now, now.” Vic clucked his tongue. “Hardly fitting language for the newly anointed heir, now is it?”

“I hate you.”

“You’ll learn to love me again. Give him a shot. You won’t regret it.”

“You’re a liar and an asshole.” Ashton sighed, risking a glance back, peering around his high-backed leather chair. The man—Brand, Brand *Forsythe* according to the resume on Ashton’s desk—was practically a statue, barely even breathing. “I should go.”

“…he’s standing right there, isn’t he?”

“Yeah.”

Vic let out a laugh that bordered on a cackle. “Oh my God, Ash. Go. Jesus fucking Christ, you cheeky little bugger. Get your shit straight.”

“I’m *trying*,” Ashton snarled, then slammed this thumb down on the screen and ended the call. Taking a deep breath, he tried to exhale his scowl like smoke, smoothing his expression, forcing a smile—then spun his chair once more.

Forsythe eyed him with one brow lofted as he meticulously adjusted the perfectly, blindingly white cuff of his shirt, just barely visible past the crisp lines of a precisely tailored black three-piece suit. The man was so sharply put together it was as though his edges had been cut out with scissors, the streamlined, graceful flow of his suit giving his bulk taper and trim.

Even if he was still imposing as fuck.

He had to be at least six foot four, maybe more, his shoulders all broad, hard angles tapering down to a narrow waist and long legs. The subtle, quiet grace of his angular features was offset by a stubborn, clean-shaven jaw, the glasses at odds with his brutish body to give him a quiet, formal, bookish appearance made only more severe by the white gloves on his long, graceful hands. The late afternoon sunlight through the office's windows glinted off his glasses, and gave a subtle gloss to the backsweep of smoothly combed, glossy hair in a muted, soft pale golden brown touched at the temples and scattered throughout with threads of silver.

With deliberated calm, he settled his shirt cuff, refastened his cufflink, then folded his hands together behind his back. His icy regard fixed on Ashton again, dark green eyes cool. "I assume my credentials have checked out, then," he said smoothly.

Where Vic's British accent made everything he said sound posh and polite, no matter how rude it might be…Brand Forsythe's accent added a note of cultured, chilly disdain, deep and rolling with lyrical inflections. Ashton flushed, resisting the urge to reach up and pull his uncomfortable suit collar away from his burning-hot neck.

That…would probably be a bad idea, anyway.

Considering he still had a bite-mark bruised against his throat from the man he'd kicked out of bed this afternoon without even asking his name, so Ash could throw on something decent and make it to this interview on time.

"Sorry about that," he mumbled, then swore at himself mentally. He was the one in charge here, wasn't he? But God, this man had to be almost twice his age, and he was looking at Ash like he was *dirt*. Fuck. Ashton cleared his throat, straightening in his chair. "Er. I mean. I simply had to check one of your references."

"I understand you and young Master Victor have been acquainted since boarding school," Brand replied neutrally.

"Uh. Yeah. How did you know I was talking to hi—nevermind." Ash swallowed, lifting his chin. Calm. Composure. Right. "So how long have you worked as a personal assistant, then?"

"Valet," Forsythe replied stiffly.

"Pardon?"

"The position is referred to as a valet, where I am from." Forsythe arched one pointed brow, sweeping Ash over with an assessing look. "It is a position of some station. More than merely a 'personal assistant.'"

"Here, it's someone who parks cars," Ashton

retorted, then reined himself in. Him and his fucking tongue. He took another deep breath, then continued, "All right. How long have you worked as a valet?"

"Approximately twenty-two years."

Ashton stared. "How old are you?"

"Forty-one."

"So you started when you were nineteen?"

"Dedication begins early," Forsythe answered obliquely, with another up-and-down look. "In most cases."

Ashton's ears burned. He knew how he looked—this twenty-three-year-old piece of shit in an expensive suit that didn't fit right because he'd never bothered to get it tailored, wet around the nose and ears, sitting in this oversized chair meant for men with more stature than him. He didn't belong in this chair, and he damned well knew it. He hadn't asked for this. He hadn't asked for the fifty phone calls a day until he shut the ringer off on his phone. He hadn't asked for the screaming newspaper headlines, the stack of newsprint on his desk right now charting the chaos and speculation while everyone from *Forbes* to *The Daily Smut Shinedown* guessed how long it would take him to crash, burn, and ruin everything his father had worked to build.

But he was stuck with it, and he was going to *try* to stop fucking up and do this right before he ran his father's business into the ground.

Which meant he couldn't let Forsythe get to him, when he hadn't even hired the man yet. Ashton cleared his throat, folding his hands in his lap and trying to keep his voice stern. Authoritative. He didn't have the same presence his father had, reverberating and commanding a room, but everyone had to start somewhere.

Maybe he'd grow into it.

"How much did Vic tell you about my situation, Mr. Forsythe?" he asked.

Forsythe's eyes narrowed, considering. Then he recited, "Your father, magnate of Harrington Steel, Incorporated, has recently taken ill with bone cancer and is currently in hospice." He recited the words so coldly, as if each one didn't carry the weight of ten tons of steel rebar dropped on Ashton's heart. "With your father currently in a comatose state and incapable of making decisions, the provisions in his living will naming you as heir and Chief Executive Officer took legal effect. You, however, have been too busy with your post-university gap year, carousing about with scantily clad young men, to consider anything business-minded, and are woefully unprepared to take the reins or even to function as an adult." A touch of cold contempt on those words, and Forsythe straightened his shoulders, looking down his gracefully aquiline nose at Ashton. "Therefore, you require an assistant to help you…what were young Master Victor's words to me? Ah, yes. 'Get your shit together before you fuck it all up.'"

The hot burn of mortification scouring through Ash was nothing compared to the sick, heavy, nauseating feeling in his gut. The phantom echoes in his memory of that fucking respirator, wheeze in, wheeze out—and that awful sick death smell of the hospice center. It didn't matter that it was the best, most expensive hospice center in New York state.

It was still a fucking *hospice center*.

It was still a mausoleum where you shuffled the dead off to wait until they finally stopped breathing.

Rather than look at Forsythe, he fingered the stack of face-down tabloid papers on his desk, fidgeting them, flipping the edge of one up—but the sight of his own alcohol-flushed face wasn't any better. Blank-eyed, reeling, he'd been caught draped on Andrew, a casual not-quite-friend who was easy-come, easy-go, no strings attached, no questions, everything he wanted clear in his open shirt and the way his hands grasped so possessively onto Ash's body in the photograph.

Ash stared at his own empty, vapid face, then slammed the paper down and pressed his lips together. He fought against the lump in his throat to speak, forcing himself to find words, strangled and small. "Yeah," he said, averting his stinging eyes. "Something like that."

"I apologize if my words about your father were insensitive," Forsythe replied, formal and inflectionless.

"It's the fucking truth, isn't it?" Ash shot back, sucking in a wet, hoarse, rattling breath. "I'm a rich spoiled fuckup and I'm not ready for this. But my Dad's dying and he wanted me to do right by his company, so I'm gonna try. You know what the job is. You know what it pays. Are you going to help me, or not?"

Forsythe remained silent for so long Ashton thought he wouldn't answer, at first. He glanced back at the man, who watched him with unreadable eyes shielded behind the glint of his glasses.

Then Forsythe swept a bow, inclining forward with the grace of a man much smaller, agile and smooth.

"Ask of me," he said, something in his rich, rolling voice trailing velvet shivers over Ashton's skin, "and it shall be done, young Master Harrington."

BRAND FORSYTHE STOOD IN THE doorway of the suite he had been assigned in the Harrington household. Frankly, after a stony, silent ride in the back of Harrington's hired car—Brand would be putting a stop to *that* quite soon—he was mildly startled Harrington hadn't consigned him to a broom closet. Not immodest in size, the suite was rather tastefully furnished in earth tones and linens, textured muslins making up much of the upholstery. Tall French doors to one side of the suite opened onto a private paved patio, looking out over the lush gardens of the massive enclosed estate. All in all, it was a rather expansive accoutrement for a newly hired valet.

He turned his head, looking down at his new charge.

"No," he said.

Ashton Harrington—young Master Harrington—blinked up at him, his long-lashed blue eyes wide and puzzled. He was barely more than a wet-eyed pup, his hair a wild disarray of inky black, pale golden freckles scattered across soft amber skin and dotting his fine, delicate nose. Brand had been informed the young Master was a tender twenty-three.

With his lean, wiry frame dwarfed inside an ill-fitted suit at least two sizes too large for him, he looked practically *twelve*.

And wholly unprepared to deal with Brand, let alone the intricacies of managing a multibillion-dollar global business.

The young Master blinked again. "No?" he repeated.

"No," Brand said again. "Where are your chambers?"

"Um." Harrington glanced away, raking a hand

through his hair. "I…I was living in the pool house. I haven't moved up to the main house yet."

In that awkward admission was an unspoken cry of youthful rebellion. Some attempt at independence, when this man-child had never known a moment of independence or self-sufficiency in his life. He was accustomed to being told what to do, Brand thought—and while he might resist, perhaps sulk a touch, in the end he *would* do as he was told.

Only now, with his father ill and—from the tabloid rumors—his mother apparently long divorced and returned to her home country of Japan, there was no one to tell Ashton anything. He was spinning. Flailing.

And waiting for someone to point him toward something resembling north.

Brand sighed, folding his arms over his chest. "Choose a master suite. One with adjoining servants' chambers."

Harrington's gaze flew back to him. "Wh-what? Why?"

"If I am to be your valet, I must be available to you at all hours. When you call, I come. It makes for a more convenient arrangement if my room adjoins yours."

A faint flush darkened Harrington's cheeks. "I don't…know if there are any rooms like that in the house."

"It is your house. Find out."

The boy scowled. The slight inner folds of his eyes, evidence of his mother's influence, drew tight, turning his angled eyes into irritated slits. "I didn't hire you to boss me around."

"You hired me," Brand pointed out, "to get your affairs in order. Since you do not seem to have a plan for doing so, it falls on me to make the decisions until you are ready to do so yourself."

"How do you know I don't have a plan?"

Brand arched a brow. "Do you?"

Harrington's lips parted. His mouth was rather pouty, pink and sullen, and for a moment the tip of his tongue darted over his lips before retreating, disappearing, as he slumped. "…no."

"When you have one, I will take it under advisement," Brand said. "Until then, young Master Harrington, I would thank you to trust me to do my job."

"Yeah. Sure." Sighing, Harrington curled a hand against the back of his neck, gaze fixed on the floor. "I'll talk to the housekeeper. She'll know."

"I'll need to be introduced to her as well, along with any other staff. You'll need to inform me of their pay schedules and employment records. Are their payments managed by direct deposit, or by check?"

"I don't know!" Harrington flared. "I don't know any

of this, okay?"

"I suggest you find out."

"I *will!*" Harrington shot him a glare. His voice became thick, heavy. "Look, two days ago my Dad was right here handling all this. Now he's…he's fucking…he had cancer for *three years* and he didn't even tell me, he just…he just *left* me here to deal with all this shit and you think I can just pick everything up and act like nothing's happening when he could be—he could be—"

His smooth, pretty face crumpled. His mouth trembled, then drew tight; he sniffled, rubbing the back of his hand against his nose roughly and then abruptly turning away—but not before Brand caught the wet gleam of his eyes. Harrington's shoulders were stiff, his breaths raspy, sounds muffled as if he was trying to force it down. He had pride, then.

Pride, if nothing else.

At the very least, Brand understood pride.

He curled his hand against Harrington's shoulder. "Direct me to the housekeeper. I will attend to what matters I can. Tomorrow, we may regroup to discuss a plan."

That slim shoulder stiffened under his touch, before a hand knocked hard against his wrist, pushing it away. Harrington turned on him, cheeks wet, looking up at him with hard, flashing eyes.

"Don't," he bit off, voice choked. "Don't you ever fucking pity me." His throat worked, and he sniffled, looking away once more, glaring mutinously at the wall with his lower lip thrust out. "Fine. Tomorrow. You decide where we're gonna sleep, I guess. But after this, I make the decisions."

"Can you?" Brand challenged softly.

Harrington only fixed him with a furious, hateful look that did little to mask the hurt glimmering in his eyes.

The hurt, and a quiet, aching need—one that sparked something inside Brand, a pull like gravity.

But Harrington turned and walked away, leaving Brand alone in the cavernous, empty white hallway of smooth white stone and open archways.

Well.

That was an interesting reaction, indeed.

Brand lingered, leaning against the door of the room, tapping his thumb against his lower lip. He had his work cut out for him, he thought. He would start first thing in the morning.

For now, he supposed it was time to introduce himself to the staff.

One way or another, he would bring the Harrington household back into some semblance of order.

With or without his young Master's cooperation, apparently.

Chapter Two

ASH WASN'T USED TO WAKING before sunset.

Nor was he used to waking to the sound of drawers opening and closing, doors slamming, people moving around the pool house with shuffling footsteps and calling voices. He couldn't make out what they were saying, but every formless word drilled into his skull, stabbing through his eardrums into his throbbing, hungover brain.

He'd shut himself in the pool house with a bottle of champagne, last night. There were still two dozen bottles in the fridge, sitting there forlorn after his father's collapse had cancelled a fundraiser soiree he'd meant to host…last night, Ash had realized as he'd sat on his bed in the middle of rumpled covers, stared bleakly out the night-locked window, and swilled bitterly at the bottle. Last night the grand hall of the house was meant to be decked out in lights and brilliance, people swirling about like scraps of pretty colored paper, while his father presided over them with his kindly smile and plied rich useless things with enough champagne to loosen their pocketbooks in the name of charity—while Ash eyed other young shiftless sons of powerful men, and wondered which he'd be making headlines with tonight.

Instead his father was lying in a bed dying, and that fucking will meant Ash couldn't even be there with him.

He had to be here, instead. Holding everything together as if, if he did everything right, he'd keep everything from falling apart so it would be okay when his father came back.

As if, if he managed not to fail at this…he'd pass some test, and his reward would be Calvin Harrington standing in front of him, hale and whole, a heavy hand resting to the top of Ashton's head in warm approval because for once, somehow, he'd done *something* right and fixed this entire fucking mess.

He didn't remember falling asleep. He'd meant to call for a car, go out, maybe hit a club, find one of his usuals who understood no strings but also understood the comfort of familiarity…but he only remembered champagne flavored by the taste of tears, the world swimming, blurring, until the lamps lining the garden pathway outside were just hazes of gold moving like foo-lights beckoning him into the dark. He'd muttered something under his breath about Forsythe being a fucking *asshole*, and then everything had gone dark.

Until everything was suddenly far too bright, as there came a sound of rustling curtains, curtain rings sliding, and then sunlight stabbing against the backs of his eyelids.

Swearing, Ash rolled over and buried his face into the pillows. "What in the *fuck?*" he mumbled groggily.

"Get up, young Master," Brand Forsythe's icy voice demanded. "Eight in the morning is late enough to lie abed."

Ash tensed.

Oh, this asshole was *so* fired.

He creaked one eye open. His head throbbed, a sledgehammer symphony inside his skull, and the intrusion of morning light added a few sword stabs right into the center of his brain. He stared blearily at the blurry shapes moving through his field of vision—until he recognized the gardener and his crew, quite busy emptying the drawers lining one wall of the open, terraced space into boxes and carting them outside. What the fu—

"Coffee," Forsythe said, suddenly inserting himself into Ashton's line of sight with an insulated silver mug, that stern, unforgiving face filling his vision. Forsythe sank to one knee next to the bed, one white-gloved hand draped against his thigh, the other brandishing the mug like a demand. Cutting green eyes drilled into Ashton. "I presume you will be too hungover to function without it."

"Fuck. You." Jesus fucking Christ, Ash was going to kill Vic. He pushed himself up on one aching arm just enough to snatch the coffee mug, the covers falling down to his waist. He took a testing sip, then grimaced at the overly sweetened, overly creamed, thick mess and thrust it back at Forsythe. “I like mine black.”

Forsythe tilted his head, taking the mug. “My apologies for presuming. Most children prefer sweets to bitters.”

Ash grit his teeth. “You trying to set a record for getting fired? Jesus fuck, what are you doing? What are they doing with my *stuff?*”

“Moving your things to the master suite,” Forsythe replied, as if it was perfectly natural, and Ash scowled, grasping up a knotted handful of blankets and pulling them up to his chest.

“Goddammit, Forsythe, I’m *naked!*”

That cool glance slid over him, tracing over his bare chest as if trailing ice cubes in shivering pathways over his skin, dipping down to the barrier of the blanket against his hips before meeting his gaze once more. “I hadn’t noticed.”

“Get out,” Ash bit off.

“Get dressed,” Forsythe countered smoothly.

“Not with you standing over me!”

Forsythe sighed with weary patience and pushed his glasses up his narrow nose with one long, white-gloved finger. “Young Master,” he said, as if it should be perfectly obvious, “I am here to *help* you get dressed.”

Ash froze. “…what?” Heat flushed through his

cheeks. He stared at Forsythe. Was he for fucking serious? Was he supposed to stand here naked and let this man dress him? *Touch* him like he wasn't stark ass-out? "That's…not in your job description."

"You did not give me a job description." Forsythe's lips pursed. He flicked an invisible speck off his sleeve. "I know my duties quite well. And if you do not, apparently your servants have been lax in your care."

"I don't fucking like relying on servants."

"That would belie the reason you hired me."

A frustrated growl welled in the back of Ash's throat. "I hired you to help me organize the business side of things. I'm not so helpless I can't dress myself."

"You cannot even wear clothing appropriately sized for you."

"Oh, you can fuck *right* off."

"That," Forsythe retorted, rising to his feet and setting the coffee mug aside on the nightstand with an almost ludicrously precise touch, "would be one thing that is not in my job description."

Ash glared at him, wrinkling his nose.

Then rolled over and plunked face-down back into the pillows, hugging them to his chest.

To hell with this.

His head was *killing* him.

He'd be responsible tomorrow.

Forsythe sighed. Ash's only warning was the faint hint of pressure as fingers curled in the duvet—before it suddenly whipped away along with the top sheet, cool morning air whooshing over his bare skin and practically slapping against his naked ass.

"Get up," Forsythe said, an edge of steel entering his voice.

Ash yelped, scrambling to grab the fitted sheet, ripping it off one side of the mattress and dragging it over his hips before twisting upright into a sitting position, glaring at Forsythe. He thought he caught a snicker from one of the gardening crew passing through with another batch of boxes, and fire bloomed under his skin, simmering until his temples throbbed, ears burning.

"You fucking ass," he bit off. "What the fuck are you trying to pull?"

"We have a day of work ahead of us." Forsythe dropped the bundle of duvet and sheet pointedly to the floor. His gaze flicked for a moment to Ash's throat, and Ash realized with a mortified shiver that Forsythe was eyeing the fading bite-mark on his neck. "I would like to assess first the state of Harrington Steel, then the state of the house, and appraise what business matters have been halted since your father is…indisposed. For that, you need to get up." And for all the harsh, unyielding demand in that flinty stare…for a moment, that rolling, cultured baritone gentled just a touch. "You will have to take his place, young Master Harrington. There are empty spaces at Harrington Steel, and we must ascertain how you are to fit into them."

That reminder hit with a more sickening slug than the post-champagne lurch in Ash's stomach, draining his anger into a gray, hollow slurry that rolled in his gut. The retort on his tongue died, and he lowered his eyes, staring down at his fingers clutched in the fine linen of the sheets, gripping them up until the fibers strained.

"…yeah."

He waited for another cutting remark from Forsythe. Another accusation. Another reminder of how inadequate he was. He'd managed to prove that in just a few days, with Harington Steel's stocks down by more than half and investor faith dropping on speculation about how he'd run the business into the ground when his father inevitably died. He didn't have to be on top of the business world to hear the rumors, to get the frantic shareholder emails he didn't reply to because he didn't know what to say.

But Forsythe remained silent, save for the faint sound of his polished shoes on the gleaming wooden flooring—drifting away, then returning, before the man's tall, formidable bulk sank down on the edge of the bed, weighing it down enough to tilt Ash toward the heat he gave off, a faint scent of something earthy and cool and dark clinging to him. A gloved hand extended to Ash, offering four Tylenol in an open palm; the other hand proffered a fizzing glass of seltzer water.

"Perhaps you would find this more agreeable to your hangover," Forsythe said quietly.

Ash lifted his head, searching Forsythe's face. Dark green eyes looked back at him, frank and unflinching, yet revealing nothing. Ash didn't know what he was looking for. He'd just hired this asshole yesterday, and he was already riding roughshod over Ash, spinning him into a whirlwind until Ash didn't even know if he should stop him or just let him have his way.

And he didn't know what he thought he'd see, in that impassive gaze.

It was pathetic to be so desperate for approval he'd turn to a stranger who only owed him as much as a paycheck bought, anyway.

He lowered his eyes again, scraping the Tylenol from Forsythe's palm and into his own, then tossing the pills back in a dry swallow that lodged in his throat before taking the glass and washing them down with a deep drink.

"Thank you," he forced himself to say, passing the glass back to Forsythe. "How did you even know I'd be hungover?"

"I hazarded an educated guess. Now." Forsythe held up a pair of Ash's boxer-briefs, just a tiny swatch of black fabric, and shook them out briskly between his hands. "If you would be so kind as to give me your legs."

Ash's eyes widened. His stomach dropped—and this time there was no mistaking the snicker from the stream of people passing in and out of the pool house. Scowling, he snatched the boxer-briefs from Forsythe's hands. "*Give me those,*" he hissed, then darted a glance over his shoulder, hiding the underwear under the sheet quickly. "And get out. I'll dress myself."

"But—"

"*Get out,*" he repeated, then flung a glare toward the gardening crew. "All of you get the hell out. For fuck's sake, can I get dressed in peace?"

"Today," Forsythe answered, the single word practically a threat, his eyes glinting darkly as he rose to his feet and swept another of those infuriating bows, deep and yet utterly mocking. "I'll have a car brought around when you're ready, young Master."

"I don't see you leaving."

For a moment, he'd swear a ghost of a smile flitted across Forsythe's mouth.

"As you command," Forsythe said, and turned and walked from the pool house, lifting one hand in a quiet but imperious snap.

The gardening crew, who had frozen mid-task, hadn't moved—hadn't left, not even when Ash had demanded it.

But at that snap they turned to file out, hefting boxes and leaving in subdued silence, practically an entourage in Forsythe's wake.

Ash stared after them, then groaned and flopped back against the pillows.

"Fuck my life," he muttered, then tightened the sheet around his hips and rolled out of bed.

He'd finished yanking the curtains closed and pulling the French doors shut for some semblance of privacy before he realized Forsythe had laid his clothing out over the rattan chair near the bed. On the table next to the chair, he'd left a tray with a few slices of toast, scrambled eggs, half a grapefruit, a tall glass of orange juice—and a spraying pink and orange tiger lily decorating the tray in delicate accent, fresh-cut and its petals still glistening with beads of moisture. Ash stared.

He felt like a fucking toddler being fed and dressed for school.

And he wasn't sure if he wanted to fire Forsythe or kiss him, when he flung himself down in the chair and scooped up a bite of the eggs. He'd never tasted simple scrambled eggs so good in his *life*—and he knew damned well the house chef hadn't made them. Richard was such a snot about gourmet gluten-free food he couldn't do *simple* to save his life, and the last time he'd tried scrambled eggs he'd somehow managed to make them both rubbery *and* runny. These were light, fluffy, perfectly seasoned with just a touch of pepper, almost melting in Ash's mouth, and he let out a relieved groan as he devoured bite after bite and let the food settle the roaring in his skull until he no longer thought it would *crack*.

He lingered over the toast and orange juice, closing his eyes and making himself settle, breathe, smooth his hackles. That was one fuck of a way to wake up…but it didn't mean Forsythe was wrong.

He just didn't have to be such a dick about it.

But if Ash was going to get his shit together…

No more sleeping until sunset. No more losing himself in the arms of strangers, half-drunk and not even caring if they only wanted him because they knew who he was and how much money was riding on his shoulders and just how likely it was they'd get their moment of fame when the next morning saw their faces splashed in the tabloids. Ash smiled bitterly, pressing his lips against the cool rim of the glass.

He practically kept the tabloids in business.

If he shut himself away and refused to do his job, half the publishing industry might grind to a halt. At least last night he'd been too drunk to wake up with company.

Forsythe probably would have flashed his one-night

stand's ass everywhere, too.

Sighing, he finished his orange juice, stole five minutes in a quick shower, and rose to pull on his clothing. One of his old single-breasted suits in deep navy, nearly black, with subtle pinstripes; he didn't even remember what he'd bought it for, probably one of his father's fundraisers, but he didn't recall it fitting this comfortably, as he settled the coat over his button-down…and he *distinctly* recalled the over-long pants legs catching on his heels all night at the event, his draping suit cuff dipping into food trays as he browsed the refreshments. But the pants legs fell perfectly now, stopping just at the tops of his shoes, and the sleeves ended neatly a precise half-inch above the cuff off his shirt sleeve.

Staring, Ash fingered the hem, then flipped it back over his wrist. The stitching there was definitely new, neat and precise in nearly militant lines. Holy fuck.

Had Forsythe fucking tailored his clothing?

How did the man even know his *fit?*

And when the fuck had he even…?

He looked quickly over his shoulder, half expecting the man to pop out of nowhere to answer a question he hadn't even spoken out loud. The pool house was silent, drawers hanging open, everything in disarray. No sign of Forsythe.

But the specter of the man was *present*, practically breathing down the back of Ashton's neck.

That man was a *demon*.

Ash let out an incredulous laugh, tucked his wallet into his pocket, and headed outside and into morning sunshine tinted that watery color that promised autumn was loosening its last hold and the brisk, nippy chill to the air would soon become pure and biting ice. Slipping his hand into his pockets, Ash followed the main walk through the garden and up to the front drive of the sprawling, palatial yet minimalist Mediterranean style mansion in smooth white that threw the sun back in a blinding glare. The red brick of the courtyard was like spilled blood in contrast, while the gleaming Mercedes pulled into the drive was a blot of black ink in the center.

Forsythe stood at attention next to the car, and as Ash rounded the house, Forsythe dipped another of those bows and pulled the back door open. Ash eyed him, but sighed and slipped into the backseat. As soon as he was settled, Forsythe closed the door firmly, then rounded the car to the driver's seat and slid in. Smoothly, he started the Mercedes and pulled it forward, easing out of the courtyard and into the long, winding, tree-shrouded drive that coiled from the Harrington estate toward the main streets of New York. Ash watched the back of Forsythe's head for a moment, then sighed, looking away, watching the tree-light reflections dappling against the windows.

"Are you driving me because you think you're my jailer?" he murmured. "Don't trust me to show up on my own?"

"I am driving you because this, too, is part of a valet's job," Forsythe replied crisply. For a moment his eyes, in the reflection in the rear view mirror, flicked to Ash. "Your comfort and safety are my utmost priority. That includes ensuring you are safely conveyed to your destinations." He shifted flawlessly as the Mercedes eased onto the public streets, the rumble and hum of the finely-tuned vehicle changing around them into a soothing growl. "From this point forward, I will not allow a stranger to be entrusted with your safety. You can either hire a driver I will personally screen, or allow me to drive you."

Ash arched a brow. "Were you this bossy with Vic's family?"

"I did not need to be," Forsythe replied pointedly.

Ash grit his teeth, but let it go.

The annoying part was that the bastard was right.

Silence held, on the drive through New York. Silence was better. Safer. He didn't know what to say to Forsythe, anyway, and Ash had other things on his mind.

Like the tall, glossy spear of glass and silver thrusting against the New York City skyline, reflective surface painted in the colors of the day and sun-flare blinding off the tall brushed-steel *HS* emblazoned vertically down the side of the building.

If Harrington Steel was a kingdom and the home a palace…the real throne was here. The Tower, people tended to call it. The seat of power. And right now that seat was occupied by a pretender prince, its king gone.

He was just keeping the seat warm for his father, he told himself.

That was all.

And he nearly cringed when Forsythe parked the car, let them both out, and led him to the door—only for the doorman to scramble to open it for him, dipping his head and tipping his cap in deference.

"Mr. Harrington," the doorman said respectfully.

Ash nodded and forced a frozen smile. And managed to keep it, as they moved through the lobby to the elevator surrounded by double-taking stares, scrambled greetings of "Mr. Harrington" repeated over and over again until he wanted to scream *I'm not Mr. Harrington. I'm Ash. I'm not ready to* ***be*** *Mr. Harrington.*

But Forsythe's watchful presence, hovering at his shoulder, kept him silent.

The elevator let them off on the top floor, and the vaulted, open spaces of the glass and steel CEO suite. The airy reception area was empty save for Ms. Vernon, settled primly behind her desk and tapping away so rapidly that the few slim, dark braids that slipped loose from their tight bun swayed into her smoothly burnished brown face with the force of her keystrokes. She didn't even pause, fingers a blur, as she glanced up with a warm, polite smile, her dark brown eyes shrewd but her assessment pleasant.

"Good morning, Ashton," she said. She'd never called Ashton anything *but* that for as long as she'd worked for his father, and he felt his shoulders coming down from around his ears even as she transferred her gaze to Forsythe. "Mr. Forsythe. Welcome to your first day on the job."

"Believe me," Forsythe said dryly, "my first day started before the ink was even dry on the contract."

Ash shot him a foul look. Ms. Vernon only chuckled. "Ashton, I've held all your calls this morning and promised a return within the next twenty-four hours. If you'd like to get settled, I'll forward your correspondence."

"You can forward it to me," Forsythe interrupted. "I will handle preparing the young Master's daily diary, and will report his calendar to you for reference in screening correspondence."

Ms. Vernon blinked. So did Ash, before he scowled at Forsythe. "You don't even have an email address on the company intranet yet."

"Yes, I do," Forsythe corrected smoothly, then turned and walked away, practically sailing down the polished slate floor and through the double doors, into the CEO's office.

Ash stared after him. So did Ms. Vernon, before she arched both brows, canting her head with a soft whistle through her teeth.

"I know," Ash groaned, as the door banged closed. "I *know*."

Her lips tightened in a clear struggle not to laugh. "I didn't say a word, Ashton."

"You didn't *have* to." He took a deep breath and squared his shoulders. "Wish me luck."

Ms. Vernon's soft, gentle laughter chased him through the heavy slate doors, which pulled open with the weight of all the responsibility crushing down on him and closed with the finality of a prison sentence.

Forsythe had already settled himself at the broad desk of weathered, graying, repurposed railway wood bolted together with old rail ties; he'd hauled one of the chairs from the other side of the desk and positioned it next to the high-backed leather chair, and had a laptop flipped open in front of him, the Harrington Steel decal stuck on the corner. It was clearly brand new, probably even a newer model than the one Ash had left closed on the desk last night.

Ash blinked. "Where did you get that?"

"I already requisitioned it from IT," Forsythe murmured distractedly, large hands moving with speed and dexterity across the keyboard, the sound of typing softened by the white kid gloves. The laptop screen reflected in his glasses.

"*When?*"

A pointed glance flicked up over the top of the laptop screen. "While you were in bed this morning."

"And they gave it to you without my approval?"

That pointed look lingered, then dropped back down to the screen. "They appeared relieved that someone else was stepping in."

Hurt was a hard shot to the center of Ash's chest, the kind of blow that could stop a heart and then start it again. Fuck. *Fuck,* what was he even trying to do? He was useless. He wasn't cut out for this. Everyone knew that. Every last person bobbing and ducking and ass-kissing calling him *Mr. Harrington* knew he was just a fucking waste of space, and they were just waiting for either his Dad to come back or to just die so the Board of Directors could declare Ash incompetent, remove him, and replace him with someone who could actually *do* this.

Letting himself dance around in this puppet show was just asking to humiliate himself.

"Fuck this," he ground out around the lump in his throat. "I'm leaving."

Forsythe went stone-still. "Where do you think you are going?"

"Out. Nobody needs me here anyway, right?" Ash glared at Forsythe. Everything inside him *ached* with an awful and pulling tension that felt like it would snap and unravel him into nothing but a pathetic pile of threads. He turned away, yanking at the door. "So is it your fucking business where I go?"

No man as large as Forsythe should move as quickly as he did. One moment Ash was pulling at the door—and the next Forsythe had rounded the desk. His gloved hand covered Ash's, stilling it on the handle, pushing the door firmly closed.

And holding it there, as Forsythe braced his hand against the door over Ash's head, pinning the door in its frame and trapping Ash between a wall of slate and a wall of man so overpowering and intimidating that his shadow turned the glassy light of the sun-filled room into darkness.

"It is entirely my business," Forsythe bit off, pinning Ash with a fierce look. "How do you think I knew the entirety of your history and dilemma without being told?" The gaze that raked over Ash was harsh, scoring. "You are constantly tarnishing your family's reputation in the papers. You have been notorious since you returned from boarding school and appeared in the public eye—even more since your father's sudden illness. What do you think it would do for your family's standing if you were to be seen carousing about with your…*gyrating paramours* with your father in his current state and his business affairs unattended?"

"I don't *care!*" Ash shot back, breathing in great, hoarse, heaving gasps that he wouldn't let turn into sobs. This fucking asshole—this asshole crowding him, acting like Ash was supposed to obey him like some fucking child, talking to him like this when he just…he just…

He hadn't even had time to *hurt* before he was thrown into this.

He hadn't even had time to cope with the world falling down around his ears before everyone was waiting for him to put it back together, and judging if he placed so much as one stone out of place in the million stones it took to made an empire.

Gulping back another harsh breath, he glared at Forsythe. "Is it so fucking wrong of me to want a distraction?"

Forsythe's eyes narrowed. He studied Ash in measuring silence, before inclining his head, then straightening, his hand falling away from the door. He slipped his fingers under the hem of one glove and peeled it off precisely, revealing a long, angular hand with crude knuckles and a certain brutish grace and finesse to it.

"Very well," he said—then caught the fingertip of the second glove in his teeth, his stern, firm-lipped mouth moving against the white fabric as he tugged the glove away from his other hand.

Confusion roiled in Ash's gut. His gaze darted from Forsythe's eyes to his mouth, those hands, then back again. "…what?"

"Since male attention is the distraction you so often seem to desire," Forsythe replied calmly, "I shall oblige."

Neatly, meticulously, he tucked his gloves into his suit coat pocket.

Then captured Ash's face in the heated coarseness of palms worn work-rough and capable, tilted his head up, and leaned down to claim his mouth in the hard and undeniable command of those cruel and unsmiling lips.

Where Forsythe's words were ice, his mouth was fire, burning and wild—and Ash went hot in a trembling flush from his fingertips to the twisting breathless depths of his stomach, burning in a liquid wash as if he'd plunged into a sea of molten flame. That searing ocean stole the air from his lungs and swallowed him deep, in over his head before he'd even known he was drowning.

Forsythe took command of his lips the same way he'd taken command of Ash's life, and while Ash gasped and floundered and clutched at Forsythe's arms, at the hard-hewn strength concealed beneath the lie of the smoothly tailored suit...Forsythe showed him with languid, domineering control exactly what he meant to *oblige* with every soft, taunting graze of his teeth and every flick of a tongue that licked and teased at Ash's throbbing, sensitized mouth.

For a breath, he couldn't stop himself from going boneless, from arching against Forsythe. His usual distractions were boys his own age—college boys with football bodies and rich clothing and easy, shit-eating grins. He'd never been kissed before by a man who knew what he was doing with such certainty that he made Ash feel small and vulnerable and new, suddenly not so sure of himself at all, trembling and overwhelmed and completely swept up in the sheer magnetic force of Forsythe's absolute control.

God, he tasted like liquor and sharp steel edges, tasted weathered and wild all at once, and the size and heat of his body, the feeling of muscle tested and worn by time, were turning Ash's blood heavy and hot and dark. Every time he tried to steal a breath around that deep, dominating kiss it drew every part of his body up tight until he felt the smallest inhalation pulling at the base of his achingly hard cock.

This was what he needed. What could make the pure

shit of his life go away for a while. What could make him forget he was so goddamned pathetic he didn't even know where to start with his Dad's pride and joy before he'd already halfway run the business into the ground. What could let him ignore that just to be able to get up in the morning, he'd had to hire someone—

Hire someone.

And that someone was currently kissing him like a whirlwind.

The heat in Ash's blood turned cold. He tore away from Forsythe's mouth, jerking his face to the side, and shoved against his chest, thrusting himself back against the door with a gasp. "Forsythe!"

Forsythe stilled as if his off switch had been flipped, only to shift into motion again, his hands slowly falling away from Ash's face and leaving the ghostly burn of their afterimpression behind. He regarded Ash coolly, as though Forsythe's chest wasn't subtly heaving, his mouth parted and glistened and reddened. As if this were just another duty, and now it had been done.

"Do you find me unattractive, then?" he asked.

"N-no, it's not that, I—I—"

Ash was going to throw up. He glared at Forsythe, his lips trembling; this felt all *wrong*, and even worse was that some deep frightened part of him wanted it back. Wanted that feeling of letting go of control and letting

Forsythe take over and make him feel small and sheltered and hot and pleasured and completely at his mercy. No. No. *Fuck* no, he just…just…he might be a fucking spoiled shit, but he wasn't *that* kind of person.

His fingers curled into fists, nails biting into his palms. "Fuck, you think I want sex to be some kind of transaction like this?" he demanded. "You're my fucking employee, so you're just humoring my fucking libido for a paycheck?"

Forsythe's calm regard didn't waver. As if this was nothing; as if…as if… "I have every intention of being your faithful servant in all things."

"Not that," Ash hissed. "*Not that.*"

Forsythe started to step closer, one hand lifting—but Ash jerked away, sliding to the side and away from the door, edging back toward his desk.

"Don't," he said. "Don't, I just…" Bitterness made his mouth feel like a tight, sour pucker, drawing down. "Fine. I won't go anywhere. I'll…" He tore his gaze away from Forsythe, but ended up staring at the desk. The desk that would always be his father's desk, and Ash was too small to fill its seat. He folded his arms over his chest, hugging them to himself. "…just…give me a little space for a while."

"As you wish," Forsythe replied smoothly.

The faintest whisper of stone on stone hinted at the

door pulling open—but it didn't shut. No sound of small echoes from patent leather footsteps. Then:

"I apologize if I made you feel in any way violated," Forsythe murmured.

"No. It's not that." Fuck, if anything it was the opposite. Ash…Ash was the one who'd crossed a line here, even if he hadn't started it. He hunched into his shoulders. "But thank you for apologizing."

"Young Master," Forsythe replied.

Then the door swung closed, soft sigh of settling hinges, faint click of the latch.

And Ash was alone.

Just a speck of dust, floating inside this hollow, empty space.

Chapter Three

BRAND TOOK THE TIME FOR a coffee and to run a few necessary errands before he took himself back to the Harrington Steel tower and his young Master's office.

In truth, he needed a touch of time to compose himself as well. While he had not intended to in any way test the young Master, simply obliging him in a more private manner than his usual tabloid scandals…

He had not expected Ashton Harrington to push him away.

Particularly not for those reasons.

Pride *and* ethics.

Perhaps the young Master was not as the papers had painted him.

He smiled to himself faintly, finished the last of his coffee, and dropped the cup in the bin just inside the top-floor reception area before exchanging a nod with Ms. Vernon and crossing the room to the office door.

He rapped his knuckles briefly to announce himself, then slipped inside. Harrington made a small and miserable bundle in the massive desk chair, but he was still *there*, frowning at the screen of his laptop, puzzlement clear on his pretty, rather princely features. When Brand stepped inside, the young Master froze, glancing up at him almost guiltily, before looking away with a quite fetching blush and scowling at the screen.

"You appear confused, young Master," Brand said. "What are you looking at?"

"I…" Harrington's voice broke on the first try; he cleared his throat and began again. "I'm not sure. I think it's an overseas supply contract with a company in India…it…was supposed to take effect yesterday but it doesn't look like anything's been done or shipped out. I can't tell."

"It's possible there was an issue with customs, or something was awaiting your signature." Brand rounded the desk, reclaimed his chair, and reached over to tilt the laptop so they could both read. "Let me see."

Harrington froze, staring at him sidelong, his blush deepening.

Before he lifted his chin with clear pride, and fixed his gaze firmly back on the screen.

Very well, Brand thought with a touch of amusement. If his young Master didn't want to discuss it, then far be it from him to press the matter.

"I'm not sure this is the best place to start unraveling everything," Harrington mumbled. "But it was the first thing I could halfway make sense of. Got to start somewhere, right?"

"Somewhere is better than nowhere, young Master," Brand murmured.

And that was that.

Somewhere turned out to be a spaghetti tangle of maritime shipping laws and some kind of problem with the containers, delaying shipment until a replacement could be found. The sourcing department had been on top of it, quickly finding a supplier for new containers, but a purchase that large had required a Harrington to sign—and there had been no Harrington in residence to do so.

Brand walked Ashton Harrington through everything, ensuring that rather than simply signing off on things without reading, he *understood* why this mattered—how it impacted the entire business, when one late shipment took time away from other things that must be done on a tight schedule to fulfill a number of global contracts. Rather like a game of Jenga…pull the wrong block loose, and everything came tumbling down until there was nothing left to do but stack up again and start over.

"Is that how bad it's gotten in a few days?" Harrington asked, staring morosely at the dozen documents open on his screen. "I just…let everything fall apart, and now we have to rebuild?"

"Not yet," Brand said. "But the tower is teetering. Be very careful where you pull, young Master."

Wide, almost frightened blue eyes flicked to him. Harrington swallowed. "I don't know where to pull. I…show me?" His soft lips pressed together, the shape of teeth pushing from the inside, their plushness briefly drawing Brand's eye and reminding him of that moment when Harrington had gone soft against him with his mouth ripe and wet, a sweet darkness waiting to be explored. "Really show me. Show me what it means. Don't just tell me what to do."

"Ah," Brand replied, and bit back his smile again. "As my young Master wishes."

And so they spent the day: navigating through a tangled mess of contracts and schedules and trade agreements, researching maritime trade law, sending emails, dashing off signatures. Harrington looked as if he'd break down crying at any moment, but every time he started to falter something went stiff in his spine and his mouth tightened and he glared at the laptop screen. Brand tactfully kept his mouth shut, and only gave him those moments to collect himself—and for today, Brand took on the task of making calls the young Master should be making, speaking as his representative and soothing ruffled hackles and offering adjusted timelines and favorable easements on contract terms to keep them from being cancelled altogether.

Over twenty years as the right hand of a global

business mandate were sorely tested today—and by the time close of business came, even Brand was starting to feel the strain around his eyes. They'd not even stopped for lunch, despite scheduling no fewer than nine business luncheons in the coming weeks so that key political players in the trade market could meet the new young prince of steel and make their obligatory obeisances. The young Master was, quite frankly, looking rather pale.

But he kept doggedly reading, the note pad at his side scribbled down with messy, scrawling handwriting jabbed in the notes he'd been taking all day. Master Harrington had taken his suit jacket off, draped it over the back of his chair, loosened his tie in a most disgraceful way, and rolled up his shirt sleeves. Brand lingered on his profile, on the lines of determination written in his fiercely pretty features, a touch of youthful fire shining through his misery and despair.

He'd had his whinge, worked through his feelings…but he wasn't giving up, Brand thought.

And so Brand held his tongue, and only bowed his head over his own work, organizing a tentative schedule over the coming months to restructure production to meet the most high-priority deadlines and reallocate materials for more critical projects until order could be restored.

However, he could only allow this to continue for so much longer—and when he heard the sound of a vacuum running in the reception room, he glanced up, pushing his glasses up to pinch the bridge of his nose and glancing out the window. The New York city skyline was all jewels on black velvet, bright colors glimmering and winking against dark silhouettes, the sky a bed of blue.

Bloody hell, it was after ten.

He saved the file he was working on, closed his laptop, and stood, touching Harrington's shoulder.

"Young Master," he said. "It's well past time we leave. We'll be in the way of the cleaning staff."

Harrington jerked, rubbing at heavy, shadowed eyes, blinking slowly before looking owlishly at Brand. "What?" His dulled, tired gaze flicked between the laptop screen and Brand. "But…I'm not done…"

"It will hold," Brand said gently, and reached across Harrington to save and exit the program on his desktop, before carefully closing the laptop lid. "When you're this tired and you've not eaten, you'll make mistakes. Come. I'll take you home."

Harrington looked as if he might argue, but then he nodded, sighing heavily and dragging to his feet. "You're right. We can finish in the morning."

"Indeed," Brand replied, and bent forward in a bow, gesturing toward the door. "After you."

The young Master was subdued, on the drive home. Brand watched him in the rear view mirror; Harrington leaned his elbow against the windowsill and stared out the window, his expression withdrawn, fingers curled against parted lips that never said a word. Brand had the feeling that today had been a bit of a wake-up call. Perhaps the young Master had had an inkling of the work ahead of him—hence seeking Brand's assistance—but today had truly driven home the enormity of it. The reality of it, too.

And particularly, the reality of the circumstances that had brought him to this point.

Brand made a mental note to schedule a visit to the hospice center in the young Master's diary in the next few days.

It was, after all, part of his job to see to *all* aspects of his Master's well-being.

At the house, Brand barely put the car into Park before Harrington was out of the backseat and heading for the path toward the pool house.

"Young Master," Brand called softly, then bowed and nodded toward the front door to the main house.

Harrington faltered, his expression falling briefly, before settling into resigned defeat. "…right. Of course."

Brand kept a respectful distance as he trailed Harrington into the house and toward the darkened open kitchen, where he shrugged out of his suit coat, draped it over one of the stools ringing the kitchen island, and rolled his sleeves up.

"I'll have your supper together in less than twenty minutes," he said, pulling the massive double-doored refrigerator open—only for Harrington to duck under his arm, reach inside, and snare one of over a dozen bottles of champagne before turning and stalking down the hall.

"Don't bother," drifted back, the line of Harrington's shoulders tense.

Brand sighed, watching him go until he was just a shadow vanishing into the night-locked hallways of white stone arches and lightless niches.

"As you wish, young Master," he murmured.

Then promptly uncorked every last remaining bottle of champagne in the refrigerator, and poured them out in the stainless steel sink.

Satisfied, he draped his coat over his arm and retired to his chambers.

He would take on the liquor cabinet in the morning, if he had to.

His rooms adjoining the master suite had their own entrance, as well as the entrance accessible through the young Master's rooms. Brand lingered in the hallway outside his door, listening to the sounds of the young Master moving around the spacious grand suite, noise reckless and worrisome but at least he was *there*. The shadows crossing the faint light seeping beneath the door gave no hint as to what he was doing, but as long as he wasn't destroying the place then Brand would let him be.

The rooms had *just* been refurbished.

He'd hate to make more work for the housekeeping staff.

He let himself into his own suite—smaller than the rooms he'd originally been assigned, but he didn't need much. Like the rest of the house the décor itself was a study in neutral colors and minimalism, making the most of even small spaces with delicate touches, much of the furniture made of reclaimed wood and Brand's bedframe itself a thing of precisely contoured and sanded driftwood in a weathered shade of gray. He stripped down, folding his suit away for a proper steam cleaning later, and replaced it with a pair of loose pajama pants before settling into the cool, comfortable linens to sleep.

Only to sigh as his feet slipped over the foot of the queen-sized bed.

Another item for tomorrow, perhaps. A larger bed.

He would deal, otherwise.

Tucking himself on his side so he could draw his legs up, Brand set his alarm for four in the morning, slipped his phone into the charger he'd left on the nightstand, and let himself drop off into sleep, sliding easily into the dark.

Until the door creaked open, faint enough that he almost slept through it—but over twenty years of listening for his Master's slightest need keyed his senses to high alert immediately. He tensed, opening one eye, but didn't move, just listening. A light tread, one he was beginning to recognize as Harrington's; bare feet, he thought, against cool stone. Then another creak as the door closed, the sound of a latch clicking so slowly it could only be an attempt at silence, secrecy.

Then the hiss of cloth and skin on sheets, a feather's weight pressing into his bed.

And the warmth of a lithe body pressed against his back. Pajama-clad legs bumping against the backs of his thighs. Slim hands curled against his shoulder blades.

Soft breaths against his spine, as with a hitching sound Ashton Harrington buried his face against Brand's back.

Brand stiffened. "Young Master…?" he asked softly.

Harrington shook his head, his dark shock of hair teasing and feathering against Brand's skin. "Don't say anything," he answered in a choked whisper. "I don't want anything from you. Not like that. Just…just…" That rough, hurting sound again. "…just let me be here. Let me…let me not be alone."

Brand started to look over his shoulder, unable to help himself when that aching, rough edge to the young Master's voice caught at the quiet strings of his heart and pulled at them to the point of pain. But Harrington hunched into himself, pressing his hands harder against

Brand's back, then curling them into fists.

"Don't," Harrington pleaded, rasping and thick. "Don't turn around. Just…just stay like this."

For a moment, Brand remained as he was, taking in the hints of Harrington's profile he could see in the dark—before he turned to face forward once more, settling into the pillow with the candleglow warmth of his young Master cradled against his back.

"As you wish, young Master Harrington," he murmured.

Harrington remained silent for several shaky breaths, then, "…Ashton. Ash."

"Young Master Ashton."

The bed shook faintly as Ash let out a near-soundless, bitter laugh. "…that'll work."

Brand said nothing.

He only let things be, and listened long into the dark of the night as Ashton's rattling, raspy, tear-filled breaths quieted one at a time.

And slowly, sweetly slipped into the quiet respite of sleep.

Chapter Four

Ash woke to an empty, unfamiliar bed.

Not that he didn't wake that way all the time...but he was usually half as hung over, twice as sore, and not in his own house.

Even if, right now, he wasn't in his own *bed*. He was confused for a moment—the master suite was new to him, and *that* didn't feel like his bed either when he'd moved out to the pool house the moment he'd returned to the States, and never come back. He'd tried to lie there in the master suite last night, looking up at the vaulted ceilings and listening to the night come in through the windows, cricket-sounds and leaf-whisper riding the breeze, the bed too large for him and everything making him think it should be his father in that room, not him.

Even if his father had never used the grand master suite, either. He slept in a room off his office in the east wing of the house.

Sometimes Ash thought it was no coincidence that that room was as far as it could possibly be from the pool house, letting them circle around each other without their orbits ever intersecting.

That was what they were, he'd thought last night—staring at the mindless eyes of the ceiling's stucco dots through a haze of champagne that he'd only swilled halfheartedly, the fizzy taste and alcoholic bite doing nothing to chase away a feeling that left him all wrong in his own skin, ill-fitted and his limbs sticking wrong. He and his father were planets in orbits that never overlapped, circling a darkness without even the warmth of a single star.

Maybe that was why Ash always tried to burn himself out, living fast and living hard.

He just wanted the warmth of one bright star, burning in the darkness of his night.

It was that which had chased him from bed, last night—and to the only human warmth close by. Maybe if he'd been sober he wouldn't have done it. Maybe if he'd been thinking straight, he'd have remembered those cold, cutting green eyes and the contempt with which Forsythe regarded him. Maybe if he hadn't been hurting all the way down to the marrow of his bones, he'd have thought of that kiss he didn't understand, and that boundary that shouldn't have been crossed.

But he hadn't been sober. He hadn't been thinking straight. He'd been hurting to the point where it was a physical thing knotted inside him, choking off his air.

So he'd ended up curled up against Brand Forsythe's

back, falling asleep with the man's body heat cradling him, safe so long as Forsythe didn't look at him and see him for how small and cowardly he really was.

And now he was waking up alone in Forsythe's bed, the smell of fresh-cut grass drifting in on the breeze that ruffled the linen curtains over open patio doors. The door between the adjoining master suite and Forsythe's was open. The man himself was nowhere to be found.

Ash groaned, burying his face in the pillows—pillows that had a faint trace of that earthy scent that had surrounded him as he'd fallen asleep, that scent that had seemed to block out the world and say everything would be okay as long as he let Forsythe take care of anything he needed.

Take care of *him*.

What was he *doing*?

What had he been thinking, crawling into the man's bed and curling against him for comfort like some kind of small child?

Maybe he could blame it on the alcohol.

And order Forsythe not to ever speak a word about this again.

"Young Master," Forsythe said smoothly, his voice so close Ash nearly jumped when he hadn't heard him come back into the room at all, soundless as a cat.

He flushed hotly and peered over his bare arm.

Forsythe stood in the door with one of Ash's suits draped over one arm, a long linen napkin folded over the other, a tray balanced in both hands, piled with croissants dripping with melted blue cheese and what looked like slivers of beef. It smelled at once mouthwatering and nauseating, when his head was on fire *again* and his blood alcohol content was low enough to make him want to puke. He eyed Forsythe, then grumbled and buried his face into the pillow again.

"…I guess I can't tell you to get out when it's your room."

"And my bed," Forsythe replied archly. "At least you had the decency to be clothed this time."

"I wasn't going to get into your bed naked!"

Forsythe said nothing. Ash risked another peek over his arm, but Forsythe was still only watching him with that immovable calm, one sardonic brow arched, completely unreadable.

While Ash was trying not to think about getting into Forsythe's bed *naked* when he still remembered how the man tasted.

Like still-burning embers on his tongue, scorching into him without end.

That flush seared deeper until he felt on fire from inside, and he pressed his cheek against his arm, clearing his throat. "…*anyway*." He wasn't talking about this.

Wasn't thinking about it, or the fact that he knew the feeling of the broad, taut muscles of Forsythe's back moving underneath his palms, his cheek, with every slow inhalation and exhalation.

"If you would like to sit up," Forsythe said, "you may eat, and then you should dress so that we might be on our way."

"Another day of contracts?"

"And quite a few phone calls."

"Great."

Sighing, Ash pushed himself up and leaned against the headboard, taking in the room while Forsythe settled the tray across his lap. He'd never been in any of the servants' quarters throughout the house, let alone any of those adjoining the master suites, unless he had tumbled through them as a child and just forgotten the memory. This house had never really felt like home, not when he'd been sent off to Liverpool and boarding school so young, but even after barely more than a day Forsythe had added a few touches that made the room feel *lived in*, when so much of the echoing mansion didn't. A plaid casual shirt draped over a rattan chair, shoes lined up neatly just outside the closet, several ties laid over the bureau, cufflinks shining in a tray. Books lined on the top row of a shelf, the other shelves empty but several neatly labeled cardboard boxes stacked underneath. Ash squinted, leaning forward a little, trying to read the gilded spines; what did Forsythe like to rea—

"Young Master Ashton." Forsythe cleared his throat pointedly. "You are not eating."

Ash jerked his gaze back to his valet, wide-eyed, then ducked his head and picked up one of the croissants. "…sorry," he mumbled, then took a bite—only to nearly moan as marinated beef and blue cheese and buttery croissant practically melted on his tongue. "Oh my God," he managed around another mouthful. "Richard made this?"

"Please do not talk with your mouth full. It's unseemly." Forsythe's lips thinned as he bent to lay the linen napkin precisely along the side of Ash's tray. Sheepishly, Ash picked up the napkin and wiped at his mouth, catching Forsythe's gaze sidelong. "And no. He did not. He wanted to feed you some sort of gluten-free claptrap, and I decided otherwise. He was rather incensed."

Ash made himself swallow before he let himself smile. "Richard mostly cooks to feed himself. I'm never here, and Dad usually eats—"

He caught himself on the present tense, heart sinking. Fuck. He stared down at his tray, then made himself take another bite of croissants that suddenly had no taste at all.

At least Forsythe had the tact not to say anything.

And Ash didn't want to talk anymore.

Wonder why.

It was an odd twenty minutes, spent eating breakfast in Forsythe's bed while the man moved about the room, laying out Ash's clothing on the foot of the bed and tidying his own personal effects in silence. Ash took that time to study him surreptitiously from under his lashes, distracting himself from his morbid thoughts. Forty-eight hours and Forsythe had already invaded his life, taken it over, twisted it up, and Ash was still trying to find balance and figure the man out. Nothing about him made sense. From how easily he'd accepted the job to the way he always seemed to anticipate Ash's every need, to why he hadn't even *asked* about Ash crawling into his bed.

Or that kiss.

No, that kiss definitely did not make one goddamned bit of sense.

Ash stole a sip of the coffee from the steaming mug on the tray. Black, bitter this time, and the tight tremor of his lips managed to relax into a faint smile.

"Black," he said softly, lifting the mug.

"I do listen," Forsythe replied, smoothing out a tie atop the suit laid on the bed, then straightening and dusting off his gloved hands. "Would you prefer to bathe in my bathroom, or yours?"

"Eh? Oh. Um, yours is fine? The one off the master

bedroom doesn't have a shower. Just, like, a swimming pool."

"You prefer showers, then?"

"Yeah."

Forsythe adjusted his glasses, pushing them up with one middle finger. "Temperature?"

"Uh?" Ash blinked. "Usually hot as it'll go, but—hey!"

He was talking to Forsythe's back.

Then to nothing at all, as Forsythe disappeared into the bathroom.

"Uh…?" Ash called. "You don't have to run my shower for me!"

The only answer was the creak of the faucet—then the sound of running, spraying water.

Ash sank back against the pillows, cradling the mug in both hands, just…blinking.

Having a valet was *weird.*

The throbbing in his skull had gone down, at least, by the time he topped off his last few bites of croissant and chased them with the Tylenol waiting neatly inside a napkin folded into a little flower cup. He slid out of the bed gingerly, padding toward the bathroom, and started to peer inside—only to bump right into Forsythe as he was emerging, planting almost nose-first in his broad chest.

With a yelp, Ash retreated, staring up at the man. Forsythe cast a long shadow, dwarfing him, that feeling of being *small* once more, and Ash's stomach tightened strangely. He swallowed, licking his lips. "Um, I'll…be right out."

"Leave your clothing over the door and I'll have it laundered," was all Forsythe said, before ducking around him.

Ash slipped into the bathroom, body almost grazing Forsythe's bulk, a tingling whisper of body heat licking over his skin and leaving him shivering as he shut the bathroom door behind him and then slumped against it.

Demon. Fucking *demon.*

Quickly, he stripped down and opened the door just enough to drape his pajama pants over it before shutting it again and slipping into the glass-walled shower. He scrubbed himself off quickly, letting the spray scour and steam him until he felt at least human again, closing his eyes and losing himself in the relaxing heat. He ducked his head under the spray briefly, raking his fingers through his hair, then shook it off, shut the water off, and turned to reach for the shower door.

Only to find Forsythe standing outside the shower stall, a large, fluffy white towel spread and waiting between his hands.

Ash fucking *shrieked,* stumbling back and grabbing

at the shower head to keep from slipping, his heart turning over.

Then immediately grabbing at his groin to cover himself, glaring at Forsythe, his face fucking *boiling* so much it was a miracle the water didn't steam right off his cheeks.

"Goddammit, Forsythe, I'm naked!"

"I," Forsythe deadpanned, "am trying to remedy that."

"Oh my fucking God. Get *out*."

"It is my bathroom, and you are not yet dry."

"It's my *house*, now leave the towel and get out!"

Forsythe's lips thinned. "No."

Ash stared. "*No?*"

"I will not be derelict in my duty," Forsythe said, an edge of something darkening his voice, commanding and sharp. "Step out of the shower. Allow me to dry and dress you, and then we will be on our way."

There it was again—that *way* Forsythe had about him that made Ash just want to go belly-up, this small and helpless thing in Forsythe's hands. Part of him simmered, wanting to rebel…but his knees were weak and his gut felt strange and there was a tight pulling feeling in his inner thighs that he didn't understand, a flutter in his chest that left him confused and meek. And after a frustrated, flustered moment he ducked his head, keeping his hands over his hips as he stepped dripping and naked out of the shower.

The towel—thick and soft and heavy and warm as if it had just come out of the dryer—enveloped him. So did Forsythe's arms, folding around him and caging him as the man wrapped him up in soft Egyptian cotton, shrouding him until he was at least decent, and began to gently work the towel over Ash's body. Ash tucked his arms around himself and made himself hold still as strong, capable hands touched him everywhere, their heat hardly muted through the thick layer of the towel and Forsythe's gloves, stroking over him with a surety and confidence that seemed to *know* him.

And the entire time Forsythe said nothing, the only sounds the faint rasp of cloth on skin and the wild beat of Ash's heart. He risked a glance upward, expecting to find Forsythe preoccupied, gaze on his hands.

Only to find those dark green eyes locked right on him, watching him with a quiet intensity that stole his breath.

Forsythe held his gaze unwaveringly, trapping him like a cobra mesmerizing a mouse, as he stepped forward—and with measured, deliberated strides, backed Ash from the bathroom and into the bedroom, the sheer bulk of his body herding him. Clutching at the towel, Ash stumbled back, retreating, but Forsythe never let more than an inch of space flow between them as Ash wobbled into the bedroom, then bumped up against the post at the foot of the bed. He froze, staring up at Forsythe as the man leaned in, that crushing bulk nearly pressing into him.

And leaning around him to pluck a pair of clean boxer-briefs from the clothing laid out on the bed, before drawing back.

Forsythe arched a brow, the glint in his eyes bordering on amused, as he sank down to one knee. Ash groaned, closing his eyes, and thunked his head back against the bed post.

That man wasn't a demon.

He was the fucking devil himself.

He didn't resist as Forsythe gently encircled one ankle, lifted it, and guided Ash's foot into the boxer-briefs, then the other, before skimming them up his calves and thighs. For a moment heavy hands framed his hips as Forsythe settled the boxer-briefs into place, gripping as if in possessive claim…before falling away to tug the towel from Ash's unresisting fingers and drape it across the footboard. His undershirt pulled over his head, next, then a white and crisply starched button-down—and Ash looked up at Forsythe with his thoughts a formless, wordless knot of confusion and wondered at his own obedience as he raised his arms so Forsythe could slip them into the sleeves.

As Forsythe began to button the shirt, his gloved knuckles grazing against Ash's skin through the undershirt, he murmured, "You are staring at me, young Master Ashton." That pointed brow again, darkened eyes drilling. "You have *been* staring at me."

"I'm practically naked. You're dressing me," Ash managed to force out, throat dry. His entire body felt too tight, and only drew tighter as that touch grazed higher. "And you *kissed* me yesterday."

"I am aware," Forsythe responded blandly, as if reciting his appointments for the day. "Did you think I had forgotten?"

"I don't know!" Ash spluttered. "I...is...like is that an English thing?" He didn't know what he was saying, words coming out jumbled and all wrong. "Valets are also like...personal concubines?"

Forsythe's mouth curved slightly at the corners. He buttoned the top button underneath Ash's chin, then pulled away to catch his trousers next, holding them so Ash could step into them. Forsythe pulled them up around his hips, deft fingers teasing against Ash's waist as Forsythe tucked his shirt in—only to make him gasp, stomach dropping out, as Forsythe briefly jerked him forward by his grasp on the waistband, before dragging the zipper up and firmly slipping the button closed.

Only to frown, immediately unbutton and unzip

Ash's slacks again, and drop to his knees.

Ash froze. "Forsythe!"

"Your button is loose," Forsythe said, as if the button had personally offended him, and tugged at the slacks—giving Ash no choice but to stumble out of them. "And to answer your question, no. That is not 'an English thing.' And I doubt it was even in the days when valets were commonplace, rather than an increasing and archaic rarity."

That…really didn't answer anything at all.

It just left Ash staring at Forsythe, just as confused as before, as the man slipped his hand into his pocket and retrieved a little paper card with several needles stuck into it, one end wound with different colors of thread.

"I shall mend it," Forsythe pronounced, already selecting a needle, "and you can have it back."

"You keep a needle and thread in your pocket?"

"A proper valet is prepared for anything." And Forsythe was already picking out a slim length of thread, black to match the slacks, and deftly inserting it through the eye of a needle.

Suspicion pricked at Ash. He eyed Forsythe. "Including your employer wanting to duck out in the middle of the day for a hookup?"

"Precisely," Forsythe said without missing a beat, and stabbed the needle into a buttonhole.

Ash let out a startled laugh. “That was an asshole move,” he said, and Forsythe’s lips curved—dark, pleased, almost certainly *smug*, but a quiet smile nonetheless.

“It worked.”

The next beat of Ash’s heart came erratic and strange. “…you smiled.”

For a moment, Forsythe’s gaze darted up to him. A glimmer of warmth darkened them…or was Ash imagining that, in the reflections off his glasses?

“You gave me reason to,” Forsythe murmured.

“Oh.” Ash dropped numbly to sit on the edge of the bed, leaning back on his hands. “I…” He didn’t know what to say. Fuck, he’d been a prickly mess since the moment Forsythe walked into his office. *Before*. He stole a shy glance at the man, then offered, “I…I’m not trying to be a disappointment. I’m not trying to be a fuckup. Really, I’m not. I swear.”

“No?”

“No.” Ash bit his lip. “I’m just…scared. I thought I’d have time before this happened. I thought I’d have forever. Me taking over the company was just *one day*, but suddenly it’s *now*—and I’m scared.”

“So you run,” Forsythe observed, fingers working deftly with the needle, thread looping and then tightening in tiny black arcs.

"Run. Check out mentally. Shut down. You name it, I do it."

"If you run, there is a guarantee that you will fail." Forsythe looped the thread into a little knot, tied it off, then bit the end off with a quick snap of his teeth, sensuous lips gliding against the thread momentarily. The needle vanished into his pocket. "If you try, it is only a possibility." He drew closer, then, smoothing the creases in the slacks, before sinking to one knee and gently gripping Ash's ankle to guide his foot into the leg of the slacks, gloves grazing soft against his skin. He looked like some strange knight kneeling before a lady, or a prince offering Cinderella her glass slipper, and those dark eyes were strange and warm and quiet and searching as he looked up at Ash. "*Try*, young Master."

Ash smiled faintly. "Are you actually trying to encourage me?"

"I believe that, too, is in my job description."

Sighing, Ash shook his head, shifting to make it easier for Forsythe to slide the slacks up his legs. "You confuse me, Forsythe."

"You have known me for two days." Suddenly rough hands had him by the hips, dragging him forward with undeniable strength and not so much as an if-you-please, Ash's stomach flipping as Forsythe's grasp lifted him to his feet, positioning him until he stood with Forsythe kneeling at his feet, so close that the man's breaths stirred warm through his shirt as he murmured, "It takes at least three before I am an open book to my employer."

"Funny," Ash rasped, and that brief smile flitted across Forsythe's lips again.

"Here." He tucked Ash's shirt quickly, neatly into his waistband, then zipped Ash up again and rose to his feet. "Much better."

He guided Ash into a tie, next, fitting and looping it neatly into a Windsor knot, then a soft, dark gray waistcoat and the matching black suit coat. They, too, fit perfectly, and Ash once more checked the cuffs for that tell-tale line of fresh stitching.

When did Forsythe find the *time?*

Forsythe smoothed the suit coat over Ash's shoulders, settling it into place. There was something soothing about the touch, about feeling like Forsythe had put him together one piece at a time until he was ready to face the day. Ash offered a faint smile. "Thank you."

"You are welcome, young Master." With a brief bow, Forsythe stepped back. "Now if you are prepared, you are due at the office for a Board meeting in approximately twenty-seven minutes."

Panic laced, sharp and shrill, through him. "*What?* When were you going to tell me that?"

"I put it in your email calendar last night."

"I didn't check that!"

"Why not?" Forsythe asked pointedly.

"Oh my God, you are *such* an asshole." Ash dragged a hand over his face—then flinched and resisted the urge to bat Forsythe away when the man came at him with a comb, sliding it into his hair and smoothing it back from his face. Fucking hell, he was going to look like his father if this kept up. "What's the meeting about?"

"Shareholder projections for the fourth quarter," Forsythe murmured. With a gentle touch he tucked a lock of Ash's hair behind his ear, grazing the upper curve; Ash fought the urge to shiver and jerked away. Forsythe was just full of too many mixed signals—hard claiming kisses and cold demanding words and careful attentive care and fucking asshole surprises, leaving Ash to flounder only to offer a hand before he drowned.

He just…he couldn't deal with this right now, whatever game Forsythe was playing.

"I don't even know what that *means*," he deflected.

"You may want to learn quickly." Forsythe's hand vanished inside his coat with the comb, and re-emerged with a dark brown expanding file, laced closed with a snap of black elastic. He offered it to Ash with a brief bow. "You can read it in the car."

Ash took the folder, unlooped the elastic, and spilled out several pages of printed bullet points and charts.

"…what's this?"

"A cheat sheet, as it were. Enough talking points to get you through."

Frowning, Ash paged through the notes, rifling the printouts quickly. "When did you make this?"

"Last night, as well." Forsythe inclined his head. "I would not let my young Master go in unprepared."

With a sigh, Ash flipped the folder closed. "I can't tell if you're trying to break me, or build me up."

"What if one must occur for the other to be possible?"

"…I'm too hung over to answer tha—"

He broke off as, this time, a fresh bottle of water appeared from inside that bottomless coat; Forsythe offered it expectantly. Ash exhaled, unable to help a rueful smile. Hydrate a hangover. Right. And of course Forsythe had the answer right there.

"Thank you."

The only acknowledgment Forsythe gave was a sharp gleam in his eyes, a pointed glance. "I would thank you to break this pattern, and be sober tomorrow morning."

"Then stop driving me to drink," Ash said dryly.

"I make no promises," Forsythe retorted, and swept that deeply mocking bow once more, extending his arm toward the door. "I follow where my young Master leads."

"Asshole," Ash said.

Forsythe's low, velvet-and-sand laughter chased him from the room, a near-sinister purr. One that seemed to promise Forsythe knew something Ash didn't. Some end game played by all the wrong rules.

And Ash wasn't sure he wanted to know what would happen if he lost.

CHAPTER FIVE

BY THE TIME THE BOARD meeting was over, Ash wasn't sure he hadn't lost already.

Especially when he was bent over in the private bathroom in the CEO suite, losing his breakfast in the toilet while Forsythe rubbed his back and murmured soft, soothing things as if that could ease the raw, terrified nerves turning his stomach into a pit of churning acid.

That room full of stiff, balding, suit-stuffed men had eviscerated him. The cheat sheet hadn't been worth a damned thing when they had barely even let him talk. They'd barraged him with questions, rapid-fire and accusatory, and before he'd even finished half a sentence in stammered response another would start up. If this was a trial by fire, he'd been completely and utterly burned—and only Forsythe's hand against the small of his back, concealed by his chair, had kept him from running from the room in the first five minutes.

He coughed one last time, then straightened and flushed, wiping at his mouth—only to find Forsythe watching him, obligingly holding out a damp folded cloth and a little paper cup full of blue mouthwash, the scent so strong it stung his nose.

“Here, young Master Ashton. This should help.”

Ash took the cup and swigged it back, swishing it around his mouth before slipping past Forsythe to spit into the sink, then rinsing with water and dabbing clean with the cloth. “Don’t tell me where you were hiding that,” he said—only to turn and find Forsythe offering a plastic-wrapped toothbrush and a travel tube of toothpaste that seemed to have materialized from nowhere. Ash sighed. “Or that.”

“As I said, a proper valet is always prepared.”

Ash leaned his hip against the wide counter, the same slate as the floors and walls, and ripped the plastic off the toothbrush. He felt hollow, and not just because he’d just emptied himself out. “So you knew I was going to come running out of that meeting ready to puke.”

“I had an idea it would not go well, preparations or not.”

“They hate me,” Ash said miserably, then laid a strip of toothpaste on the brush and stuck it in his mouth, mumbling around the bristles. “They want me to fail.”

“They want to make money.” Forsythe leaned his bulk against the counter next to Ash, folding his arms over his chest and tilting his head back to regard the ceiling contemplatively, dimmed white fluorescents reflecting from the lenses of his glasses. “Right now, they do not believe you are capable of accomplishing that goal."

Ash wrinkled his nose, then finished scrubbing his mouth out, spat, and rinsed before drying his face on one of the towels stacked to the side of the sink. "They're probably right."

"Are they?"

He eyed Forsythe sidelong. "You think they aren't?"

Forsythe shrugged, so close one massive shoulder brushed against Ash. "You are here, when you could be running away."

"That's nothing. Being here doesn't matter if I don't do anything useful while I'm here."

"Then let us be useful, young Master." Forsythe straightened, pressing a hand to his chest in one of those light bows, even if it was significantly less mocking this time. And Ash might almost think there was actual *concern* in his gaze, as Forsythe fixed him with a searching, lingering look. "Are you well enough to work? Do you need medication?"

"No." Ash shook his head, drying his hands and dropping the towel. "No, let's get to it."

"I am at your disposal."

Ash managed a faint smile. "Going to be the Alfred to my Bruce Wayne?"

Jaw tightening, Forsythe scowled. "I am neither that old nor that wrinkled."

With a grin, Ash folded his arms over his chest. "Are you insulted that I think you're old?"

"You do not think I am old." That scowl faded into another penetrating look—knowing, as if reminding Ash how he'd clutched at Forsythe's arms, how he'd melted and gasped and arched when the man had kissed him like a tempest. And that tempest seemed to sweep over him in a rush of body heat as Forsythe brushed past him, sliding body to body in the narrow space for a moment before breaking free, voice drifting over his shoulder. "And I think you rather find my age appealing."

Heat suffused Ash's face and crawled down his neck. He stared after him. "…Forsythe!"

Pausing to hold the bathroom door, Forsythe turned a dark glance over his shoulder. "For my wisdom and experience, of course."

"I…" Ash gulped, straggling after him—then scowled, resisting the urge to fucking *shove* that broad back. "Of course."

Asshole, he muttered mentally.

Fucking *demon.*

ASH HAD BARELY SETTLED AT his desk and pulled the

laptop up on a new email with the meeting minutes—Ms. Vernon had been the only person besides Forsythe in the room *not* grilling him—for his review when his cellphone buzzed in his pocket.

He fished it out and winced at Andrew's name on the text preview. He flashed a guilty glance at Forsythe, but the man was fixed on his own laptop, typing rapidly, long fingers elegant on the keys in efficient drumbeat notes. Ash swiveled his chair away a little, then swiped his unlock code and read the text.

Hey haven't seen you for a few days

Followed by:

Wanna hook up tonight

Ash scrunched his nose. Just yesterday he might have said *yes* in a heartbeat. Andrew was easy, uncomplicated, handsome in a sort of overly tanned Ken doll way, their relationship completely shallow. They weren't even friends, not really—not like Vic, whom Ash had known since boarding school. Andrew was just another bratty rich kid who always said yes, didn't ask questions, didn't get personal, and didn't want Ash to stick around until morning. They were a habit for each other, when a hookup was too much work.

And for some reason, the idea of Andrew made Ash feel bizarrely ill.

Maybe because Andrew didn't taste like embers and

calm, quiet command.

With a surreptitious glance for Forsythe, Ash dropped his phone back in his pocket and settled back to work.

And ignored his phone when it buzzed again ten minutes later—and again not long after, before the ringtone chimed. He grit his teeth and reached into his pocket to mute his phone without even looking at the screen. Even if it wasn't Andrew, he didn't have time for Vic right now. Or for some tabloid reporter who'd managed to get his number. Or for demanding phone calls from business partners he had no idea what to say to. He had an entire fucking mess on his desk with a contractor build dispute and some labor union threatening a lawsuit when he didn't know a goddamned fucking thing about New York unions and labor laws, and of course Forsythe chose now to be bizarrely silent and withdrawn instead of a know-it-all telling him everything before he even asked—

A polite knock came at the door, muted through the heavy slab of slate. Forsythe's rapid-fire typing stopped; Ash glanced up as the door swung open. Ms. Vernon peered around almost tentatively, her warmth subdued, her dark skin subtly ashen.

"Mr. Harrington?" she ventured…and that was when Ash's stomach sank. She never called him that. And she met his eyes, her own dark and aching, as she continued, "…Ashton. I…it's the hospice center. They've been trying to reach you. I've got them on line two."

For a moment Ash couldn't breathe. His lungs were stone, and he couldn't move, couldn't speak, everything choking inside him.

Then Forsythe's hand curled against his wrist, clasping it against the arm of the chair—and Ash realized he was gripping at the leather in a white-knuckled grasp with both hands. But that touch seemed to free him from his frozen spell. Mouth dry, he managed to rasp, "Thank you, Ms. Vernon."

She nodded, offering him a wan smile, and slipped out, pulling the door tactfully closed. Ash stared at the desk phone, at the red light for line two, that gentle hand on his wrist the only thing keeping him from bolting. He lifted his gaze to Forsythe's; Forsythe nodded, silent encouragement, and somehow it felt as though through that touch he bled his strength into Ash, giving him the courage to pick up the receiver from its cradle and tap the button to take the call.

"Hello?" he croaked.

"Mr. Ashton Harrington?" an authoritative, not unkind female voice said.

"Y-yes, that's me."

"This is Nurse Failia Hawkins as Fairways Hospice.

It…it's about your father." Her voice softened. "There's no easy way to say this."

Ash closed his eyes. His throat knotted, trying to strangle his voice, his breath. "He's not…?"

"Not yet," she assured him, yet the next words were anything but reassuring. "But his vitals are low. It may not be long, if you can come."

Ash nodded—then cursed himself. Like she could fucking see him. "I…I…" He had to speak. Had to keep himself under control. Had to be the adult here, and act like he knew how to handle any of this at all. "I'm coming right now. Thank you," he managed.

Then dropped the phone back in its cradle before he could hear her response.

That hand on his wrist tightened. He opened his eyes, staring at Forsythe.

"Forsythe…"

"I'll bring the car around immediately," Forsythe promised, that deep, rolling voice soft with understanding.

"Thank you," Ash repeated numbly.

Forsythe said nothing.

But at first he didn't leave, either.

He only shifted that grip on Ash's wrist to cover his hand, enveloping it in his own, resting there for a moment of reassurance as though that massive hand had the strength and surety to hold Ash's crumbling world into place.

Then he stood and, with one lingering look, left Ash alone.

Alone and free to curl in his chair, burying his face in his thighs with a grieving, miserable keen.

HE'D MANAGED TO SPEND HIMSELF in dry sobs by the time Forsythe came back up for him; Ash refused to walk outside for the brief few steps from the tower to the car with his face streaked with tears, not when he'd probably be giving a hovering reporter a feature shoot that would further embarrass his father's name. He was grateful for Forsythe's rather obvious shifts to place his body between Ash and any particularly open lines of sight, as he escorted him to the car.

And he was grateful to Forsythe for not expecting anything of him, not even a single word, as he drove them through New York City's busy traffic and into the quieter, winding suburban roads leading out to Fairways Hospice Center.

Set against low, unassuming hills of well-tended green and made up of multiple private little cottages scattered around the main building, Fairways didn't look like somewhere where people were dumped off to die in peace. Every last one of those cottages was just a cozy little mausoleum.

The bodies inside just didn't yet know they were dead.

The gate guard waved them through after checking Ash's ID. Forsythe parked in the main lot, let Ash out of the back of the car, then hung back, clearly waiting. Ash stared across the almost violently green grass—so offensively bright and *alive*—toward his father's cottage, tucked away behind a few others. He'd only been here once, the first day after the collapse, and suddenly lawyers were talking about living wills and making decisions that flew over Ash's head like a cloud of buzzing gnats while he watched his father be transferred from a gurney to a quilt-laden bed, unmoving and barely breathing, tubes shoved up his nose and down his throat.

Ash had wanted to scream at him, so much. Wanted to scream because his father had *planned* for this, so efficiently that the second he collapsed this machine kicked into place ejecting Calvin Harrington into this retirement home for the dead and kidnapping Ash into a kingship he'd never asked for, never wanted.

And right now, Ash didn't trust that if he walked in there he wouldn't start screaming anyway.

"Young Master," Forsythe urged gently.

"I know," Ash said around the lump in his throat. "I know. I just…need a second."

"Of course."

Ash stood there for long moments, staring across the grass, letting his eyes unfocus until he could only see the blue of sky and the dark hard line of trees seaming the earth to the clouds far distant. Like this, when the entire world was blurred, the wet film of tears masking his eyes didn't have to be real.

It was just an illusion of the skyline, the strange dreaming curve of the world.

He stayed like that for several long breaths, until he could inhale without tasting salt and his chest didn't feel like a hollow death's rattle.

Then he set off across the paved walks cutting the grass into puzzle pieces, Forsythe an ever attentive shadow in his wake.

All was silent inside his father's cottage, save for that awful wheeze of the respirator—the curtains drawn, the lights dimmed as if already in mourning, the room so tastefully and lushly appointed it looked like a funeral parlor with his father already laid out in state for the wake—if not for the slow, shallow, almost invisible rise and fall of his chest. A nurse in floral patterned scrubs hovered over the bed, adjusting Calvin Harrington's breathing tube with gentle hands, but as Ash eased the door open and slipped into that terrible rotting death-smell mixed with the desperate scent of cleansers and fresh-cut flowers, she excused herself with an almost deferential nod.

Then the door closed, and it was only Ash, Forsythe…and the thin wisp of flesh in the bed that he used to call his father.

He almost didn't recognize Calvin Harrington. His father had looked weak and frail when he'd seen him just a few days ago, but now…now he was almost nonexistent, so translucent Ash imagined he could see the rusty color of the sheets shining through his body. His bones were knobs threatening to punch through filmy parchment skin, his cheeks sunken in until the outlines of his teeth pressed against his flesh, his eyes recessed so deep they were just pits, shadows, in his skull.

That wasn't his father.

That was a skeleton trying to crawl free from its flesh sack, a nightmare trying to come to life.

He still remembered his father standing tall in elegant suits, powerful yet with a casual ease that put people off their guard around him, his graying hair and weathered hands seeming to speak of both wisdom and temperance, kindness and surety. Whatever life had filled that man had fled, leaving behind only this husk like a shed skin.

Ash took one step closer to the bed, then stopped, rooted to the spot. His mouth twisted and trembled in this awful, hurtful way that he couldn't stop, screwing up no matter how he tried to control it, and a terrible bark coughed up his throat only to catch against his palms as he clapped them over his mouth. Everything turned stinging and hot and runny, colors blurring together until he couldn't see that terrible thing in the bed anymore. He couldn't see anything but the colors of heartbreak, melting and running down the inner walls of his chest.

"Young Master?" Forsythe asked softly—tactful inquiry, unspoken question:

Shall I go?

He knew what Forsythe was doing. What he was asking. If Ash wanted to be alone with this; if he wanted to save his pride.

All he wanted was for this to not be happening. Not now. Not yet. Not *ever*.

And he turned, before he could stop himself…and flung himself against Forsythe's chest, gripping up handfuls of his suit jacket.

"Forsythe," he gulped out, burying his face against his broad chest, every breath coming out on a sob. "*Brand.*"

After several moments, Brand's arms came around him. Brand was so *large*, this fortress of a man, and with those arms around him it felt like Ash was on the inside and the world was on the outside and if he just held on hard enough, Brand's bulk could wall the pain away. Brand enveloped him in solid, quiet, stable warmth, in the scents of cool earth and musky darkness that eased away the scents of death, and for just these moments Ash closed his eyes and let himself *hide*.

"I know, young Master," Brand murmured, that lilt to his voice gentle, his breaths stirring Ash's hair. "I know."

No matter how Ash tried, he couldn't stop crying. He'd cried so fucking much since that phone call, but every time he thought he'd emptied himself out some new reservoir of pain inside him punctured and bled out in a fresh wash of tears. Every time he'd cried alone, shoving away from anyone before they could see more than a few faint trickles of tears.

But Brand let him not be alone, in these moments.

And Ash clung to that, for what small comfort it was—until the flood finally slowed. Until he could breathe again without feeling like the stitches binding him whole would snap. Until he could find his voice, and not just another wretched, keening cry of pain. Taking several shaky breaths, he scrubbed his nose against his wrist, then curled his fingers in Brand's coat again and rested his cheek to his chest.

"Stay?" he whispered. "Stay with me."

"Of course," Brand answered—as if there could be no other answer.

Ash didn't resist, as Brand guided him to the deeply upholstered sofa positioned against the wall near the bed. Gently, Brand eased him down, then settled next to him with one heavy arm draped around Ash, holding him against his side. Ash leaned into him, biting his lip, forcing himself to look at the fragile shape of his father in the bed once more—then looking away again, whimpering and shaking his head in denial and hiding his face against Brand's side.

He would feel guilty for this later, knowing he had essentially bought the man's comfort and compassion, but right now he didn't have it in him to feel anything but the ache of impending loss—and relief that someone, anyone was here, rather than leaving him to face this alone.

Leaving him to stand vigil on his own, when every miniscule breath was like the second hand ticking down, down, down to the hour of his father's death.

He didn't know how long they sat there—the only sound the respirator, Ash's sniffles, and the strong, steady beat of Brand's heart against his cheek. Ash felt like something was building up inside him, something that would come out as a scream if he didn't wrench it down into something more tame, more sensible, pressing against the insides of his lips until he couldn't take it anymore and let it spill out in words.

"I don't know how to deal with this." His voice was a scratchy mess, an invasion on the almost sacramental stillness of this death-watch, and he winced, bowing his head, staring down at his knees. "I…I know it has to happen to everyone someday. We're not immortal. But you imagine this slow thing, you know? Every day they're a little bit less of themselves, and you have time to cope with them slipping away. Years of grains falling through the hourglass." He rubbed at his aching throat. "But for me…one moment he was there, and the next his hourglass was shattered with only a few grains left." His lips trembled, and he pressed them together, fighting against that warning of fresh tears and shaking his head. "It's too sudden."

"I know."

Something about the hush in Brand's voice, the edge to it, made Ash look up—but the man wasn't looking at him. He was staring at the bed, at Calvin Harrington, but his eyes were distant behind his glasses, green unfocused and far away, seeing other things.

"Forsythe…?"

Brand shook himself, then looked down at Ash. He looked almost confused for a moment, something strange flickering across his face, before he admitted, "My parents died when I was eight." He said it with the same blunt calm with which he said everything else—but those depthless eyes told a different story, strange and deep with unspoken thoughts, glimmering. “An automobile crash. I was the only survivor, save an older sister who wasn’t in the car that night.” He hesitated, lips parted in silence for long moments, before he continued, “As you said…too sudden. The hourglass, shattered.” His gaze strayed away from Ash once more, and he adjusted his glasses absently. “It changes your life in an instant.”

“I’m sorry.” As deeply as Ash ached…there was room in him to ache for Brand, too, he found. And he didn’t know what to do, so he did what felt right—and shifted to lean harder against Brand’s side, resting his head to his shoulder. “What…happened after that? If it’s okay for me to ask.”

Brand turned his head toward Ash; his cheek brushed warm against Ash’s hair. “I stopped up with my sister. She was a nanny for the Newcombs.”

“The Newcombs…? Vic’s parents?”

“One generation back, young Master.” A touch of amusement. “His grandparents. His father was one of my sister’s charges, for all that he was older than I at the time. The Newcombs were kind enough to allow her to take me in with no charge for room and board, so I learned to make myself useful around the house.” Brand shrugged lightly, powerful shoulders moving beneath the suit coat, shifting Ash's weight. "I found comfort, I think, in taking care of things. As if, if I took enough proper care, they would not be taken away from me."

Ash bit his lip. He didn't know what to say. Brand Forsythe was a stranger to him; over the past few days he'd managed to stitch himself into the fabric of Ash's life, but he'd put himself in a role as ubiquitous and yet colorless as furniture, as utensils.

These words—quietly, rawly, yet so freely given—made him a person, rich with life and color.

And Ash didn't know what to do with that, so he only curled his arms around Brand's arm, leaning in close, and listened.

"After a time," Brand continued softly, "it became natural. And when I was nineteen, a young Mr. Newcomb—lost much as you are, soon to be married with no idea what to do with an estate and an inheritance—offered me a formal position in the household."

"Doesn't that bother you?" Ash ventured. "Living for someone else, instead of for yourself?"

Brand smiled faintly. "What makes you think I don't live for myself?"

"I just…" Fumbling, Ash shook his head. "Isn't there anything else you've ever wanted?"

"Someone to care for." And then those darkened eyes were on him again—locking on him, holding him, drawing him in until the terrible mausoleum of a room fell away and there was only an unspoken question swimming in eyes as dark a green as a still deep pond at night, glimmering beneath firefly-light. "Nearly everyone I loved was taken from me in an instant, young Master Ashton. Is it so strange that what I should want most in the world is to keep the people I care for comfortable and safe?"

"But…how can your care for people who are paying you to do it?"

"Sometimes it is not about the money." That warm, reassuring arm tightened around him. "Do you think I would not care for you if you did not pay me?"

Ash's breaths caught. He—fuck, he was too emotional right now, and this…this was hitting him hard, gutting him in ways he couldn't handle. He ducked his head, staring down at his lap. "…I think you wouldn't be here if I wasn't paying you. It's your job, and you can't care for someone you've known for three days."

"I came to you under terms of employment, yes," Brand countered. "Money would not have been enough to make me stay. Not even for these few short days."

Something in that rich, velvety voice, something compelling and soft, drew Ash to look up at him again. He didn't *understand* Brand Forsythe, when something seemed laid bare and naked on that elegant face—but it was written in a language Ash didn't know how to read.

"Forsythe…?"

"Brand," he corrected softly.

"…Brand." He swallowed back the lump in his throat. "I don't—"

"…A-Ash…?" drifted across the room—low, creaking, whispery as a ghost.

But familiar as the sound of Ash's own voice, cutting through him with a knife's keen edge.

He jerked his head up. "Dad…?" His heart stopped, then started again.

His father's eyes were open.

His eyes were open, and he was struggling to speak, coughing and choking around the respirator tube feeding down his throat.

"*Dad!*"

Ash shot to his feet, flinging himself toward the bed, fumbling at the thing in his father's throat, fingers clumsy, his breaths coming so short and tight he might as well be choking on the goddamned tube himself. It was suddenly too noisy in the room, devices beeping and shrilling and clanking in alarm, the sounds crushing in on Ash and ramping his panic to shrieking levels. Then Brand was there—nudging him gently out of the way, his skilled hands gripping the respirator tube, easing it back, slipping it past his father's lips. Calvin Harrington coughed, his entire body racking, jerking, before he sank to the bed, breathing in deep, heaving, but clean gasps. Ash gripped the edge of the bed rail desperately, blurring beads of wetness turning his vision into burning prisms, silently begging this wasn't it—the last moment before his father slipped away.

But his father only settled against the bed, blinking muzzily, breathing hard until it began to slow. His gaze darted around, then landed on Ash, a bit cloudy but *there*, life and presence in dark blue eyes shadowed by the tangle of iron-gray hair falling across his brow.

"...Ash," he rasped, as if confirming something to himself. His voice was thready, weak, but God, he was talking, making *sense*— "Where...am I? And why—" He broke off in another cough, hollow and deep, but brief. "Wh-why...do I feel like I've been hit by a truck?"

Ash couldn't help a bark of laughter that was more of a sob as his eyes spilled over, hot trails scorching down his cheeks. "You're in the hospice center *you* fucking arranged because you didn't tell me you had cancer, and you've been in a coma for almost a fucking week."

His father blinked quizzically. "Oh," he said, rather blankly. "That sounds about right. Explains why you're looking at me like I was dying."

Ash grinned. He couldn't help it. He was fucking terrified, afraid his father was about to close his eyes for the last time right now after a few final words, but God he was *awake* and talking and lucid, and that had to be something, right?

"You *were* dying, you dick."

Calvin Harrington let out a measured sigh, then shifted himself subtly, as if testing his body, before settling. "…not yet, I think. Not if I get a choice. Also, your language is atrocious." Then he frowned, wrinkling his nose. "Do I have to stay here?"

"I see where young Master Ashton gets it from," Brand said flatly.

Calvin Harrington's gaze darted past Ash to Brand. "Who are you?"

"The valet."

His father arched one dark brow. "So the company's still in one piece."

"Hey!" Ash spluttered, then laughed weakly and scrubbed at his cheeks. "Fuck. Barely. You dumped a lot on me, Dad. Including, you know, fucking *dying*."

With an amused sound, his father fixed a wry look on Ash, gaze warm, tired. "And I don't doubt you had it in you to handle it." His emaciated shoulders bunched beneath his pajamas as he gathered his arms under himself. "But I think the obituary's a bit premature. If you don't mind—"

Ash realized he was struggling to get up—and too

weak, but still trying, his entire body straining as if he'd snap himself like a twig in his stubbornness. Swearing, Ash gripped his shoulders gently, trying to push him back down.

"Lie down," he said firmly—but his father only scowled and struggled against him weakly. "Dad, lie down!" Goddammit, he didn't know how to do this without hurting his father, and he loosened his grip, flinging Brand a helpless look. "Brand—"

Eyes glinting almost in warning, Brand leaned over the bed and gently pressed his the flats of his palms to Calvin Harrington's shoulders, holding him down with careful but inexorable strength. "Go fetch the doctor," he said firmly. "Someone should be here by now, and they are being extremely lax in their duties. I'll watch your father."

Nodding quickly, breathlessly, Ash retreated from the bed and darted for the door—but not without catching his father's sardonically irritated voice drifting after him.

"From my son's keeper to my jailer," Calvin Harrington said. "And I don't even know your name."

"Brand Forsythe."

"The Newcombs' man."

"Young Master Ashton's man, now," Brand corrected.

"I see," was all his father said—before Ash ducked

from the room and pelted across the grass, his heart pumping furiously as he ran for the main building.

Because he was afraid if he wasn't fast enough, if he didn't find the doctor and bring her back to tell him for sure his father would be okay…

The man would slip away, and Ash wouldn't even be there to see him go.

Chapter Six

BRAND FORSYTHE DID NOT LIKE being useless.

But that was how he felt, as he stood against the wall in an unobtrusive place and watched as the elder Master Harrington was bundled into a wheelchair by attentive nurses. The man was a fragile bundle of sticks, clearly exhausted, drowsing and listing in his chair. Even Brand was worn out; it was almost dawn, after a long night of extensive testing, examinations, monitoring, and negotiating with the facility staff and doctors. Were the patient anyone else but one of the richest men in New York, the elder Harrington likely would have been told to go to bed and wait until morning and normal hours.

But Calvin Harrington wanted to leave, despite his frail and weakened state—and so Calvin Harrington intended to leave, even with his son watching him with worried eyes and fretting his hands, clearly torn between urging his father back into bed and wanting to get him out of this place.

Frankly, Brand doubted the wisdom of this. The elder Harrington looked as if he would collapse again at any moment, and his sudden return to consciousness didn't necessarily indicate he was actually healthy, or his prognosis was any better.

But it wasn't Brand's place to say. Nor was he here to attend to Harrington the elder.

His concern was Harrington the younger, and at the moment Ashton looked as if he was on the verge of collapse himself. Hollows of exhaustion darkened his eyes, his pale, gold-tinged skin turned so ashen his pink mouth stood out like a bruise, his posture heavy and slumped. He'd tossed his coat off hours ago, leaving him pacing in his trim, well-fitted waistcoat, an elegant and graceful figure despite his agitated tension. More than once he'd nearly started arguments with the doctors, with his father, with Brand, before snapping his mouth shut and subsiding to restless silence full of simmering, muted glances. Resentment.

If his young Master didn't collapse, Brand thought, he might well explode.

And there was nothing Brand could do about it—and he hated it.

Ash was too keyed up, not to mention focused on his father; the one time Brand had attempted to soothe and calm him, Ash had turned on him with a snarl and pulled away in a way that shouldn't hurt as much as it did. Brand…did not feel right, at the moment. Something inside him felt strange and shaken, and it was tied directly to the hot-eyed, impetuous young man currently hovering over his father's wheelchair while the nurses packed Calvin Harrington's suitcase.

Brand was not accustomed to talking about himself, he thought. His life had been spent with the same family; his sister was still head housekeeper at the Newcomb estate in Liverpool. When one served with the same family since childhood, there was little need to disclose details that everyone knew as intimately as their own entangled life stories. And Brand…Brand was not prone to relationships. Not when few relationships could survive the level of service and attentive dedication required of a valet. The few dalliances he engaged in to explore physical urges and learn his own desires? Meaningless. They required no personal disclosure, no attachment, no loyalty.

They were nothing against the devotion he saved for his Masters, young and old alike.

And so Brand had never had occasion to speak of himself this way. To tell another his life, his thoughts, his feelings, and have them look up at him with wide, vulnerable eyes that seemed to need those bits of himself, vouchsafed and precious, to offer some anchor point in an unmoored world. He didn't think Ashton would ever understand how shaken it had left Brand, to speak of such things and have his young Master lay his head to his shoulder and simply, quietly take them into himself.

He didn't think Ashton understood many things, but Brand doubted the wisdom of telling him. Not when, at the moment, if he chose to act…he might do something reckless.

Like pick Ashton up in his arms right here, right now, in front of his father and the nurses alike—and carry him from this place and home, so that Brand could force him to rest.

It was setting his teeth on edge, watching Ash reel with exhaustion and be able to do nothing about it. To leave Ashton's needs unattended, to stand here a stiff and useless statue, was anathema to Brand's very existence. And if this took much longer, he didn't know if he would be able to control himself.

Ash glanced up from watching the nurses and caught Brand's eye, before offering a wan smile and looking away again. Brand grit his teeth, hands slowly clenching into fists behind his back.

Ten more minutes, and he was putting an end to this whether Calvin Harrington was ready to depart or not.

He closed his eyes, taking a slow, measured breath and attempting to settle the snarling agitation under his skin. This…wasn't like him. He was being irrational. Unreasonable. *Possessive.* He wasn't even sure why, yet young Master Ashton…

There was something *in* Ashton. A quiet and aching need, a wordless plea that seemed to have gone unanswered for years. A question, searching in those dark blue eyes, and raising a buried and hungry thing inside Brand that whispered an answer.

Even after he had told Ashton exactly what it meant to him to serve…no, he didn't think the young Master understood.

Brand was not whole unless he was shepherd to a lamb, and right now every soft and tender and vulnerable thing about Ashton Harrington was begging for Brand to protect him, possess him, do for him so that he might never need do for himself again. That hungry thing inside Brand needed someone to *depend* on him. He'd never wholly understood it—if it was about care or about control or about something else.

He only knew that it roused with a fierce and demanding need to young Master Ashton, in ways it had never roused to anyone else.

"There," the nurse said, and snapped the suitcase closed. Her smile was skeptical, her voice dubious, but she remained pleasant and polite, expression almost frozen. "All ready. Your checkout paperwork is finished, Mr. Harrington, so you're free to go. We'll forward your records of care here to your regular physician."

Calvin Harrington only made a tired sound, nodding

forward in his chair. Brand stepped forward without thinking to take the handles of the wheelchair, but Ash shoved his body in the way with a fierce look.

"I've got it," he hissed, and took the handles to ease the wheelchair forward.

Brand inclined in a bow. "As my young Master wishes," he said, and exchanged a nod with the nurse as he took the suitcase, instead.

As long as they were getting out of here and getting Ash home, he didn't care.

They made a quiet procession, moving across the dew-dampened sidewalks in the chill predawn gloom, the sky that strange luminous shade of washed-out night that came when the stars had set but the sun was just beginning to whisper golden morning-song. Ash pushed the wheelchair almost too slow, as if he was afraid of pitching his father forward, but before long they were in the lot—where a sudden bright flash nearly blinded the night.

A camera.

Ash jerked, flinching; Calvin Harrington didn't even respond. Brand hissed under his breath, positioning his body to shield the Harringtons as he pulled the back door of the Mercedes open.

"Get in," he said, pressing his hand to the small of Ash's back.

Ash balked. "But Dad—"

"I will handle your father," Brand said, as another camera flash went off in the dark, from somewhere beyond the bushes ringing the main drive. "*Get in.*"

Ash watched him with doubtful eyes for one moment longer, then ducked into the car. Brand bent to carefully bundle Calvin Harrington into his arms, lifting him from the wheelchair and easing him as quickly as he could into the backseat without jostling him when he felt as though he were made of straw, thin and ready to snap. Harrington stirred enough to fix him with an irritable look, but seemed to understand the necessity when he kept his mouth shut and didn't struggle as Brand buckled him in, then slammed the door shut.

A few more flashes came as Brand folded the wheelchair and stowed it in the boot along with the elder Harrington's suitcase. He shut the boot, straightened, and flung a searching look toward the source of those bright bursts of light. He couldn't make anyone out, but he knew they were *there*.

Bloody vultures.

He slid into the driver's seat, started the car, and backed the Mercedes out of the drive. The drive back into the city was as silent as a funeral march, and when he glanced in the rear view mirror he found the elder Harrington asleep, Ash staring out the window with a brooding and vacant stare, the faint gold of sunrise washing him in the colors of whatever memories haunted his heavy brow.

It was nearly seven by the time Brand turned the Mercedes in at the estate and pulled it through the roundabout. An unfamiliar car was in the drive, a little blue Prius with a rental sticker on the bumper. He frowned, but busied himself with helping Calvin Harrington out of the car and into his wheelchair. The moment the elder Harrington was safely settled, Ash took the wheelchair again with possessive insistence.

Brand sighed, gathered the suitcase from the boot, and followed his young Master up the walk.

Yet before they reached the front door, it opened; a woman stepped out, small and plump and trim in a neat pencil skirt and stylish leather boots and a slouching cashmere sweater. Her graying black hair was swept up out of her amber face, but a few tendrils drifted across her brow, swaying with her rushed, pattering steps as she came tumbling down the steps and pulled Ashton into her arms.

"*Ash,*" she said softly, her accent making a lyrical sigh of his name.

Ashton went stiff, arms held out from his side, eyes wide; they darted to Brand as if pleading with him for help, before he finally creaked into motion and wrapped his arms awkwardly around the woman.

"…okaasan?" he croaked, while Calvin Harrington stirred, lifting his head, staring at the woman with haunted eyes.

"…Amiko?"

Ah. So this was the runaway mother who had made such headlines over a decade ago, when she'd publicly abandoned Calvin Harrington and her son to return home to Japan. Brand had been in the UK at the time, but the scandals of American new royalty tended to make even the gossip rags back in the old country; he'd thought little of it at the time, the stories sensationalized to make her sound quite terrible indeed. It was hard to see the salacious rumors in the warm, smiling woman who stood on the red stone cobbles and hugged her son so tightly.

It was easy to see much of her in Ash's features, though, and in a certain softness to his mannerisms—but little else, as if her well-known departure had left him devoid of an entire half of his cultural heritage, his mannerisms and speech so entirely Western. Brand wondered if Ash ever felt the absence. If he ever felt disconnected from himself. If—

If perhaps Brand should stop fixating on his young Master, before the ache within him grew too overwhelming to bear.

If he were to be entirely honest with himself, it was disturbing. This sudden, sharp sense of need, attraction, possession. And no doubt, were his young Master to know of the dark and covetous thing rearing its head inside Brand…Ashton Harrington would be more than disturbed. He would be incensed, possibly even frightened, when such craving bordered on obsession.

And it made no *sense*.

Brand forced his mind back onto his responsibilities, and dutifully hung back, waiting until the Harringtons finished their conversation. Ashton's mother pulled back enough to look at him, smiling and cupping his cheek.

"You look too much like your father when you make that face, little Ash," Amiko said, then laughed. "Both of you, please close your mouths. And stop staring, you're embarrassing me." Her sharp black eyes suddenly snapped to Brand, curious and inquisitive. "Who is this?"

"Brand Forsythe, Ms. Harrington." Brand dipped briefly, bowing his head. "Personal valet to the younger Master Harrington."

Amiko answered with a similar bow, almost mocking him with the laughter in her eyes. "It's a pleasure. Though it's Miss Arakawa now."

"Apologies for the indiscretion."

"*Amiko,*" Calvin Harrington repeated, raw and desperate, staring at Amiko Arakawa like a man in the desert shown an oasis of water.

Amiko regarded Calvin Harrington thoughtfully,

before something softened in her eyes—something Brand couldn't quite read, before she sighed and rested her hands on her hips. "Don't you start. You're the one who let me go," she said with fond exasperation—then nudged Ash out of the way and took the handles of the wheelchair. "Now come, I can already see you're tiring yourself out."

The elder Harrington craned back so that he never took his eyes from the pert little woman fussing over him, even as she wheeled him up the walk—and deftly tipped the wheelchair up the short front steps and into the house.

Leaving Brand and Ash alone, standing on the walk and staring after them.

"I…am not certain I understand what just took place," Brand said.

Ash shook himself, running a hand through his hair and spiking it up in a tired thatch of black everywhere. "My parents have a really complicated relationship," he said, drifting closer to Brand. His warmth was a thing like soft prickles, reaching out to touch Brand as he stopped, brushing almost arm to arm. "Dad still loves Mom. She still loves him too, just…not the same way. So she comes, she stays for a little while…and then she runs again." He shrugged. "I think he holds on to her too hard, and it makes her run away. But they're still friends. She cares enough to come see him when he's sick." A weary smile flitted across his lips. "Sometimes love doesn't work the way you want it to, but it doesn't have to turn into hate."

Brand lingered on that smile, on the ache in it that went deeper than just this night.

And how much of your mother's son are you, then?

If someone tried to hold on to you too hard, would you run?

"That was a remarkably astute observation," Brand murmured.

Ash snorted. "You don't have to say 'remarkably.'" At Brand's flat look, he made an indignant sound. "You don't! I'm not that much of an oblivious little shit!"

Brand bit his tongue and held back a smile. "Far be it from me to disagree with my young Master."

Ash eyed him sidelong, the faint tug at his lips almost coy. He leaned over enough to bump Brand's arm with his shoulder. "Why do I pay you?"

"You could stop."

"Mm." Ash straightened, settling once more, hands in his pockets as he tipped his head back to look up at the brightening sky. "Would you leave if I did?"

"I haven't decided yet," Brand answered, and Ash grinned.

"Let me know when you do," he said, and tossed his head toward the house. "Come on. Let's go get Dad settled now that he's back home."

"Getting Calvin Harrington settled" mostly involved Brand leaving the suitcase in the elder Harrington's suite of rooms before both he and Ashton were bullied out by Amiko Arakawa, leaving them both standing bemused outside the door to Harrington's rooms while it closed in their faces.

Brand glanced at Ashton. Ashton looked back at him, then shrugged ruefully. "That's my mom," he said, and that was the end of that.

At least, this morning, Brand didn't have to fight Ashton to usher him into a shower and dress him afterward. If anything Ashton was almost too docile, withdrawn into himself, the haze of exhaustion a near palpable cloud around him. Brand had to avert his eyes as Ashton began stripping down without a second thought, just a moment's impropriety letting Brand linger on the smooth curves of pale golden shoulders dotted with sun-freckles like spatters of cinnamon, begging to be bitten.

Before he fixed his gaze on the wall beyond Ashton's shoulder—and didn't look back until his young Master had once more stolen Brand's bathroom and was safely in the shower, the glass fogged nearly opaque with steam.

The urge to *look*, to devour Ashton with a single

glance and imprint the image of his lissome, willowy frame on Brand's memory, pulled magnetic in his blood.

He excused himself to the kitchen, and busied himself making the young Master's breakfast.

By the time he returned with a tray and the morning paper, Ashton had extricated himself from the shower, wrapped himself in a towel, and dressed in his underwear and socks. He smelled of soap and shower-warmed skin and something sweetly enticing, as Brand leaned close to slip him into his suit. There was a quiet pleasure in the way Ash lifted his delicate chin for him as Brand knotted his tie and settled it smoothly against his chest; a certain satisfaction in how Ash's pulse jumped against Brand's touch as his knuckles grazed his throat; a certain allure in how Ash cocked his head with his lips parted as if waiting in invitation for Brand to rediscover the soft melted candy taste of him, the sweetness and trembling of his mouth. It meant nothing, he knew.

Yet he took his small pleasures where he could.

That, too, was part of being a valet.

Ash settled quietly onto the edge of Brand's bed to eat; apparently Brand's room was Ashton's as well, now, as long as Ashton meant to make use of his shower. Keeping his smile to himself, Brand retrieved the newspaper he'd fetched from the front stoop and laid it next to his plate, unobtrusively folded to the finance section.

"Share prices are up this morning," he murmured.

"Because Dad's out of hospice," Ash said dryly, glancing disinterestedly at the numbers. "Not because of anything I did. Those reporters move fast."

"They do."

Ash fell still, toying a toast point between his fingers, silent, gaze unfocused. "It's been a long night," he murmured, shoulders sagging. "A long week. And it's only Wednesday."

"It's Thursday, young Master," Brand pointed out, and Ash flinched.

"Seriously?" He grimaced. "Fuck. And I still have to go to the office, don't I?"

"Your father is still incapacitated. You are still the head of Harrington Steel." But Brand relented, leaning over to pick up the napkin from Ashton's tray and dabbing at a crumb at the corner of his mouth. "You can nap in the car."

Ash glanced at him quickly, that startled wide-eyed look he had when Brand did something he didn't expect, like a deer caught out in the woods by a hunter's straying light. His eyes widened further still as Brand drew the napkin away—and gave in to temptation, for just a moment. He let his thumb glide over the soft, plump bow of Ashton's lower lip, feeling how it gave to the touch, its warm, plush, velvety texture. To wipe away another crumb, of course…yet for a moment his gut went tight and hot as he caught the faintest hitch of Ashton's breaths, before Brand forced himself to remember what was proper and pull away as if he had done nothing.

Ashton stared at him, brows knitted together, before he lowered his eyes, exhaling heavily. "…yeah." He put the toast point down, uneaten, and took a long sip of his coffee before standing, smoothing his fingers over his suit coat. "I need to do something first." Then he paused, giving Brand a strange look, before looking away. "…alone. Sorry."

That stung, oddly. Brand parted his lips, then closed them again and bowed his head in acquiescence. "Of course, young Master. I shall wait for you at the car."

"Are you even safe to drive?" Ash asked. "Aren't you tired?"

"I have gone longer without sleep."

When Ash said nothing, Brand lifted his head, meeting dark eyes turned soft with worry—and Brand's heart gave a low and quiet beat, stumbling and irregular. Was his young Master actually *concerned* for him?

"Maybe we'll call it early today," Ash murmured.

"We will stop," Brand said firmly, "when the work for the day is done."

A laugh broke through Ash's tired apathy. "You like

bossing me around a little too much, Brand."

"Do you really mind it?"

"No." Ash's laughter faded into a smile, small and thoughtful and withdrawn and almost, dare he say, flirtatious. "Not really." Then he laughed again and bumped Brand with his elbow, before turning and striding from his room with a wave over his shoulder. "See you in a bit, Brand," he called back.

Leaving Brand alone, looking after him…

And wondering things he had no business wondering.

No business wondering at all.

ASH STOOD OUTSIDE THE DOOR to his father's suite and wondered why he was afraid to knock.

He could probably count the number of times he'd been in these rooms in the past twenty-three years on one hand, and wouldn't even need every finger on both hands to count how many times he'd been in the adjoining offices.

"I can see your shadow under the door," Calvin Harrington called through dryly, and Ash's heart jumped. "Your mother's in the kitchen, if you're looking for her."

Closing his eyes, Ash breathed in deep—and almost

wished for Brand's steadying presence here to give him courage, but fuck…he had to do this himself. No one could push his orbit into intersecting with his father's but himself.

He just hoped he wasn't about to push them into a collision, just because he was trying to…to…

He didn't even know what he was trying to do.

Be *present*, maybe.

Not something he'd ever really been good at.

He opened his eyes, squared his shoulders, and pushed the door open. "I'm not looking for Mom," he said. "I'm looking for you."

Calvin Harrington's rooms were simple, utilitarian, his furniture all chosen with a purpose, unlike the other, more opulently furnished rooms in the house; his bed was a small and simple walnut four-poster—and he was currently propped in it, changed into clean pajamas and nearly buried in quilts, a move that had Amiko Arakawa's handiwork all over it. He looked tired, but *better*; as if, in his own bed instead of that hospice bed, he was still a living man and not just a ghost that had forgotten it was dead.

He'd been staring toward the open windows, but now Calvin Harrington turned a thoughtful look on Ash, tilting his head back against the headboard. "Ah? I thought you'd avoid me for at least a week," he said. His voice was no longer quite so weak and thready, picking up some of that ringing timbre that could command attention in a boardroom. “Direct. I’m impressed.”

Ash closed the door, then leaned against it, fidgeting his hands together behind his back. “Not so direct that I know what to say to you.”

“We never have known what to say to each other, have we.” His father smiled, lines seaming in his square, blunt-featured face, wrinkles that didn’t seem to have been there just weeks ago practically collapsing in on each other. “Don’t just hover there, son. Sit. Let’s talk.”

Biting his lip, Ash ventured closer, then stole the wicker chair next to the bed and sank down into it. “You’re looking better. Your color’s good.”

His father barked out a snorting laugh. “No, I’m just flushed with irritation. Your mother’s a tyrant.”

“Because she loves you.”

“I’m lucky she’s still willing to, aren’t I.” A touch of pain flickered across his father’s face, old and etched in deep. “Lucky you’re still willing to, as well.” His eyes cleared, focusing on Ash with a frank, clear regard. Even if his body was so clearly weak, his hands clutched and trembling against the quilts, those eyes were still sharp, intelligent, incisive. “We don’t know each other very well, do we, son?”

“No,” Ash admitted softly, and wondered why it hurt

to say something they'd both known their entire damned lives. "Not really."

"I shouldn't have waited this long to change that." Calvin Harrington's gaze was haunted, before it shuttered as he lowered his eyes to the shaking claws his hands made, bone white through skin. "It's odd how two strangers can love each other even when they don't really know each other, isn't it?"

"You're still my father." Ash smiled faintly. Only his father would find such a fucking backwards way to say he loved him, but God…had he ever, before this? "You haven't been bad to me."

"I haven't been overly good to you, either. Being too permissive out of guilt isn't the same as being good." Stick-thin shoulders heaved in a deep sigh. "I was young, when Amiko left. I didn't know what to do with a child on my own. And I thought…" Dark blue eyes pleaded for understanding. "I thought I might break you."

"I wasn't a toy you could break, Dad."

"I know that now." Calvin Harrington hesitated, his shriveled, dried lips working, before he murmured, "But I thought maybe it would be better if I sent you away where I couldn't damage you while I figured out what I was doing."

Ash shrugged stiffly. "Boarding school wasn't so bad. Met Vic. Made good friends."

"Lost a father."

The words hit like a slap—the sharp sting of days of terror, fear of losing someone he'd never really had and never really would if his father's last sands slipped through that broken hourglass. Ash swallowed, looking at his father tentatively. "Have I lost you?"

"I'd like to think not." His father pried a hand free from the duvet and held it out—clearly with great effort, his entire arm shaking as if the weight of the hand at the end of it was too much. "Do you think we could be good friends?"

Ash couldn't stand it. Couldn't stand that shaking hand, and he pushed himself forward quickly, taking it, steadying it, curling it in his own. His father's hand was so cool, his skin waxy and fragile, and Ash's throat tried to close; he wouldn't let it, making himself speak, making himself steady his voice.

"It could be a start," he forced out.

"It's a start I'd like." His father's hand tightened weakly on his. "If you'd like that, too."

"I…I think I would." *If we even have that kind of time*. The frailty of that hand in his own drove home how unlikely that was. Ash took a hitching breath, looking down at his father's hand, tracing his thumb over knuckles turned into sharp, bony spikes. He smiled weakly. "I don't resent you, Dad. I really don't. It's…not like we were ever that far apart. You're just…more like that awkward uncle I see on holidays or something." He laughed under his breath. "And Mom's that awkward aunt."

"Better than being that asshole who shipped you off to boarding school and forgot you."

"I stopped calling you that before I spent four years fucking my way through college on your dime."

His father laughed, sharp and startled—then broke into raw, rough coughs, doubling forward, his hand tightening convulsively on Ash's until the finger-points of his bones dug into Ash's knuckles painfully. Panic laced through Ash, binding him tight in its coils, and he leaned forward, reaching helplessly.

"Oh—oh fuck, are you okay?"

Calvin Harrington held up his free hand to forestall him. He hacked a few more times, then rasped, "I'm fine. I'm fine." He pressed his hand to his chest, then took a few more deep breaths. "Just need to rest, that's all."

Ash sank back into his chair, then realized just how tight he was holding his father's hand and eased his grip with an apologetic wince. "Are you sure? Can I get anything for you?"

"If I let you, your mother would be mortally offended." His father smiled faintly. "It's fine, son. And I think I'm keeping you from work." He flicked his gaze over Ash. "You wear that suit well."

"I feel like a little boy in Daddy's clothes. I think I need a few more years to grow into it."

"I think you wear it just fine your own way."

Ash searched his father's face, realization sinking in with a heavy and somber weight. "…you're never coming back to Harrington Steel, are you."

"No, son," Calvin Harrington said regretfully. "I'm sorry to throw this at you without preparing you…but it's yours, now. I…do you hate me for that?"

"No." Ash dragged a smile up from somewhere and patted his father's hand, cradling it in both of his own. "I've always known it would be mine one day. I've always accepted that, I…I even wanted it one day, when I was ready. I just wasn't expecting to have to be ready so soon."

"Life never goes according to plan." His father's tight grip loosened—then slipped away, fingers slipping from between Ash's. "Go, son. That valet of yours is waiting for you, no doubt."

The thought of Brand made a faint flush heat beneath Ash's collar. He almost wanted to ask…but…fuck, they didn't really have that kind of relationship, did they? Where he could say *hey Dad my valet kissed me and let me sleep in his bed and held me while I cried, and I get kind of funny feelings when he does certain things.*

Yeah. No.

Hard pass on that conversation.

So he only shrugged, pushing himself to his feet. "I'd better go before he has an aneurysm. He's a fucking drill sergeant."

"I'm sure he is." Calvin Harrington chuckled, then trailed off, eyeing Ash thoughtfully. "You know you can tell me anything, don't you, son?"

"Like you told me about having bone cancer?"

It fell off Ash's tongue without thinking, and he flinched as if he'd cut himself with the barbed edges. Fuck. Fuck, he hadn't meant—

His father's face crumpled, then smoothed as he gathered himself with that classic Calvin Harrington dignity. "…fair. I deserved that."

"No, you didn't." Ash dragged his fingers through his hair. "I'm sorry. I just…"

"If there was anything you could have done, I'd have told you. When there was nothing…why burden you with it?" The sound of defeat in his father's voice was crushing. "I've tried so many treatments. I tried. I *fought*. I didn't just lie down and give up, son." He made a bitter sound. "But sometimes you fight with everything in you, and you still lose."

"What about a bone marrow transplant?" Ash pleaded.

"From who?" his father countered. "It has to be a

sibling or an exact match. I'm an only child."

"But I—"

"Likely wouldn't be a match, son." Calvin Harrington cut him off. "I wouldn't put you through that kind of pain to even ask."

"But Dad—"

"Ash." His mother's voice interrupted from behind, yanking him up short enough to choke the breath from him. "Let him rest."

Ash stared helplessly between his parents. These *strangers,* standing there making decisions over his head, asking him to be an adult and yet refusing to treat him like one while they just…just…

Gave up, without even letting him try.

He couldn't stay in here. He pressed his lips together, then turned away—not even looking at his father again, when he couldn't. Couldn't stand the entreaty in his eyes, or the pull on Ash's heart when no man who was nearly a stranger had the right to make him hurt this much.

He brushed past his mother, out into the hall—but stopped when she followed him, her soft hand falling gently between his shoulder blades. Hers was a touch that was more the echo of a memory than anything he *knew,* but it was enough to halt him in his tracks.

"So I'm your awkward aunt, am I?" she teased sadly.

"Yeah," he choked out, staring straight forward.

"Kinda."

"Ash." She pressed against his back, soft and gentle, and slipped her arms around him. He wasn't particularly tall, but she barely came up to his shoulders, her cheek laid against the nape of his neck. "You know I miss you, don't you?"

"I know."

"Honestly…I don't understand how you don't hate both me and your father."

"I guess when I'm right in the middle of my own young fuckups, I can't hate you for yours."

"You were never a fuckup." She tightened her hold, then gripped at him lightly, urging him with her touch around to face her, to look down into her smiling face and sad eyes. "How we handled what to do with you after our own mistakes? Hai. That was a mistake." She curled her knuckles to his cheek. "Anou…and then there came a point when…" She shook her head. "It seemed like you didn't even need us. And we didn't know how to fix that."

He looked down at her in silence. It was strange to see someone who looked so *much* like him, and yet her expressions were so different, her body language, like watching a stranger wear his face.

"Did you want me to need you?" he asked.

Her brows drew together. "I'm your mother, Ash."

"…yeah." He caught her hand, held it against his

cheek…then drew it away, letting go, retreating out of her reach. "I love you," he said. "I just…got used to not having you."

To not having anyone, he thought, as he walked away from her. And right back to…

Right back to Brand.

It was only natural, he told himself. Brand was waiting for him at the car anyway, and he had to drag himself back to Harrington Steel and fit himself into his father's place and try to make it mold around him somehow, someway, to make this last. Yet he couldn't stop the feeling of relief that bloomed in his chest, as he stepped out the front door of the house and found Brand waiting, leaning against the car, idly toying with his cufflinks. He'd found the time to change into a fresh suit, but he wasn't quite as crisp as normal, his hair a touch mussed, his buttons not quite perfect, his eyelids heavy with an exhaustion Ash understood when he felt it mirrored in his bones.

He liked Brand like this, he thought. It made him look more human.

Brand looked up as Ash approached, and straightened to reach for the passenger's side door—but subsided when Ash shifted to lean against the car next to him.

Silence held between them for long moments. Ash stared at the house. It looked like a show home to him, something people looked at but didn't live in. He wanted to change that, he thought. He wanted to…to not be his parents. These people who made a life and didn't live in it. He might not ever have kids of his own, but he just…

He wanted more than this, he realized.

This cardboard cutout of a life with no real connections. No real warmth. No real bonds that held humans together, instead of just occasionally crashing into each other when their orbits intersected.

He wanted the kind of gravity that pulled people together so hard they couldn't drift apart. Not the way his mother and father had.

And not with anyone caught as collateral damage in between.

He glanced at Brand; the man's eyes were impossible to read behind the glint of his glasses, but Ash thought for a moment Brand had been watching him, too. He traced the gilding of sunlight over the man's aquiline, elegant profile, then looked away again.

"They let him come home, but it's only a temporary reprieve, isn't it," he murmured. "He still has bone cancer. He's still dying. And it won't be long. All this means is he'll die here instead of in hospice. With his eyes open, instead of slipping away without even knowing what's happening."

Brand bowed his head, looking down, his lips set

pensively. "Young Master…do you wish for a comforting answer, or an honest one?"

"I don't even know." Ash laughed humorlessly. "Say whatever you feel like saying."

"It is his choice," Brand replied. "Everything up to this point has been his choice. There is little to do to change the consequences, now. There is only honoring his wishes, and making him comfortable."

The breath knocked from Ash's lungs. Whatever he'd thought Brand would say in that rolling, deeply inflected voice…it wasn't that. He'd…he'd wanted Brand to *fix* it, he realized. Wanted him to have some sort of practical solution like he always did, some perfect right answer.

Not…not *this*.

"But—" Ash struggled for words around his choking, halting breaths. "If I could—"

"It's not your decision, young Master Ashton," Brand said softly, reaching for him. "Sometimes you have to accept tha—"

Ash jerked free from the warm hand that fell on his arm. "Let me go," he bit off—then skittered back a few steps when Brand straightened, that hand still outstretched. Ash shook his head sharply, glaring at him. "No. Just…just…fuck, just go away. I need five minutes of my life without you breathing down the back of my neck." He couldn't stop the vicious, hateful torrent spilling past his lips—all his confusion and hurt and frustration condensed down into piercing bullets and spitting out of him at Brand. "I haven't had a fucking minute alone since I hired you. Just…if you're not going to help, just fucking leave me alone."

Ash spun on his heel, turning away. He didn't even know where he was going—just that he was running. Running away from Brand, from that confused, almost wounded look on the supposedly impenetrable man's face. Running away from the specter of death that hadn't just faded; it had only followed them home, and spread its wings over the Harrington house.

Running away from himself, when he was too useless to fix anything.

"Ashton!" Brand called, raw, almost desperate, but Ash wouldn't stop.

He just closed his eyes, closed his ears, and *ran.*

Chapter Seven

Brand stood helplessly in the drive, watching as Ashton vanished down the road. Everything in him wanted to chase him—to drag him back, to hold him here, to keep him safe.

But Ashton had said no, leaving Brand locked and frozen and not even sure what had happened or why he felt as if he'd been struck a violent and bone-shaking blow.

"He has my temper," a soft, gently accented voice said from behind him. "My fears, too."

Brand glanced over his shoulder. Amiko Arakawa leaned in the doorway of the house, watching him with a sort of melancholy amusement, though not unkind.

"Miss Arakawa…?"

"Amiko," she corrected wryly. "I've spent enough time in the West that I'm used to it." She pushed away from the door, descending the steps on light, delicate steps to stop before him, looking up at him assessingly. "Ash runs when he's afraid, Mr. Forsythe. Just like me. And he has quite a bit to fear, right now."

"I…" Brand curled his fists helplessly. "I am

supposed to be with him. I am supposed to be *there* for him."

"And you would hold him down to do so?"

Yes, Brand realized with a sharp and sudden ferocity. If Ashton wanted him to. If that *something* inside Ashton that pulled on Brand was really twin to the unnamed thing coiled and waiting inside him.

Was that what this was?

Recognizing a kindred spirit, and hoping beyond hope that someone, that *Ashton* could understand and crave this need inside Brand, this yearning he didn't even have the words to articulate?

He let his gaze drift toward the road, and the spot where Ashton had last disappeared. "If he would let me," he murmured.

"That's between the two of you," Amiko murmured. "But it would only make me run farther…though Ash may be like me, but he isn't me. It's strange to know him so well, and not know him at all." She tucked her hair back primly. "I used to come back to Calvin, once…before I stopped coming back at all."

"What made you come back, before you stopped?"

"Knowing that he would always be waiting for me."

Brand returned his full attention to the petite woman at his side. "Then…young Master Ashton needs to know that I am waiting for him?"

"I have a feeling he already does." Amiko lingered on Brand, studying him, seeming to weigh and measure him. "…you want to be something more to my son than simply his manservant, don't you?"

"I…" Brand struggled, fists clenching once more, fingernails digging into his palms. "I don't…know. I have been in his employ for approximately three days. But I will say I am drawn to him. As if some part of me recognizes some part of him. Yet I know my place, and I know I must remain in it."

"You're blunt. Honest." Amiko chuckled. "I should disapprove. I don't."

"I value honesty, Madame."

"Then I will be honest with you." Amiko sighed, gaze drifting away from him. "Sometimes you just…feel things. And they don't have an explanation. They don't follow logical sense. One day you can wake up and realize you're in love with your best friend…or you're out of love with your husband. You can be indifferent to someone one day, and then the light catches them just right the next day and they take your breath away, and they're all you can think about. I could tell the moment I met you that my son consumes your thoughts—and you are so busy trying to figure out why that by the time you finally do, he'll be gone."

"That may be for the best," Brand said.

"It might. But if you feel like reading tonight…perhaps read about the red string of fate." Amiko smiled faintly. "It's a story I know quite well."

"The red string of fate?"

"Hai—ah, look it up, I think perhaps someone else would explain better." She reached over and patted his arm. "But perhaps it's just the two of you tugging at each other's strings, and it doesn't have to make sense at all. The red string has no understanding of days, hours, minutes, even years. It just is, and it pulls when those holding either end of it are close enough to each other to hear each other's heartbeats."

Brand frowned, turning that over. It sounded quite terribly impractical. "Thank you, Miss Ara—Amiko." He supposed he had a good deal to think about, if nothing else—least of all the oddity of having this conversation with Ashton's mother, even if it was in veiled terms. "If he returns to the house, would you tell him that I am at the office?"

"Of course." Amiko's eyes glittered brightly as she fluttered her fingers at him. "Go. Shoo. You look like the workaholic type."

"Madame," Brand said, pushing his glasses up the bridge of his nose, "you have no idea."

Ash ran until his waistcoat threatened to cut his torso in half; until the slap of the pavement against his feet ached through his dress shoes; until his entire body pinched and he doubled over and struggled to breathe as he hunched on the shoulder of the winding suburban highway in the shade of the overhanging trees.

Fuck. *Fuck.* What had he thought he was going to do? Run all the way to the inner city in his fucking polished Italian leather shoes?

The bitingly cold air sliced into his lungs. He pressed his hands against his thighs, straightening, and glanced back the way he'd come. At least Brand hadn't chased him down and dragged him back.

So why, then, did he feel a faint twinge of disappointment?

It didn't matter. Brand was just going to drag him back to more work. Nothing had changed now that his father was home; nothing at all. Ash was still the completely unprepared CEO of a global megacorporation.

And his father—this figurehead in his life who was half stranger, half everything he loved—was still dying.

They'd just changed the scenery.

Maybe Ash was the one who needed a change of

scenery. He fished his phone from his pocket and pulled up the black car service app he'd used before Brand had taken over as his driver, and put in a request for pickup.

Within ten minutes he was settled in the back of a sleek black SUV with blackout windows, leaning against the door and watching the roads slide by, blending from slick suburban blacktop into patched and potholed city streets. The driver said nothing, practically a voiceless automaton, and Ash kept his mouth shut. If he said anything, there would be no tart rejoinders, no gentle mockery.

Who would have thought Ash would miss that?

He had the driver drop him off on the sidewalk at Central Park. Considering he hadn't picked up anyone watching him as he'd run from the estate, it wasn't likely Ash had been tailed—and considering his past haunts, wild yacht parties and burning through the gorgeous young men at expensive bars frequented only by the rich, he doubted any nosy paparazzi would even think to look for him here.

Nor did he think anyone would recognize him, making it safe to take his shoes off, tuck his socks into his pockets, and walk barefoot through the grass.

It wasn't anything he could remember ever doing in his life. As a child he might have played on the lawns at the Harrington estate now and then, but he couldn't recall.

Such things hadn't been allowed at his Liverpool boarding school, the boys kept tightly in hand. And when he'd come breaking out of Liverpool and into liquor-soaked years at university…

There'd been a certain expectation. Living fast, living hard, glitz and glamour and money spent everywhere. No time for simplicity.

No time for savoring the crunch of autumn leaves beneath his bare soles, and the ticklish feeling of grass poking up between his toes.

Yet as he lingered, looking up at the wan autumnal sun and the pale, watery sky, he wondered if he would ever be able to coax his father to walk through the park like this with him, one day. Just father and son learning how to *be* father and son in a simple and quiet moment. He didn't even know if his father would be able to stand again, let alone walk with him, talk with him.

And just like that, the bitter pain in the pit of his stomach was back, chasing him from the park and through the city streets.

He didn't know how long he wandered. The bustle of continuous pedestrian traffic was a blessing, letting him blend in, get lost, be no one on his way to nowhere.

Even if "nowhere" ended up being a quiet hotel bar, dim-lit where he could hide himself in the shadows and sink himself into shot after shot of vodka.

He tried to take it slow, pace himself…but what the fuck did it matter? Maybe he'd follow in his dad's footsteps. Give himself liver cancer. Not tell anyone about it until he was almost dead, but who the fuck would even mourn him? He didn't have an ex-wife or a kid or anyone but a valet who didn't even *like* him; he just coddled Ash for a paycheck, and before the week was up Brand would probably figure out working for Ash wasn't worth it and just…quit.

And then he'd have no one.

No one except Vic looking at him with pity, and the people whose beds he shuffled through just to pass the time.

There was Andrew. Andrew wasn't anyone, and he wasn't anyone to Andrew.

But if he was with Andrew tonight, he wouldn't feel so alone.

He wasn't sober enough to be making this decision. But he wasn't sober enough to stop himself, either, and as he paid his tab and wove out of the bar, he called for another black car pickup. He saw the world through a haze of street lights, running in the vodka blur like a city seen through a rain-fogged window, as the car took him out to the waterfront bank of ridiculously high-priced condominiums where Andrew lived on his mother's pension. Hell, he might not even be home. Ash didn't know what he'd do, then. Go home, maybe.

Go home, and wait until Brand Forsythe fell asleep before slipping into his bed, pressing against his back, and begging the man not to look at him, not to make him feel ashamed of this quiet and lonely need.

The black SUV let him off outside Andrew's gate, tall wrought-iron that creaked open to Ash's touch. The lights were on upstairs in the sleek modern-deco townhouse, and when he slouched against the entryway and pressed the doorbell, the echoing chime inside was followed by Andrew's call of "Coming!" and the heavy clatter of feet on the stairs.

Then he was there—handsome and familiar and easy, and his face lit up with a touch of curious interest as he saw Ash. "Ash, hey—thought when you didn't answer my text—"

"I had shit going on," Ash said.

He bit his lip, looking up at Andrew—tanned and boyish and disarming, utterly shallow and vapid and perfect for what he wanted right now and all wrong for what he needed. Andrew was so *passive,* always went along with what Ash wanted…and until now, he'd always thought that was exactly what he craved.

Only now he wasn't sure what he wanted at all.

Only that it was easy to forget with Andrew, and he'd take that if nothing else.

"I'm drunk," he said, then stepped closer, curling his fingers in Andrew's shirt and jerking him close. "And I want you."

He stretched up on his toes and pressed his mouth to Andrew's. Andrew made a startled sound—one that melted into an eager murmur as he leaned in, his hands grasping at Ash, rough and clumsy and fumbling at his clothing.

"Oh hell yeah," Andrew gasped, dragging Ash inside and into the foyer, his tongue tracing Ash's mouth and then teasing inside. Ash almost thrust away right then and there; he was used to Andrew's fumbling, sloppy kisses, but he didn't want Andrew *inside* him like that, knowing him, making it intimate. He tore his mouth from Andrew's and distracted himself by pressing his lips to his strong, tanned throat, kissing and licking and biting. Groaning, Andrew went limp—and didn't protest when Ash shoved him against the wall inside the foyer, slipping his hands under his clothing to run his fingers over his hard, toned body, that beach-body athleticism that Ash used to find casually appealing but now felt plastic and fake.

Fuck.

Fuck.

He could feel Andrew's cock pressing against his belly, hard and hot through his jeans, but Ash?

Ash wasn't hard at all. Wasn't anything.

If anything, he felt slimy. Sick. Violated, even though he was here willingly. Even though he'd *started* this.

With a groan, he leaned into Andrew, resting his brow to his chest and slipping his hands out from under his shirt. "I'm sorry," he whispered. "I can't. I fucking can't. This is fucked up."

Andrew's hold on him tightened, then loosened and fell away. "Ash…?" he asked, voice thick with desire, breaths rushed—but Ash only shook his head, pulling away.

"I shouldn't be here."

"What…?"

"I shouldn't *be* here." Ash swallowed roughly, watching Andrew's puzzled face in complete misery. Andrew looked like a confused puppy, adorable but completely empty and without substance. "I…I shouldn't have come here just because you were easy and it would make me feel better. I'm sorry."

Andrew looked utterly lost, but just shrugged, smiling affably and scrubbing his fingers through his crop of dusty brown hair. "Hey. No strings, right? Never any hard feelings."

"I know." That didn't stop the twinge of guilt in the pit of Ash's stomach, or the ache for something else. Some*one* else. "I just can't live like this anymore." Shaking his head, he ducked around the door they'd left open, slipping outside into the night. "I gotta go."

"Hey!" Andrew stumbled after him. "Hey—you've been drinking, you shouldn't drive—"

Ash fished his phone from his pocket, and offered a faint smile over his shoulder. "I won't be," he said, and hit the first speed dial in his address book.

Before lifting his phone to his ear and waiting, heart in his throat, for the line to pick up.

Chapter Eight

Brand Forsythe was not in the office.

He'd meant to be. He'd *tried* to be, for a few distracted hours spent rescheduling meetings and sorting young Master Ashton's affairs so that his absence at the day's meetings wouldn't cause too much of a setback. Yet his entire world had stopped each time the office door opened, arresting on that unspoken hope that his *brat* of a young Master would come straggling around the door with a sheepish smile and a pout, that schoolboy sullenness that both wanted and rebelled against discipline.

Instead it was only Ms. Vernon, each time—so and so was on the line for Mr. Harrington, should she push next week's meetings as well, was Ashton coming in today?

Brand hated that he didn't have the answers.

But even more, he hated that he didn't know where the young Master *was*, and right now there was nothing he could do about it.

He checked his phone a dozen times an hour—and more than once had to push it away from himself to keep from calling, sending a text.

But it would only make me run farther, Amiko Arakawa had said.

Brand didn't want his young Master to run any farther.

He wanted him to come *back*.

So he could do his job and stop making Brand's life harder, of course. It couldn't be for any reason other than that.

For any reason such as sorting out what this craving was. This need, that had erupted so simply from one kiss and grown quietly under his skin until it felt as if it would take him over entirely.

He wasn't sure what pushed him to the break point. Perhaps yet another intrusion from Ms. Vernon. Perhaps another phone call full of demands he had no answers for, while he fought to keep his voice even and calm and soothing rather than clipped and sharp with a building temper. But somehow the massive glass-walled space was suddenly claustrophobic, and Brand needed to be out with a desperation that choked his breath from him.

He barely spared a moment to tell Ms. Vernon to hold all calls for the rest of the day before he spilled out into the afternoon sun. The air smelled like vehicle exhaust, the close pressing sweat of millions of people in an enclosed space, and the coming breath of winter. He breathed it in deep, standing there choking on each inhalation until they began to smooth and calm.

Then, slipping his hands into the pockets of his slacks, he turned down the sidewalk and let himself simply walk.

It wasn't something he did often. He rarely had time, when his role required round-the-clock service—and in his lifetime with the Newcombs, he could recall approximately three times that he had taken one of his dozens of annual allotted personal days. He didn't like feeling at loose ends. He never had.

Yet right now he needed the calm of doing nothing, while the weak and quiet sun beat its warmth down on his shoulders.

He walked for hours, following no set path…but as the sun was setting, purple and orange against a haze of clouds, he paused outside an open-front independent bookstore, bakery, and café. He followed the scents of baking pastries inside, and let himself wander the aisles, scanning titles, not looking for anything in particular. Yet when a shop girl, bright and perky in a red apron, approached and asked, "Hi there. Is there anything I can help you find?"…

…he lingered on her apron. Red. And on an impulse, asked, "Do you have any books about the Japanese concept of the red string of fate?"

She frowned thoughtfully, tapping her finger against her lower lip, then brightened. "You know, I think we just might."

And that was how Brand Forsythe ended up settled in a chair at one of the sidewalk tables, legs crossed comfortably, sipping at an espresso and Yasuko Fujiyama's *The Red Thread of Fate: A Color in Love-Story* open across his lap.

He wasn't certain he understood the story, and wondered if something had been lost in translation—but he thought he grasped, as he spent hours poring through the pages, what Amiko had been trying to tell him. The story explained that each person's soul was destined for another soul, and the gods connected them with a red thread of fate that was said to be tied around each person's pinky finger and could never be severed. Some believed the string was tied on birth, and would remain through a lifetime—while others believe it carried through life after life, reincarnation after reincarnation, two souls destined to always find each other, even if in some lives tragic fate or circumstance might keep them apart.

Brand was a staunchly atheistic man.

Yet he couldn't deny there was some merit in the concept to at least encapsulate the feeling that could happen, sometimes—of suddenly needing someone else to feel whole, and there being no rhyme or reason to who or when or how it would strike. Simply that one day that person was there…and the next, somehow, life could feel incomplete without them. It might take days to happen, or might take years…

But it was, at least, a common experience for many.

That did not mean it made sense to Brand that *he* was feeling this. Nor did it mean anything with the young Master oblivious, and likely utterly uninterested.

Yet beneath his surprise, Ashton had leaned in close when Brand kissed him, clutching at him and going soft and sweet and giving in a way that had nearly made Brand into an animal, that whispered those first tiny inklings that he might indeed be counterpart to Brand's quietly undefined and yet painfully undeniable needs.

Would an exploration of this attraction, if his young Master was amenable, be so very wrong?

Brand closed the book against his thigh, resting his hand against the cover and letting his gaze drift to the thinning streams of people moving down the sidewalk underneath the street lamps, the busy flood of day turned into a quieter flow—groups of friends laughing and chatting, lovers walking hand in hand in that way that made them lean toward each other as if pulled by some unseen yet irresistible force.

If he had an ounce of professionalism, he would put this out of his head. He had enough control over himself that young Master Ashton need never know—and it was best if he didn't. Brand had not discussed his desires with anyone, but he suspected they would be considered rather taboo. And for all his young Master's fast and loose ways…

There was an innocence about Ashton that said he was untried in the ways of darker things, and Brand was likely not the man to initiate him.

Above all, he had to put his young Master's safety and well-being over anything else.

Even over his own need to press Ashton against the wall and kiss him until he went soft again, until his slim fingers tangled in Brand's suit, until he couldn't hold himself up without Brand's arms around him and everything about the young Master turned soft and vulnerable and weak and so very, very desperately in need of protection.

Isn't there anything you've ever wanted? That soft, sighing voice, asking a question Brand had thought he knew the answer to.

He was starting to realize that, perhaps, he didn't know himself very well at all.

Sighing, he stood, unable to help tidying the empty dishes from his espresso and baklava bar for the busboy out of habit before slipping the book in its little shopping tote. He should retrieve the Mercedes from the office and return to the estate, and hope the young Master would be waiting—tired, likely, with that hangdog look of sheepish disappointment in himself, that neediness he seemed determined to refuse to allow anyone to answer.

But he'd barely made it two steps down the sidewalk before his phone murmured in his pocket—a low sound of falling chimes, delicate and silvery, that he'd set to the young Master's number. He slipped his phone out and caught the call before the first iteration of the ring had even finished.

And he didn't even get a chance to speak before Ashton's voice came over the line, soft and miserable and entreating. "…Brand?"

Ah, bloody hell. Ashton shouldn't sound like that. Brand closed his eyes. "Yes, young Master Ashton?"

"I'm not okay," Ash said, then let out a gulping sound that told Brand quite eloquently that he'd either already been crying, or was trying not to. "I'm not okay at all. If I text you an address, can you come get me?"

"You need not even ask. Simply…tell me you are unharmed?"

"I'm not hurt," Ash said, easing the tightness in Brand's chest. "I'm just…I'm just not okay and I need you to come because I don't trust myself to get home on my own."

Brand smiled faintly, even if it ached. "I will always

come to your call, young Master."

"Always?" Ashton asked, with a note of broken, sweet vulnerability that tugged at Brand's heart.

"Is that not what a valet is for?"

"...yeah." It came after a long silence, a shaky breath. "I'll see you soon?"

"I am already on my way." And Brand was already moving, retracing his steps back toward the office to fetch the car. "It is not safe or legal for me to speak to you while driving. I will be there for you shortly."

"Thank you." Ash's voice broke. "I just...thank you."

"There is never any need, my young Master," Brand said softly, then hung up the phone. It buzzed in his hand a moment later, flashing a text from Ashton with an address not far from the city center, followed by an emoji with an embarrassed smile and a sweatdrop, and another line of text:

you're like a knight in shining single-breasted wool

Brand chuckled to himself, pocketed his phone, and quickened his stride.

ASH WISHED ANDREW WOULD LEAVE him alone.

He was *hovering*, refusing to go back inside, even when Ash left his front doorstep and went to wait outside the gate. He fluttered around Ash like he'd suddenly decided now was a good time to finally be responsible, when all Ash wanted was to be left miserably alone until he could get *out* of here and leave this mistake behind him.

And in the morning, start over again.

Start trying to be the man he was supposed to be, and no more drunken recklessness.

Drinking and fucking around was just running. Before he'd been running with no definable goal in mind; maybe just running from growing up. Now, though, he was running from…running from watching his father die, and leaving the world crumbling around him.

He couldn't.

He couldn't run from that.

Not if he wanted to have any chance to know his father at all.

Tomorrow, he'd do better.

Tonight, he'd just sleep it off and try not to hate himself too much in the morning.

"Come on," Andrew said. "I don't like you hanging out here alone. At least come in and sleep it off on the couch."

"I'm fine," Ash said. He didn't even feel all that

drunk anymore; just tired and a bit blurry and wanting to be *home*. And cold; even in his full suit it was still chilly out, and he didn't think it would be long before the first snow flurries started. "My ride's going to be here any minute."

"You sure? You've been waiting a long time. I mean if the guy's gonna ditch you you can at least—"

Ash whirled on him with a grit-toothed smile. "You're sweet, Andrew," he bit off. "Really. I get that you're worried. I'm sorry I bothered you. But I'd really like it if you left me al—"

"If you will excuse me," Brand Forsythe said at his back, "I will take it from here."

The nearly embarrassing rush of relief that went through Ash was second only to the frozen look of wide-eyed terror on Andrew's face. Brand towered over them both, his face set in that cold mask of forbidding disdain that just didn't seem so cruel to Ash anymore—but to Andrew he probably looked like some nightmare apparition, an avenging devil in sharp-edged black. Brand's eyes were slits of pure ice behind his glasses.

And locked straight on Andrew, as if he would flay him to pieces with a single look.

It took everything in Ash not to fling himself against Brand. Andrew gulped, backing away. "Um. Sorry, man, sorry, I just wanted to be sure he was okay."

"Your concern is appreciated," Brand said flatly, then pressed one long, broad hand to the small of Ash's back, a star of heat burning through his clothing. "If you will come with me, young Master. Your car awaits."

Ash let himself be shepherded away with one last glance for Andrew, who stood petrified, a frozen look on his face. Ash bit back a laugh. "...he was just trying to look out for me."

"And he did, but there is no longer any need." Brand frowned. "You are shivering."

Before Ash could say anything, Brand slid out of his suit coat, revealing a sleek black waistcoat and crisp white shirt that turned his powerful body into elegant angles. He swirled the coat around Ash's shoulders, wrapping him in a layer of absorbed body heat and that earthy scent. Biting his lip, Ash clutched at the coat, making himself small inside the comforting, heavy layer of its warmth.

Suddenly, somehow...

The world felt right.

He let Brand shepherd him into the back of the Mercedes; the man's hands never quite left him, guiding him with gentle touches that seemed to hold him together and tucking him securely into the backseat. Yet Brand said nothing, as he rounded to the driver's side and settled behind the wheel. His jaw was tight, and he fixed Ash with a simmering look in the rear view mirror before shifting the car into Drive and pulling out onto the street.

Ash bit his tongue, pulling Brand's coat closer around him. What…what was that look for? Brand looked almost *angry,* and Ash guessed he should be when Ash had ducked out on his responsibilities again, but this was almost—

Oh.

Oh.

He flushed, shrinking down in the seat. "…Brand?"

"Yes, young Master?" Brand replied, deceptively mild.

"I…I hope I didn't give you the wrong impression." He darted his tongue nervously over his lips. "If that was why you were angry with Andrew. He…didn't do anything. Or hurt me. I just…" Ash struggled for words. "I said yes, then I said no…and then I wanted to leave."

Brand remained silent for so long Ash thought he wouldn't respond. Then, tight, clipped, "He didn't force himself on you?"

"No!" Ash shook his head quickly. "No. He stopped as soon as I said no. I just…" He tore his gaze from those flinty green eyes in the rear view mirror, looking down, fingering the fine wool of the lapel of Brand's coat. "…realized I didn't want him. And it didn't feel good."

The stiff tension in Brand's body eased; the tightness of his grasp on the steering wheel relaxed so obviously there came a faint squeak of decompressing leather.

"Good," he said, and for all that it was quiet…there was something sincere, heartfelt, in that rumbling undertone, that left Ash warm. "I am glad he did not hurt you. Though I do not like that you went to him."

"…we didn't do anything."

"I still do not like it."

Ash hunched, cheeks burning. "God, Forsythe, it's not like I'm going to fuck up Dad's reputation even more."

The silence drew Ash's gaze to the mirror again, and that penetrating green gaze.

"That is not why," Brand said softly.

Ash's heart shivered into soft, rapid beats. He didn't know what to say, when Brand was looking at him that way—and he lowered his eyes, curling his fingers in that coat that smelled so much like Brand, that made him feel like he was wrapped up inside the man, sheltered and safe.

"I think a few reporters caught me," he deflected.

"It's all right," Brand said. "I will take care of it."

Ash lingered, meeting Brand's gaze in the mirror, his chest tight, his stomach filled with strange slow flutters. "You take care of everything, don't you?"

"Including you," Brand replied.

Ash only ducked his head, heat flushing through him

with a slow and quiet warmth, and said nothing at all.

The night passed by in silence, on the drive back to the house. The mansion was dark, as they pulled in through the gate and Brand parked the car. Ash tried to open the back door and step out by himself—but he misjudged the distance and caught his foot wrong, turning underneath him and spilling him toward the cobbles.

And Brand was there—catching him, sweeping him up, lifting him into strong arms and off his feet. His pulse leaped in sharp staccato beats as Brand captured him against his chest, carrying him as if he weighed nothing, cradling him against a living furnace of strength and warmth…all while still wrapped in Brand's jacket. Ash stared up at him, curling his fingers in the front of Brand's waistcoat. Brand looked down at him inscrutably—then turned to carry him toward the house.

Ash didn't know what to do. But he didn't want to think about that right now, not when right now everything wrong inside him felt *right* and Brand felt *safe*. So Ash only laid his head to Brand's shoulder, closing his eyes and letting himself feel sheltered in that strong, protective embrace.

The house was quiet as a whisper, as Brand eased them inside—somehow managing to unlock the door, open it, and close it behind them without ever jostling Ash. Through the hallways, toward their adjoining rooms, and Ash bit his lip as Brand shifted him to cradle him closer; tentatively, Ash slipped one arm up around Brand's neck.

"I'm really confused right now," he whispered.

Brand tilted his head just enough to look down at him. "Why are you confused?"

"Everything's all wrong inside me all the time, but not right now," Ash admitted. "Not with you. You feel good. You feel safe."

A faint, warm smile curled Brand's lips. "That is all I ever strive to be for you, young Master."

Brand elbowed the door to Ash's room open and carried him inside the master suite. Ash still couldn't think of it as his, even with his clothing in the drawers and his books on the shelves, his personal effects tossed around. And the bed felt too large for him alone, when Brand bent over it to lay him down against the duvet with such care, shifting his grip to cradle Ash's head in one large hand as he laid him against the pillow.

In the darkness of the room, moonlight faint and pale through the thin linen curtains, Brand was gold, silver, and shadow—the only color that spark of green behind his glasses. His darkened gaze held Ash's, even as he sank down the length of Ash's body to fall to his knees next to the bed. One at a time, with almost ritual solemnity, he slipped first one of Ash's shoes off, then the other, followed by his socks—before he rose once more, bracing one knee against the mattress. His graceful bulk bowed over Ash as gloved fingers gently brushed both Brand's coat and Ash's aside, before beginning to flick the buttons of Ash's waistcoat open.

Ash worried at his trembling lip. He'd tumbled into bed with a dozen men, but no drunken sex had ever felt as intimate, as vulnerable, as lying here while his valet undressed him. He felt naked even before his waistcoat was fully opened, those strong, knowing hands smoothing it to either side and then slipping up to finger his tie. Ash's breaths caught, his pulse throbbing loud. His mouth felt hot, remembering the taste of a kiss that had consumed him, that had taken all control away from him to leave him sweetly helpless, surrendering.

And he wanted it again.

Again and again and again, until he couldn't think of anything but Brand and everything Brand demanded of him, wanted of him.

If only the man didn't thrust him away, and retreat behind that icy, proper façade.

His tie loosened, then slipped from around his throat like a licking tongue. Ash reached up with a shaking hand, and brushed his fingertips to the unforgiving, stern line of Brand's mouth.

"Brand," he whispered.

Brand stilled, gaze darting to his face. His lips parted against Ash's fingers…before he continued undressing him, flicking over the buttons of his shirt one at a time. "Yes, young Master?" he murmured, each word a kiss to Ash's fingertips.

Before he could lose his nerve, Ash pushed himself up, letting both coats and waistcoat fall away.

And kissed Brand, pressing his mouth soft and questioning against the older man's, just a single light brush before he pulled back quickly, trembling, waiting to be thrust away.

Brand regarded him quietly, fingers paused over a button just below his ribs. He tilted his head, gaze flicking down to Ash's mouth; in the silence Ash's heartbeat was a roaring drum, a wild primal beat that made him feel as though the earth turned and moved to his rhythm. Brand's hands fell away, falling to the bed to either side of Ash's hips.

"Ah," he said, a rough, husky edge in his voice. "So that's how it's to be, then."

Before he caught Ash's chin gently in gloved fingers, tilted his head up, and captured his mouth with those stern and commanding lips.

That feeling came rushing back—that feeling when Brand had pinned him against the door and drowned him in almost oppressive heat, dominating Ash with his sheer bulk alone. That feeling of being weak and yet not afraid; of being overpowered and so entirely overwhelmed. It shot through Ash in warm, sighing sparks, until he felt as though he were flesh stitched from fireflies—and each slow, plying caress of Brand's lips made the light inside him burn, until he was all warmth and melting softness to that firm and dominating touch.

He tilted his head, fitting his mouth to Brand's—only for Brand to still him with a tighter grasp on his chin, fingers unfurling to cup his jaw and hold just tight enough for a warning, just tight enough to keep Ash in his place with a promise of strength held in check. Shivering, Ash kept himself still, pliant, yielding, letting Brand do what he wished as Brand kissed him in slow, intimate invasions. One shuddering breath at a time, Brand delved deeper and deeper into his mouth; one slick stroke after another he tasted Ash, explored him, exposed every depth of him to a teasing tongue and the sharp sting of teeth that nipped and tormented his mouth until pain became sensitive pleasure and every throbbing pulse of his lips radiated out to every heated point of sensation on his body.

Please, Ash begged silently—and Brand responded as if he could sense that plea in every sigh, in every gasp. With a confident touch Brand tumbled Ash back to the bed, pinning him there with his weight, his bulk, the vivid pressure of masculine heat and hard-packed muscle and the sheer size of him that made him a mountain next to the small and whispered grain of sand Ash felt like. Ash arched against him just to feel that bulk pinning him, only to tense, biting back a cry as Brand's mouth marked firm, claiming bites, suckling kisses, from his jaw to his throat. Those hands took control of him again, firmly slipping the last buttons of his shirt free, tearing it away, ripping his undershirt over his head until his chest was bare to the touch of gloved fingers.

The roughened fabric of the kid gloves made fire and wildness of his skin with slow, skimming touches that trailed down his ribs, his waist. Pure torment, winding him tight as a string around a spool as Brand explored him with an almost mocking delicacy. Where Ash was gasping and eager, Brand was slow and deliberated, drawing out every moment as his fingertips shaped the planes of Ash's trembling, sensitive stomach; the contours of his pectorals, the hardening rises of his nipples. Every touch shot electric through him, rousing him with a need he couldn't endure when he just…he just…

He just didn't want to feel *alone* right now.

"Brand," he begged, burying his face against that soft wash of sandy hair, tangling his fingers in cool strands, grazing his mouth against the curve of Brand's ear. "*Brand.*"

The older man stilled, fingertips just brushing the lower curves of Ash's nipples. He pushed himself up, looking down at him through gleaming lenses that caught the moonlight and threw it back in cold edges. He slipped one hand downward—feathering, taunting, ever teasing and controlled…only to mold his hand between Ash's thighs.

"As you wish, young Master," Brand rumbled—before those devious fingers went to work.

If Ash had thought Brand was a demon before—he was Lucifer himself now, as he teased and tortured Ash through the fabric of his slacks. The friction of fine weave turned every caress into a rough and dragging torment as deft fingers stroked his entire length, searching, seeking, leaving him writhing, pressing his thighs together as if he could make the hot, almost painful lances of pleasure shooting up inside him *stop*. But that only trapped Brand's hand against him, pressure firming only to ease, erratic and leaving him strung on edge, never knowing when Brand would tease him with light, sharp-shock shivers or the tight, controlling grip of a firm palm that knew just how much pressure was too much pressure, and just how much pressure skated that thin edge to leave Ash *keening*.

He moved helplessly beneath Brand, catching whimpers behind his clenched teeth as each stroke left him slicker and slicker with pre-come, making his boxer-briefs and slacks glide against him, dripping down the length of his cock to lick in sensitive runnels over his skin. He felt so *empty* inside, a tight deep throbbing, and every touch only made it worse. Brand…Brand was *learning* him, he realized—exploring with his strokes and, every time he found something that made Ash toss his head back and claw his fingers against Brand's scalp and cry out in breathless gasps…doing it again.

And again.

And again, until Ash was so close he nearly lost himself, hips jerking upward in sharp shudders, as Brand circled his thumb beneath the fabric-shrouded head of Ash's cock.

"*Brand!*" he pleaded, nearly sobbing. He wanted more than this—wanted that emptiness sated, wanted to feel *with* someone, but Brand had him curled in agony.

Until that touch stopped, long, strong hand curled around his cock, cradling it against fabric he'd soaked again and again with drips of pre-come so thick their musky scent burned on the air between them and he could taste himself on every shallow, indrawn breath.

He forced his eyes open, looking up at Brand—who watched him with that same inscrutable regard, yet in this moment it was a darkly dominating thing, and Ash shivered as that gaze raked over him, taking him in as though he…as though he *belonged* to Brand, as though the man were master of every inch of Ash's body.

Lightly, deliberately, Brand flicked his thumb against Ash's fabric-shrouded cock head, and Ash jerked as pleasure-pain rocked through him. Brand tilted his head, studying him coolly. "You are not articulating what you want, young Master," he breathed, a low and growling rasp. "Unless what you are trying to say is that you want me."

Nearly mewling in the back of his throat, Ash tried to pull himself together enough to find words—but then Brand flicked against him again and he could only jerk his shoulders, arching his back, lifting his hips into that touch. "I…mnhh…I w-want…I want you," he managed, his mouth aching with the words, with the need for *contact*, his tongue tracing them. "Please, Brand."

"And how do you want me, young Master?" Brand mocked—ever in control, stringing Ash along until he wanted to scream in pure frustration. "Shall I finish this now, and leave you sated? Or is there something else you want of me?"

Ash's cheeks burned. There was both desire and shame in this, in wanting so desperately, in feeling so deeply, in begging so brazenly. He lowered his eyes away from that gaze that tore into him, searched deep, sought out everything that made him feel small, that made him want to submit to that hard, hot-sculpted body arched over his. He bit his lip, stealing a shy glance at Brand, then untangled his fingers from soft hair and brushed them to Brand's lips.

"I want to feel you inside me," he whispered. "I don't want to be alone."

Firm lips traced his fingertips. Brand's hand fell away from his cock, slipping to rest on Ash's stomach, before finding the button of his slacks.

"As my young Master wishes," Brand breathed, then leaned down to kiss him once more.

Ash melted for that kiss, his mouth feeling like hot honey, his blood sweet syrup, his desire dark sugar. He was sticky wet candy for Brand to taste, and he went soft inside as that delving tongue took him over and searched deep and touched him in ways so intimate his entire body went liquid at a single slow thrust. There was something almost lewd about this, obscene, moving slow and hungry beneath Brand as the man stripped him down, left him naked, caught between cool sheets and the crisp fabric of Brand's waistcoat and slacks. But when Brand started to unbutton his waistcoat, Ash caught his hand, breaking back from the kiss for a breathless moment.

"Leave it on," he whispered.

Understanding sharpened in Brand's gaze. He turned his hand to capture Ash's—then pushed it up over his head, pinning it gently to the pillows, trapping him.

"Open yourself for me, young Master," he murmured, that possessive, claiming gaze wandering down his body.

Ash couldn't stand it. He couldn't look at Brand when he felt so exposed, vulnerable—and he turned his face aside as he spread his legs for Brand, toes curling in the sheets. He was too bare, giving himself over this way, and the sensation of being so unprotected made him burn beneath his skin.

But it was nothing to the sensation as bare skin suddenly touched his entrance—gloves gone, fingertips rough, not even the coating of something slick managing to ease their callused texture. Ash caught the faint *snick* of a bottle of lubricant closing—*a proper valet is always prepared*—before thick fingertips circled his flesh, rousing chills, then flame, then senseless nothing as slowly, with cruel deliberation, one blunt fingertip eased inside him.

He'd been fucked again and again by clumsy rutting college boys, and not one had touched him with the control and surety Brand possessed, easing that single finger into him until he felt every ridge, every knuckle, every taper of its length stroking against him from within. It bordered on violation, this slick tight pain as oil spread against his skin and Brand caressed him. Ash went stiff as he forgot how to breathe, light-headed, swimming—only to suck in a choked exhalation as that slow, deep penetration of a single finger was suddenly followed by the unexpected rough *burn* of a second thrusting in deep. He fought against that hand pinning his wrist, straining as if his arm were a tether, a leash binding him to Brand and forcing his obedience to the onslaught of swift, demanding strokes that took control of his body from the inside out.

He nearly wept with frustration, with pleasure, with something deep and wrenching that tore into him. It was everything he wanted and never enough, always stopping just short of making him feel *full* enough, hot enough, deep enough. He spread his thighs wide, straining into every plunging, intimate rush of Brand's fingers.

"Are you ready then, my young Master?" Brand lilted—and something about the way he said *my young Master* sent sweet chills up Ash's spine. He curled forward as another particularly deep thrust branched lightning inside him, wrapping his free arm around Brand's shoulders, burying his mouth against his throat.

"Please," he begged. "It…it feels like you're punishing me, *please…*"

A low, deep rumble spilled past Brand's lips, so bestial for such a cool, perfectly cultured man, as if it had been torn from him in a moment of lost control. He turned his head, mouth brushing Ash's ear, breaths hot as a predator's against his skin.

"Who says I am not?" he murmured.

Before he pinned Ash to the sheets with his body, fingers slipping from inside him, hot hands gripping his thighs, pushing them apart, drawing them up, nearly burning Ash in half as he spread him open. There came the rasp of a zipper, then the stroke of searing-hot flesh, slick and molten and dripping in musky, running trails against Ash's skin, nearly burning into him with wet body heat.

Then pressure. Pressure like nothing he'd ever known, and no stretching or preparation could prepare him for the sensation of being scorched open by slow, steady inches, his body a small thing to be broken and fragmented and remade to mold around the shape of Brand until he fit *just right.*

Pain came sharp as a slap—red-hot and splitting through him, and he fought back a scream, strangling it in his throat. He wrapped his thighs against Brand's hips, holding on to him for everything in him as Brand surged slowly, agonizingly deeper, setting him on fire with every inch and leaving only char in his wake.

Ash was shattered. Ash was shattered, small, helpless, caught in this inexorable force of nature in the shape of a man. His eyes prickled, throat burning on every ragged inhalation; he felt too *full*, as if he was on the thin trembling verge of snapping, the pain white-hot and melting deep into his flesh. He'd never had it *hurt* like this before, frightening and terrible yet sweet and intimate and delicious, and he whimpered as he turned his face into Brand's throat.

"*Ah—*" he gasped, ragged and low. "It hurts…Brand, it *hurts…*"

That admission only made Brand clutch him tighter, silent save for the subtle rough draw of his breaths, but his cock swelled and throbbed in a harsh, straining jerk inside Ash, making him cry out as it moved inside him, dragging against his stretched and swollen and torn and aching insides.

"Is it too much, my young Master?" Brand whispered.

Ash shook his head with a muted sound, burying tighter against Brand. He didn't want this to *stop,* not even if it destroyed him. "No…no, just…"

"I have you," Brand promised—and sank down hard against him, that solid weight spreading his thighs to the point of trembling pain and yet weighing him to earth, too, safe and anchoring him before he could fly apart. Brand released his captured wrist to wind both arms around him, lifting Ash up into him. "Hold fast to me."

Hold fast to me, Brand said…and as Ash wrapped his arms around his shoulders and dug his fingers into his back, began to *move.*

Slow and deep as the movements of the earth, Brand filled him—a seismic thing, the grinding of mountains, the turn of the tides, time set by the push and pull between them, until Ash could only breathe when Brand was inside him, and held himself breathless and taut each time those gliding strokes drew out. He couldn't see, his vision a haze of colors blurred through tears, turning the night-locked ceiling overhead into darkness and stars. This tide of pleasure would drown him, consume him, submerge him in a sea so dark he would never see light again…and he would let it.

He would let it because Brand felt so good inside him. So right. The pain was perfect, punishment and pleasure in one, tearing out everything that hurt inside him and replacing it with the clean bright pleasure of sensation. He ignited, each time Brand sank deep enough to make him feel as though he would fly apart, every time his depths stretched and ached and burned around the searing caress of flesh to flesh. He sobbed, each time that moment of emptiness inside him left him feeling so alone, so adrift, begging to have that feeling of joining back.

And he curled small against Brand and let the man overwhelm him, wholly giving up control to his every touch.

He wasn't sure when his lips found Brand's again. Only that they tasted of tears, and he let himself sink into a kiss that promised he need only surrender. Need only trust. Need only give all of himself, willingly and wholeheartedly, into this strange and dominating man's firm and grasping hands.

So he gave—rolling up to meet him, moving himself against him, naked flesh against fabric. He gave with his lips. He gave with the touch of his hands burying into Brand's clothing, his hair, his skin. He gave with his body, as one last stroke of teasing fabric and hard muscle against his aching cock became too much.

And he fell fully and utterly into Brand's control, as pleasure made his vision white and wet heat spilled inside him in shuddering bursts twin to his own. Tight contractions of flesh to flesh matched the rhythm of his heartbeat, and he tumbled into the dark.

With the taste of his own name sinking into him, drunk again and again from Brand Forsythe's lips.

Chapter Nine

Ash woke before the dawn, when the sky was just beginning to lighten with wan color and the crickets had stopped their singing, but the birds hadn't yet started their counterpoint harmony.

He couldn't say what woke him. He was sore and tired and warm and safe, sheltered against a hard mass of muscle that made him feel so very slight and delicate, tucked close against Brand's sleeping form.

Ash didn't remember passing out, last night. Only that there had been a quiet haze in the aftermath, dazed and gasping and aching, while Brand gently separated their bodies, carefully tended to the hurt and ache inside Ash, then cradled him close with lips pressed into his hair. Ash must have dozed off like that, curled up naked in Brand's arms.

And Brand was still here.

He must have stripped some time after Ash had fallen asleep, leaving him shirtless and shoeless, naked save for the slacks Ash could feel brushing against his legs under the covers. Brand's head rested against the pillow, his darkly ashen golden brown hair spilling across the pillow, his eyeglasses laid aside on the nightstand. Even in sleep there was something fierce and sharp about his features, brooding and dark.

Ash lingered, letting himself just *look* at him, taking in the way his lips parted on sleeping breaths, the way the moonlight pooled in the hollows beneath sharp cheekbones while shadows retreated to gather under the stubborn line of his jaw. Starting just at the base of his throat, above his collarbone, was the jagged line of what looked like an old scar, snaking diagonally down the hard-cut planes of his chest and vanishing beneath the duvet; Ash touched the scar lightly, tracing the subtly different texture, the slick waxiness of something old and long-healed. It *had* to be old, to be so smooth—and Ash wondered if it was from the car crash, so long ago when Brand had once been young.

He'd never seen Brand so *still*, before. So unguarded. Even when the man was quiet he was a bastion of tense activity ready to spring into motion at any moment. Ash liked this, he thought. Seeing Brand this way. Knowing him this way.

Even if it never should have happened.

He bit his lip, guilt washing through him. He was a selfish fuck, wasn't he? Thinking about turning over a new leaf and then immediately turning around and doing something like *this*. He shouldn't be here, tucked into Brand's arms like this, abusing the man's loyalty.

Taking advantage of the paycheck that bound Brand to him, if only for the sake of his livelihood.

Swearing under his breath, Ash closed his eyes, then gingerly shifted to extricate himself. Slowly, he eased himself out from under the heavy weight of Brand's arm, slipping a pillow into his place so as not to disturb the man, and started to swing his legs out of bed.

"If you are going to practice stealth, young Master," Brand murmured at his back, velvety with sleep, making him freeze with his stomach plummeting, "you need a good deal more practice."

Fuck.

BRAND HADN'T EXPECTED TO WAKE after his young Master—though he had risen only minutes after, he thought, even if he'd kept his stillness and his silence as Ash traced his face, his body, with a feather-light touch that soaked a pleasant, soothing warmth into his skin. But when Ash had withdrawn, Brand had opened his eyes.

Only to catch a glimpse of that crestfallen, terrible expression on Ashton's face, before the young man swung away to give him the sleek line of his back, starting to rise from the bed.

"If you are going to practice stealth, young Master," Brand said, "you need a good deal more practice."

Ash winced, hunching, slim freckled shoulders upthrust to either side of his slender neck. "…sorry." He turned a wary look over his shoulder, eyes a little too wide. "Did I wake you?"

"I was already awake." Shifting onto his stomach, Brand pushed himself up onto his elbows and reached around Ash for his glasses, then unfolded them and slid them on. "And you are attempting to sneak out as if afraid a jealous spouse will catch me in your bed."

Ash winced again, then shifted to ease back onto the bed, slipping his legs back under the covers and sitting up against the headboard. "It's not that. I just…felt like I didn't belong here."

"It is your bed."

"And you're in it. And I'm naked. And we had sex."

Brand couldn't help a faint smile. "I had not forgotten."

Nor could he forget Ashton clinging to him, flushed beneath him, slim and smooth and lovely with his lips parted on soft cries that were half-pain, half-pleasure; half begging him for more, half begging him to stop. Again and again Brand had slowed, reining himself in by the thinnest thread to let his young Master adjust, to give those soft cries a chance to become *no, stop*—but they never did.

Ash had only clutched to him harder, arched up against him, begged him with the sweat and silk of his body, with the tight heat of his flesh, with the press of desperate lips teasing sweet and soft and light against his, kisses like drops of rain against his skin.

His young Master's mouth was still swollen and red from those kisses, even as he darted his tongue over his lips and watched Brand nervously, trepidation flickering in dark blue eyes. Brand wondered, then, if his young Master had regrets. If perhaps he regretted sleeping with someone so much older; sleeping with a servant; simply sleeping with Brand, as often as they had sniped at each other.

Brand was already preparing himself to wall away behind the barrier of proper formality, if only for the sake of his young Master's dignity, when Ash blurted out, "I'm sorry."

Brand stilled, tilting his head to one side. "…I don't understand what you're apologizing for."

"Last night…" Ashton looked down, twining his fingers together, then tugging them apart, then twining them again. He swallowed audibly. "Last night wasn't right. I…I took advantage of your position, and…" He looked away, mouth trembling, and fretted a hand through his hair. "I'm sorry. It shouldn't have happened. I…I understand if you want to quit." He smiled bitterly. "Fuck. I understand if you want to sue me."

Of all the things Brand had expected…it wasn't that. It wasn't something that mature, that reasoned, that considerate of either Brand's feelings or the implications of what they'd done. It wasn't that he didn't think Ash had the capacity in him.

It was just that he didn't think to see it so soon, or that Ash would be so forthright about it.

So brave.

It only made Brand want to pull Ash into his arms and cradle him, shelter him from the storm he was tossing himself through, his emotions written on his face.

But that might, right now, complicate the matter.

He turned over his response, working through the best answer, then said, "Last night was a matter of mutual consent, young Master. You did not pressure or obligate me into anything." He searched dark blue eyes. "But if it makes you uncomfortable, we shall not speak of it again."

"Just like that?"

"Just like that," Brand promised, and told himself he wasn't aching inside, wondering.

Wondering if Ash would now pretend it had never happened, leaving Brand burning for having known the first taste of what it could be like to possess Ashton Harrington, and tie them both into this desperate need inside him.

Ash stared at him, wide eyes so very liquid, his heart an open book—though he shielded the pages by ducking his head again, the shaggy fall of his hair half-hiding his face. "It just feels weird. I've known you…three days now? Four?"

"How long did you know the men you slept with in the past before you took them to bed?"

Ash flinched, but said nothing. Brand sighed, pushing himself up and twisting to lean against the headboard; he stretched his arm along its back, offering Ash a place against his side—if he wanted it.

As much as he wanted to hold Ashton, to have him, to possess him, to control him…

He needed him to be willing, first.

"That was not meant as a barb, young Master," he said. "I only mean to reassure you that it is of no concern. If anything, it means you have the assurance of confidentiality that you did not have before."

A weak smile flickered across Ash's lips. "Practical about everything, aren't you."

"A fatal personality flaw, some might say."

"…yeah." Ash took a shaky breath. He always seemed to do that when he was nerving himself to be brave—and Brand was finding his young Master chose bravery more often than not. "What if…" Ash peeked at him from under his lashes. "What if I asked you to not be practical about it?"

Brand's breaths stilled. "Pardon?"

"I mean…you're with me every waking and sleeping moment."

Ash wrapped his arms around himself as if he could shield himself; Brand so desperately wished to be the one doing the shielding, but he couldn't. Not until he heard what Ash had to say.

"It…I…" Ash shook his head. "It's hard looking at you all the time when I can't just walk away from you after sex. Not like with everyone else. I feel weird and I don't like it, and you're being practical like it's nothing at all."

"I did not say it was nothing," Brand pointed out gently.

"No? Then ignore me." Ash's laugh was harsh, hurting. "I'm a fucking wreck and it's making me all needy. Like I said, I've known you for three or four days. A quick fuck doesn't mean anything."

"You are allowed to be 'needy,' young Master." And Brand couldn't stand it anymore. He touched his fingertips beneath Ash's chin, tipping his face up, and leaned in to kiss him. Just a moment, but for that moment Ash went deliciously soft and pliant, leaning into him, before Brand drew back. "You may be needy with me, if you wish."

In that breath Ash looked as though he might cry with relief, before he managed to pull himself together, visibly composing himself. Yet the look he fixed on Brand was filled with a naked longing Brand ached to answer, and Ash edged closer to him, eyeing him sidelong.

"Can I…?" he asked softly.

"I have been waiting."

In less than a heartbeat, he had an Ash-shaped burr stuck to him; Ash tucked against his side, curling up small and fitting himself in close, his smooth, warm skin against Brand's naked chest. Brand curled his arm around his shoulders, drawing him in closer, and Ash buried his face in Brand's chest with a little whimper and slid one arm across him.

"You could've," Ash mumbled against his skin. "You could've just…"

"Not yet." Brand brushed his lips to the top of that messy head of dark hair. "That sort of thing comes with time and familiarity. Until then, I wait for your permission."

The tension in Ash's body eased slowly, until he went more and more loose against Brand. After several shaking moments he calmed, and turned his head to rest his cheek to Brand's chest, the warmth of soft skin soaking into him. "You don't seem like you like to ask permission for much. Which is weird, for a valet."

“It is not overly in my nature with my lovers, at the very least.”

“Then why with me?”

“I want you to be ready, first.”

Ash tilted his head back, looking up at Brand with wide, shyly curious eyes. “Ready for what?”

Brand considered—considered telling him, considered *asking* him, but when this was raw and new and they didn’t know where the edges were…he thought it might not be wise. Not just yet. So he only brushed another kiss to Ash’s lips, then answered neutrally, “That depends on you.”

“Oh.” Ash’s lashes swept downward, his cheeks flushing in soft dashes of pink. “Are we lovers, then?”

“If you would like to be.”

That tension came back—subtle, yet he could feel it where body touched body, absorbing into him. “Brand…?”

“Yes?”

“Tell me what you want.” A pleading, almost frightened look darted toward him, but beneath that trepidation was a touch of ferocity. “Don’t just…give me what I want. I want to know that you…that you *want* me, not that you’re just giving in to me.”

With a sigh, Brand tightened his grip on Ashton, letting his fingers slip down his arm, stroking over smooth skin. "I have been restraining myself rather forcibly for three days, young Master."

"O-oh." Ash blinked. "I couldn't tell."

"You weren't meant to. Boundaries are boundaries." Brand smiled slightly. Leaning in closer, he rested his brow to Ash's, meeting those dark, confused eyes frankly. "Yes, Ashton. I want you. And if you are amenable, then we can be lovers."

A slow smile broke like the dawn over Ash's lips, before he laughed and pulled away, looking away and tucking his hair behind one ear. "I like that song."

"What song?"

"'*We can be lovers…we can't do that. We can be lovers…and that's a fact,*'" he sang softly, then laughed, burrowing against Brand's side. "It's the Elephant Love Medley from Moulin Rouge."

Brand arched a brow. "I've never seen that."

"We can fix that." With a groan, Ash sagged against him. "When, I don't know. We have to go to work, don't we."

"We do." But Brand gathered Ashton closer, closing his eyes and settling deeper into the bed. Deeper into Ash, learning how the young man felt against him, absorbing these feelings until he was in a better place to sort them out and understand what they meant. "But we may stay a touch longer."

"Yeah?"

"Yes."

"Good," Ashton said, and draped himself against Brand in a tangle of warmth.

Brand said nothing. He simply let it *be*, breathing in Ashton's scent and listening to the rising sound of bird-calls through the windows. He found that this was rather comfortable; rather nice. Soothing, at the very least, and easing some of the hollow, yearning feeling inside him. It wasn't quite what he ached for.

But it would serve, while he gave his young Master space to learn what he wanted from Brand.

THE SUN WAS ALMOST FULLY in the sky before Ash could bring himself to speak again.

He didn't want to break this. He wasn't quite sure how he could feel so comfortable, so *right* with a man he'd met—and hired—only three or four days ago, but with the turmoil and chaos he'd lived in for the past week he wasn't about to ruin his first moment of peace. The first moment he felt truly *good* about anything in a long time.

Yet he couldn't escape his thoughts, either. The

helplessness, the loss that had sent him running away yesterday; the frustration that still circled pointlessly through his brain when he couldn't find any solution that would delay the inevitable. His father said he hadn't given up, but he'd skipped over the idea of Ash's bone marrow without even trying. What if Ash had been a match all this time?

He swallowed, wetting his dry throat. "Brand…?"

The behemoth of a man stirred with a drowsy sound, and cracked one lazy green eye open. Despite himself Ash almost smiled; Brand after sex was a very different creature from Brand before sex, one stiff and upright and the other a melted sprawl of languid muscle and darkened eyes.

"You're going to ask me to get up and make you breakfast, aren't you, young Master?"

"No. Not yet, anyway." Ash smiled faintly and looked down, where his fingers rested splayed against the tanned ridges of Brand's stomach. "I…" He trailed into a squeak, then tried again. "If I volunteer for a bone marrow transplant, he can't stop me, right?"

Brand went very still, very quiet. When he spoke, his words were measured, careful. "They cannot force him to accept the transplant. But he also cannot stop you from being tested," Brand pointed out neutrally. "It is likely that in the course of his early treatment, they tested his bone marrow. I can obtain the number for his private physician, if you wish to seek their counsel and at the very least determine if you are a match."

"I already know her. It's Dr. Singh. She's the family doctor. He'd have gone to her, and refused to work with an oncologist without her there." He bit his lip. "Could you just…make me an appointment?"

Brand studied him discerningly—then leaned in and pressed a soothing kiss to his brow. "Of course, young Master."

DR. APARNA SINGH WAS READY to see them just after lunch. Ash wasn't so sure he was ready to see *her*. Not that soon—but she'd always been willing to drop everything for the Harrington family, as long as it didn't endanger another patient.

He'd been a fidgety mess all morning. A fidgety, *flustered* mess, when he felt like the moment he walked into the office with Brand at his back, both of them slotted back into their places as Mr. Forsythe and young Master Harrington, Ms. Vernon could *tell* with one glance that last night Ash had wrapped his legs around Brand's hips and begged the man to crush him into nothing with pain and pleasure.

Yet business churned on as normal. A thousand phone calls, more contracts to review until his eyes crossed, Brand quietly explaining everything he didn't understand and reminding him of legalities before he made catastrophic decisions.

And now and then brushing his gloved fingertips to the back of Ash's neck in passing, making him jump, his stomach coiling tight with heat and longing.

Yet it was neither heat nor longing making his stomach seasick and cold, as he and Brand stepped inside the welcoming, warmly painted lobby of Dr. Singh's private practice. She was just behind the desk with the receptionist nurse, passing charts between them and talking animatedly, but as they entered she glanced up and smiled warmly, her coppery, delicate features warming with a smile.

"Hi, Ash." She greeted him with the familiarity of the woman who used to bandage up his skinned knees and trick him with silly noises before giving him a shot; her graying bob of black hair bounced around her face as she ducked quickly from around the corner and approached with her hands outstretched. "It's good to see you."

"Hi, Dr. Singh." He took her hands and squeezed them tightly, then nodded toward Brand. "This is Brand Forsythe. My valet."

Brand dipped in one of those formal bows. "Madame."

"You would have to be British," Dr. Singh said enigmatically, eyeing Brand wryly, before turning her attention back to Ash. "Darling. I have a feeling I know why you're here."

"…you could've told me before he was in a hospice center."

"Patient confidentiality is a very serious matter, Ash." She sighed, clucking her tongue regretfully. "Even now. I know he's your father, but with him conscious and power of attorney revoked by the will…" She shook her head. "Whatever you want to know, I can't break privilege without his permission."

"You know me a little too well." He smiled regretfully. "But you can tell me patient information about myself, right?"

"Of course."

"Then if you tested my bone marrow, you could tell me if it was a match for his?"

Her eyes widened. "…Ash." She darted a glance toward Brand, as if asking if he'd put Ash up to this, then back to Ash. "Yes. Yes, I could do that, but…" She pressed her hands together. "It's only a fifty percent chance you'll match. And we're still trying to find someone through the match registry. Testing you…you know it's extremely painful, don't you? Even with local anesthetic, you'll still feel it."

"I know." He smiled faintly, bitterly. "It's Friday, right? So I'll take the weekend to rest."

Dr. Singh blinked. "You want to do it today?"

"No time like the present, right?"

"Are you sure you're ready?"

Ash glanced back at Brand. Brand watched him with that same quiet, nonjudgmental regard…but that gaze seemed to promise he would hold Ash up, if ever he should begin to fall.

That was all he needed.

"I'm sure," Ash said. "Let's do this."

HE WAS LESS SURE WHEN he was lying on an examining room table in a hospital gown, face-down with his entire left hip and part of his back numb.

At least face-down he couldn't see Dr. Singh standing at his flank, or the massive needle he knew was in her hand.

He could only see Brand, standing at the side of the table, hovering close—and reaching for his hand, letting him clutch on tight, stilling the shaking of Ash's fingers.

"Brace yourself, Ash," Dr. Singh murmured. "You won't feel it at first—but then you will."

Ash took a shaky breath and squeezed his eyes shut. "Don't let go," he whispered, his heart pounding wildly.

"I won't, young Master Ashton." And then there was a twin to his own heartbeat, as Brand lifted their clasped hands and pressed them over his chest, letting Ash feel that slow and steady thump through layers of fabric, strong and reassuring. "I'm right here. Hold on to me."

So Ash held on. First there was fear. Then there was pain. A sharp sting, then deeper, so deep it felt like it cut him right through.

But always there was Brand, holding his hand so tight even when Ash bit his lip on a scream, digging in so hard he tasted blood.

It was over in less time than Ash expected, even if he'd counted every second of pain in infinities. Even with the anesthetic it hurt to stand up, hurt to walk.

Ash felt no shame in letting Brand pick him up and carry him from the doctor's office, hiding against him from the lingering ache. Hiding from the fear that when the results came through—by Monday, Dr. Singh promised—it would have been for nothing.

And there was nothing he could do to save his father after all, no matter how hard he tried.

Chapter Ten

WORKING WEEKENDS WERE A BLESSING, Brand thought. Without them, he thought young Master Ashton might have paced a hole right through the floor of the estate.

Instead he flung himself around the office all weekend; even though most of Harrington Steel's business partners were closed until the start of the business week, Ashton took the time to catch up on paperwork, grill Brand on the intricacies of contract law, continuously Google everything he could find on New York labor unions. Brand rather admired his dedication.

Even if he knew it was only a distraction, waiting for that Monday phone call.

Brand let his young Master take what distractions he could, and only stopped him to remind him to eat.

And when Ashton fell asleep over his desk every night, working himself into a weary haze well into the evening…

Brand said nothing, as he bundled his young Master into the car, drove him home, and put him to bed.

Then stayed, when Ashton curled slim fingers in the leg of his slacks and tugged and murmured a wordless plea in a sleepy slur that asked for Brand's presence, nothing else.

A presence Brand was content to provide, slipping off to sleep with the slender, fragile form of his emotionally exhausted young Master in his arms.

How strange, that he should settle so easily into this.

But this, too, was part and parcel of being needed.

MONDAY CAME WITHOUT FANFARE, WITHOUT any grand portent of a shimmering dawn or a brilliant and thunderous storm to warn of either good or bad news. There was only a gray and leaden sky, dull and neutral and flat, as flat as the empty exhaustion leaving Ash feeling like a hollow shell, barely remembering to move.

He couldn't get anything done that morning. He just stared dully at the screen of his laptop; information wasn't going in. Brand watched him over the top of his own laptop, but he didn't think he could stand it if Brand asked anything of him right now; he was grateful when the man let him have his silence. Every time the desk phone buzzed, Ash jumped—but he couldn't bring himself to answer it. Every call that wasn't Dr. Singh tempted him to scream, and he couldn't afford to lose it on a contractor or an overseas supplier just because they weren't who he wanted to hear. Brand fielded each call smoothly, answering inquiries and setting appointments and so many mundane things that just…didn't seem to matter anymore.

But when Ash's cellphone buzzed, he nearly rocketed out of his chair, heart plummeting. He sat up, sat down, fumbled for his phone, nearly dropped it, then managed to catch the call and gasp, "Hello?"

"Ash?"

He knew before Dr. Singh said it what the answer would be. It was in her voice, that careful lilt that said she was preparing to deliver the worst news possible. Still he held out hope, even as she continued,

"I'm sorry. There's no easy way to say this."

The lump of bitterness in his throat threatened to choke him. He closed his eyes, slumping forward. "I'm not a match, am I."

"No, dear. You're not."

"Of course," Ash said hollowly. "Thank you, Dr. Singh."

"Ash…darling, if you'd like I can refer you to a good grief counsel—"

Ash ended the call. Dropped the phone.

And with a harsh sound rising up his throat as if it had been ripped from the bowels of his pain, he flung himself against Brand, nearly knocking the man out of his chair.

Brand made a startled sound, rocking back, then gathered him up—pulling Ash entirely into his lap, curling forward, wrapping around him.

"I know," Brand murmured, rubbing one soothing palm over Ash's back. "I know, young Master. I'm sorry."

Ash said nothing. He only spent himself out in frustrated, furious tears, full-body sobs that racked him like a storm. He didn't know who he was more angry with—Dr. Singh for the news, his father for being ill, himself for being incompatible. He shouldn't even be so fucking frustrated; it didn't change anything.

But that was the problem. It didn't *change* anything.

Ash was just as powerless as he'd been before. He'd always *been* powerless.

It had just never hurt this much, or cut this deep.

EVEN THOUGH ALL ASH WANTED to do was go home, curl up in bed, and cling to Brand until it didn't hurt so much…he made himself stay at the office. Made himself do something where he wasn't useless, wasn't powerless; if he couldn't help his father one way he'd help him another way, and do everything he could to get it right.

If he was struggling to understand import tax and delving into the legal structures of Harrington Steel's overseas entities, at least, he wasn't thinking about how fucking useless he was.

He was ready to pass out, by the time Brand touched his shoulder, then trailed up to curl his knuckles against Ash's throat. "Young Master. You are asleep on your feet. We should depart."

"Sure," Ash mumbled numbly, pushing to his feet—but then closing the laptop, unplugging it, and tucking it under his arm. "I can finish this at home."

He didn't miss Brand's worried look, but neither of them spoke. The silence was almost tense, as they closed up the office and headed down to the car. Ash settled in the back of the Mercedes and opened the laptop again, pulling up a page he'd saved on tax calculations in Germany, but he couldn't really focus on the information. He didn't know where his mind was; skirting around his father, drifting onto Brand, wanting to just…drop everything and disappear into the Himalayas to become a mountain goat farmer. He had a hollow burned-out feeling behind his eyes, and his brain felt like every neuron was short-circuiting in a haze of smoke each time it tried to spark a thought.

"You are thinking something, young Master."

Ash pulled from his thoughts and glanced at Brand in

the rear view mirror. He offered a small smile. “You’ve known me a week and you can read me that well?”

“I tend to pay close attention.”

Ash shrugged, looking away and out the window. “The answer’s pretty obvious, isn’t it? I wanted to do something, and I…” He creased his lips. “Even though I tried, I was useless.”

“You cannot control your genetics,” Brand pointed out. “Even if he is your father, there was always a fifty percent chance that you would not match. That’s not your fault, Ashton.”

Isn’t it?

“It’s like I was born to be useless.”

“No,” Brand said firmly. “Not at all. I know many expectations have been placed on you at a very young age, but not one of those expectations was to play God.”

“I just want to *do* something,” Ash threw back, clenching his fists in frustration. “He’s back now, but for how long?”

That steady green gaze in the mirror faltered, sliding back to the road. “I don’t know, Ashton.”

“…Brand?”

“Yes?”

“Who am I, other than the son of Calvin Harrington?” Ash pleaded. It felt selfish, to wonder that—

but that, too, was part of what was frightening him, twisting up inside him in confused and tangled knots. "I feel like I don't know that, and once he's gone…I won't even be that anymore. It's like I never got the chance to find out. I couldn't want anything that would make me someone else, because I had to leave room to be the next in line. So I made myself a blank state. A carbon copy of a reckless college student. I even majored in business instead of something I might really want, because…" He struggled for words, staring down at his knees. At the crisp starched suit that was better suited for his father than for himself. "Because I knew who I had to be. So I didn't bother trying to be anyone else."

"…young Master." A touch of soft understanding in Brand's voice. "Do you resent your father, for shaping you in this image and then leaving you behind?"

"Yes!" It came out of him in a frustrated cry, before he pulled himself back, rubbing at the ache in his chest. "Is that awful? That I'm mad at him for putting me in this position and then leaving me like it's nothing? Am I being selfish?"

"Grief is inherently selfish, when those we grieve aren't here to benefit from it. That doesn't make that selfishness wrong, my young Master."

Ash didn't realize they were home until the car was stopping. Brand got out without giving him a chance to answer, rounding the car to open Ash's door—but rather than guide him out, he slid in with Ash, crowding him over just enough to make room…and then pulling him into his arms. Pulling him exactly where he needed to be, without making Ash ask for it. Ash went to him willingly, burrowing himself into that solid, reassuring warmth.

"If you need to be selfish to make this easier to deal with," Brand murmured, the rumble of his voice rolling through Ash, "then be selfish. If that means seeking something for yourself, do so. Is there nothing you've ever been curious about? Anything you like, that you could see yourself loving?"

Ash slipped his arms around Brand's shoulders, clinging, and buried his face against his chest. "…what does it matter, when I only have time to be CEO of Harrington Steel?"

"It will not always be that way," Brand promised. "The current period of instability will not last forever. Once that is settled…" He rested his chin to the top of Ash's head, a comforting weight that made him feel enclosed, enveloped. "You don't have to be your father, young Master. Estranged from all but the company. You can find room to find yourself."

"I don't even know what that means. Finding myself."

"It means trying everything until you find the thing

that suits."

Ash didn't even know where to start. With the life he'd lived before this, jet-setting around, he'd done everything from cliff-diving in the Yucatan to drunken shots off a supermodel's abs in Milan…but it was all just part of the party scene, ridiculous things people did when they were drunk and obscenely rich and giving in to peer pressure. He couldn't think of a time when he'd done something just because it had caught his interest, and he was curious about pursuing it.

"Horseback riding," he realized, remembering a vague thought so old it likely belonged to childhood. "I've always wanted to try horseback riding. Maybe having my own stables. Breeding horses."

"Then we shall begin lessons next weekend," Brand said promptly.

"You know how to ride?"

"I am a man of many talents, young Master Ashton."

Despite himself, Ash laughed helplessly, the tightness inside him easing enough to let him breathe. "I think I'm figuring that out."

Brand's quiet chuckle echoed him, before capable hands nudged him gently. "Come. We can continue this conversation inside. Preferably in bed."

Ash let himself be gently manhandled out of the car—but then stopped, glancing at the house and then back at the car, before looking up at Brand. He didn't want to take this to bed with them…and tonight he'd rather be *with* Brand than wallowing in this helpless ache. For all that they'd agreed to be lovers, there'd been nothing since that night but a few kisses and light touches before falling asleep together. And it had been sweet, and right, and comforting, and good. But tonight, if Brand wanted to...

Ash wanted more.

But not until he'd cleared his head, and could come to bed without this third presence standing between them.

He smiled faintly. "Hey. Give me the keys and go in without me?"

With a frown, Brand offered the keyring. "Whatever for?"

"I just want to go for a quick drive. Take the Mercedes around the block to clear my head." He found it in him to grin. "Promise no running off to fuck rich jocks."

If Brand found that at all amusing, his flat glance gave no indication. "I didn't even know you had a driver's license."

"You can't learn everything about me from the tabloids, Brand."

An odd stillness went through Brand. He tilted his head, regarding Ash intently. "If I wanted to know more than the tabloids tell, would you let me?"

Brand seemed to be asking more than that simple question—but Ash couldn't tell what. Some part of him was afraid to find out, when he might be useless there, as well. Helpless. Pointless.

He lowered his eyes. "I don't know," he murmured.

"Ah." He glanced up to find Brand bowing. "Shall I wait for you in your chambers, then?"

"Yeah. Yeah, I'd like that."

"Very well, young Master."

Ash said nothing. They stood in silence for long moments, Brand watching him in that strange way he had that made Ash feel like Brand was gravity and Ash was caught in his well…before Brand turned around and walked into the house, leaving Ash standing alone next to the Mercedes, keys dangling limply from his fingers.

SOMETHING IN BRAND WARNED HIM not to let Ashton go.

He stood in the front window of the house and watched the Mercedes pull away with Ash behind the wheel. It was almost midnight, and Ash was so clearly weary to the bone. Even if Brand wanted to respect his young Master's need to be alone, he wasn't sure if he should be out driving right now. But it was too late to stop him; Brand almost wished Amiko would materialize out of nowhere to tell him what to do about her son, with his fragile emotions and sudden whims—but this late at night she was likely bedded down either in her suite or in Calvin Harrington's. Brand held himself stiffly still, fighting the urge to do something inadvisable without anyone here to stop him.

And then pushed himself into motion, bloody well stepping outside to do it anyway.

Several other cars were parked in the adjacent garage, including Amiko's rented Prius, their keys hanging on a ring just inside the door. Brand selected a quiet late-model black Ford sedan, slipped in behind the wheel, and only waited long enough for the automated garage door to open halfway before he sent the Ford rolling out into the night.

He'd just circle the block. Keep a safe distance; Ash never needed to know Brand was following him. He didn't know why it was so urgent; this wasn't that possessive need, but something darker, ramping his pulse up and tingling at him with a wash of premonition so dire it could only be pointless paranoia, set on high alert when his own emotions, he was discovering, could be just as fragile as Ashton's.

At least where Ashton himself was concerned.

There was no sign of the Mercedes, when Brand

turned onto the main road. Ashton had a bit of a head start; he might have also gone in the opposite direction. Brand would take a circle around, and if he saw nothing to be concerned over he would go back to the house and just…wait.

Yet he wasn't as far behind as he'd thought; as he guided the Ford through the winding suburban roadways, he caught tail lights up ahead, their configuration familiar, slowing at a stoplight. Brand slowed as well, keeping his distance, waiting for the light to change before he accelerated. The Mercedes pulled forward carefully as the light switched green.

And in a crunching of metal, a screaming of tires, another car came careening through the intersection and slammed right into it.

If Ash had been going a single notch faster, the Mercedes would have been T-boned. Instead the car—a flashy red truck, that was all Brand saw—slammed into the nose of the Mercedes, spinning it to the side and not even slowing down as it kept streaking past, weaving drunkenly. The Mercedes skewed wildly, then skidded to a halt. Brand's heart stopped, then leaped forward, charging ahead as quickly as the Ford as Brand slammed down on the accelerator.

He couldn't breathe. He couldn't breathe, couldn't think, couldn't do anything but let the icy fear in his veins propel him forward.

He barely let the Ford slew to a halt before he was out of it and pelting toward the Mercedes. The hood was crumpled, smoke emerging from beneath its buckled arch; he saw no sign of movement from inside. The window had cracked, but not so much that he couldn't see the motionless form slumped over the steering wheel, dangling by the seatbelt.

The world receded into a distant hollow numbness rushing down a long tunnel. He was dimly aware of his own voice echoing in that tunnel, crying *Ashton, Ashton, Ashton,* but he was disconnected from his own words, his own thoughts, his own movements even as he ripped the door open and reached inside, fumbling for the release on the seatbelt. Ash tumbled out and into his arms, motionless, this small and pathetic bundle turned hollow by the absence of the bright, sweet life that made him so animated, so engaging.

Chest so tight it was ready to snap, Brand fumbled for his young Master's collar, his throat—his pulse. Oh God, he had a *pulse,* he was unconscious but alive. Brand let out a harsh, aching sound of relief, ripping painfully from his throat, then made himself remember practicality. His phone in his pocket. 911, the operator crisp and professional and doing nothing to soothe him even as he gave the intersection and Ash's condition. He barely gave her time to confirm before he let the phone fall from numb fingers so he could curl those fingers around Ash, cradling him close.

"Please," he whispered, bowing over Ash, as if he could wrap himself around his young Master and make himself the glue to hold him together. "Ashton, my young Master…oh God, *please*."

Chapter Eleven

Ash woke to the worst headache he'd ever had in his life, and he'd once survived a weekend filled with enough Everclear and Jaegermeister to kill anyone else from alcohol poisoning.

His first impression was pain, throbbing in his skull and pulsing with quiet soreness throughout his entire body. His second impression was a horrible medicinal smell—a hospital smell, a *hospice* smell, and for a moment his lizard brain panicked that he was back in that hospice center watching his father die, and the man had never woken up at all.

But his third impression eased that fear away, when he recognized the heavy weight draped over his body.

Brand's arm, already familiar after a few short nights.

If Brand was here, holding him, nothing could be wrong.

Even if he wasn't quite sure where *here* was, until he cracked one eye open muzzily, peering past a blurry haze of pain. He was…in a hospital room? In a hospital bed, lying there surrounded by neutral blue walls and medical equipment and curtains in those weird patterns that only seemed to belong to hospital furniture and décor. Everything smelled like antiseptic and medication, except the faint, earthy scent of Brand drifting around him.

Brand…had somehow crammed himself into the hospital bed with Ashton, bulk and all, curled on his side and still fully dressed even though Ash had been stripped down to a hospital gown. Brand looked almost ready to fall off the twin-sized bed, but still he held a close grip on Ash, cradling him tight even in his sleep, lines of worry and exhaustion seamed clearly into his face. Ash's heart skipped.

He didn't know how he'd ended up here. All he remembered was a sudden bright flash, noise, pain, fear, then darkness.

Yet he'd woken up with Brand holding him as if he was something precious, and he didn't know what to make of that.

A soft throat-clearing jerked his attention away from Brand. A nurse stood at his side, and he had a feeling she'd been there the entire time but had given him enough of a chance to reorient himself before startling him. She noted something down on a chart, then offered him a dry but not unpleasant smile, tucking her pen into the tight braid of her black hair. Her scrubs stood out in pale pink, stark against her deep brown skin.

"Had an interesting night, Mr. Harrington?" she said

a touch sardonically. “Good to see you’re awake. Having any trouble with vision? Do you feel nauseated?”

“N—” His mouth as too dry to speak, and he coughed when he tried, only to wince as it made his entire sore body twinge. She quickly poured a paper cup of water from a pitcher at the bedside, then tipped it to his lips. He sipped gratefully, letting the cool water ease his parched mouth. “Thank you,” he managed. “No…not nauseated. My vision was a little blurry for a second, but it’s getting better.”

“All right. That’s less to worry about, then.” She nodded toward Brand. “Your boyfriend was losing his shit for a minute there, boo.”

“He’s not my—!” Ash realized his voice was going up, rising in pitch and volume, and caught himself with an embarrassed flush. “Uh. He’s not my…I don’t…know what we are.”

“Pain in the ass, that’s what he is. Tried to get him to leave. You try moving a man that big.” She snorted. “Wouldn’t damned well let go of you.”

“Oh,” Ash said faintly.

“You’re fine, by the way,” the nurse mocked gently. “Little bruised up, but not even a concussion—though we’d like to keep you until morning and double check with an MRI.” She pointed the chart at him meaningfully, then slotted it into the holder at the foot of the bed.

"You're lucky the other driver just clipped you. Could've been a lot worse."

"Is that what happened? Someone hit me?"

"Your not-boyfriend said it was a hit and run. Red truck ran a changing red light at an intersection."

A sick feeling chilled in Ash's gut. He could've been killed right there. Not even dying at an old age like his father, wasting away as disease ate at him.

Just gone, like that.

Barely a blink, and then blinked out.

"Oh," he said again. "I…thanks for telling me."

"Mmhm. You just use the call button if you need anything. I wouldn't try going out there on your own. I've kicked out six reporters today. Pain in my ass."

Ash winced. Of course reporters had found him here. "Sorry."

She snorted. "I'll bet you are."

He forced an apologetic smile. "I'll be out of your hair by morning."

"*If* the doc gives you the all clear." She eyed him, then patted his foot through the hospital blanket. "Get some rest until then."

"Sure," he said. "Thanks."

The nurse paused to straighten a few things, then let herself out of the room with a significant look and pulled the door closed behind her, leaving them alone. Ash turned his head toward Brand, watching him, trying to let his nearness soothe that horrible clutching feeling inside. That realization that he'd almost died, and he'd never even have seen it coming, never have had even an instant to grapple with the reality of it.

He wondered if that was better or worse than having years to stare death down, and watching it crawling toward you inch by inch.

Fuck, he was morbid right now. He guessed having a dying father and nearly dying himself would do that. He closed his eyes, biting back a low whimper in his throat, when if he let that sound out he'd start crying from the sheer shock of it.

But apparently that sound was enough to rouse Brand—because the man stiffened, his arms tightening around Ash, before he sucked in a sharp breath, lifting his head.

"Young Master." He said the words with such relief they came out as breathless and strange endearments. "You're awake—I—are you—"

To see such naked concern on that stoic face…it pulled Ash between a rapid yo-yo of emotions, this mess of confusion and fear and relief and warmth and need and a small and terrified hope for something he couldn't even name. He smiled humorlessly, shifting one aching arm to curl his hand over the arm Brand had around him.

"I'm fine," he said. "The nurse said I was a little dinged up, that's all. And that I was in a hit and run…?"

Fury lit Brand's eyes like lightning illuminating a dark night, flashing there and gone. "I have alerted the police, but yes. A reckless driver hit your car."

Ash's brows knit. "You saw it?"

Another new expression: sheepishness. Brand was just full of them tonight, as if something had ripped away whatever filter kept his emotions masked. "I…ah…I followed you."

"…why."

"I was concerned about you driving alone while so tired. Driver fatigue is one of the top causes of automobile accidents in New York, with a rate of approximately—"

"Don't—" Holding up his hand, Ash laughed—and immediately regretted it, when his ribs protested like they would snap. "I don't need the statistics. I'll be mad at you later. If I feel like it."

Brand watched him searchingly, furrows in his brow, then asked, "…do you need anything? Can I fetch anything for you?"

"Just…I…just be here with me. That's all I need." *That's all I ever need.* Ash smiled slightly, forcing one weary arm up so he could lightly thread his fingers through the mess of hair drifting across Brand's brow.

"Your hair's mussed."

Brand's shoulders stiffened. "I shall remedy that straightaway."

"Don't." Ash lingered, skimming his fingertips along the arch of Brand's eyebrow. "I like it."

"If you like it, then." Brand captured his hand and pressed his cheek into it; a faint hint of fresh stubble brushed Ash's palm, followed by the touch of warm lips. "You frightened me near to death, young Master."

"I promise it wasn't on purpose. This time."

"Unrepentant brat."

"Oversized asshole."

Brand smiled slightly—reserved, yet with a warmth that stopped Ash's heart. "So it would seem we both are," he murmured, and leaned down to kiss Ash, tracing over his lips with a grazing touch that seemed to jumpstart his frozen heart until it beat too fast—reminding him with every sensitized tangle and sweet brush that he was *alive*, until he groaned with the pure warmth of it rushing through him.

Only to break off with a hiss as Brand's kiss sank deeper, and put pressure on a split in his lower lip until it sang with a keen slice of pain.

"Ah—ah, *ow*—"

Brand retreated immediately. "Apologies, young Master."

Ash eyed him. “You are not.”

“I am,” Brand promised solemnly. “A small amount.” His gaze darkened. “Mostly, I am angry.”

“Can you yell at people when we go home?” Biting his lip, Ash reached up to tug at Brand, quietly begging him to lie down again. “I’m tired. And I still…” He exhaled a shaky breath. “I’m scared, and not quite sure I’m really here. Please, just…stay here, and then…”

Brand sank down quietly against him, fitting his body more surely to Ash’s until there was no space between them, balancing them together on the small bed. “Of course,” Brand murmured, nuzzling into Ash’s hair. “I shall begin my quest for vengeance in the morning.”

Ash choked on a small laugh. “Did you just make your very first joke?”

“You called me an oversized arsehole, not a humorless one.”

“…yeah.” Ash turned his head, resting his cheek to the pillow; his nose almost touched Brand’s. “Thank you,” he murmured.

Brand blinked quizzically. “For what?”

“For being you.” Ash forced himself to move even though it hurt, and shifted down to tuck his head underneath Brand’s chin. “Don’t question it. Just sleep.”

Brand’s snort stirred Ash’s hair, before subsiding. “As my young Master wishes.”

Ash only closed his eyes with a smile, and let himself start to drift off, giving in to his body's demands. Yet he couldn't fall asleep; not even with Brand holding him. *Especially* with Brand holding him, when suddenly he was full of questions he was afraid to ask.

But also afraid not to, when he'd almost lost the chance in a single flash of light and high-speed impact.

Now or never.

He opened his eyes, gaze fixing on the tic of Brand's pulse against his throat. "Brand?"

The deeply velvety sound of Brand's voice said he had been almost asleep. "Yes, young Master?"

"Were…" Ash struggled to figure out what to ask. What to say. "Were you like this with Vic and his parents?"

"No," Brand answered immediately. "I was always for them; they were never for me."

"It's…never been two-way for you?" Ash realized, tilting his head back to look up at Brand. "Ever?"

Brand shook his head, saying nothing, but dark eyes seeming to ask everything. An ache inside Ash crumpled, hurting deep.

"Oh. Brand…"

Rough fingertips, for once devoid of gloves, pressed to his lips gently, skirting around the split in the lower. "I'm not asking that of you, young Master."

"Why not?" Ash asked.

Brand stilled—yet it was different from his normal stillnesses. A tense thing, sharp with portent. "…what?"

Oh fuck. Fuck, he'd probably just completely stepped in it with a man twice his age who knew ten times more about the things Ash was trying to fumble with. Ash didn't *do* relationships. He'd never even met anyone he wanted a relationship with, when everyone who might be considered his peer was just as shallow and pointless as he'd spent twenty-three years pretending to be.

Just as shallow and pointless as Brand probably thought he was.

But he'd started this, so he might as well finish it—instead of leaving it hanging open-ended and waiting to ruin everything when he wasn't even sure there was a *thing* to be ruined.

"I mean…I just…why not? Why don't you want to ask that of me?" he asked. "You…you keep acting like I'm everything to you when you don't even know me. Why don't you want me to be the same toward you? Why do you want it to be that one-sided?"

"Young Master," Brand said, something low and almost dangerous in his voice, "I did not say I *wanted* it to be one-sided. Only that I am accustomed, in a way. My devotion to the Newcomb family was a different thing. It was only appropriate that such devotion should not be returned. It was part of my job."

"Am I just that, then?" Ash whispered. "Part of your job?"

Brand's lips parted, but he hesitated several breaths before he spoke. "Is this really a conversation you wish to have in the hospital?"

"Will it really be any better at home?"

"I suppose not." Yet there was something odd about Brand, something restrained that Ash could almost see hovering over him, a thing riding him and waiting to be spoken. "No," Brand said carefully. "You are not simply part of my job. But I am not certain what you are."

Ash wet his lips nervously, his skin prickling. "What do you want me to be?"

That oddness redoubled into a tight tension. "That is potentially a dangerous question, young Master."

"Why?"

"Because I am not certain I have the terms to articulate what I want you to be." That keen gaze sharpened, flicking over Ash's face, dipping to his mouth before rising to his eyes again. "Nor am I certain you will want to hear them."

Ash didn't understand. What could be so horrible that he wouldn't want to hear it? Unless…Brand was trying to tell him not to push. Not to make it more than casual sex outside the office. Ash lowered his eyes, lingering on the faint hint of the scar just barely peeking up past Brand's collar.

"...tell me, Brand. Please. If I'm not just your job...what do you want me to be?"

"I..."

That was when Ash realized that cold, proper, unflappable Brand Forsythe?

Was *nervous*.

He looked almost as though it *pained* him to be uncertain about something, and Ash couldn't help a fond smile, resting his hand to Brand's chest.

"Take your time," he teased softly. "They're not letting me out of here until morning."

"...you truly are a brat." Brand made a huffy, irritable sound, but only tightened his hold on Ash, drawing their bodies together. "I would ask something of you, first."

"I'm listening."

"Tell me how you feel, when you are with me." As blunt and straightforward as everything Brand said, yet it hinted at something unspoken, a leading edge. "Tell me why you kissed me that night."

"For the same reason I called you to come get me instead of trying to get home on my own. I..."

Ash's heart beat harder. Admitting this out loud,

trying to quantify it...he didn't know how. He didn't know how to describe the feeling he'd had since the moment Brand had taken him in hand and Ash had realized he wasn't spinning anymore, so long as Brand held him tight.

"I get confused with how I feel around you," Ash confessed. "I...no one's ever taken care of me like you do. Not really. I had discipline at boarding school and I guess that's the only reason the worst things I do are waste money and act like a shiftless asshole, but..." He shrugged helplessly. "Being a harmless waste of space isn't—it's not like—just because I'm not *bad,* it doesn't mean I'm somehow *good.* And now everyone's expecting me to be better than I really am, and part of me wants to do it. Part of me wants to stand up and do right by my dad and not disappoint everyone. Prove I can do this. Be a functioning, independent adult."

Brand curled his knuckles against Ash's cheek, roughness grazing against his skin. "Am I standing in the way of that, then?"

"No!" Ash protested. "If anything, you...you make me feel like I can do this. Which doesn't make sense, because I get this..." His pulse skipped and leaped. His stomach twisted, high with nerves, with fear, admitting this...this *thing* he felt that he didn't know how to define, hoping Brand wouldn't...laugh in his face, recoil in disgust, leave his heart in pieces on the floor. "I get all weird inside when you want to do everything for me. Because it's not like…not like a hired servant helping me. Not the way you do it. It's *different* the way you do it…like there's this entire different meaning behind it." Ash lowered his eyes; Brand was watching him so *intently*, stealing his breath, and if Ash looked at him he'd lose the courage to keep speaking. "It's like you're taking care of me because I'm…small and helpless, and I *need* it." He winced at how that came out; God, he sounded weird. "But I'm not small. I'm not helpless. I'm used to no one…taking care of me like that. My parents never did." He bit the inside of his cheek. He could barely get his voice out as more than a strangled whisper as he finished, "…so why do I get all weird and hot inside when you do?"

A full-body shudder went through Brand, so intense Ash could feel it with every inch of his body. That large, rough hand curled against the back of Ash's head, drawing him in so Brand could kiss his temple, the corner of his eye, murmuring against his skin.

"There are terms for that, but I think if I told you, you would rebel," Brand said, low and rich with a husky edge. "Suffice to say it brings me an equally deep pleasure to care for you."

Ash leaned into that warm affection as if starved for

it, soaking it in. "Are…we talking about the same kind of pleasure?"

"I should think so," Brand said—then, at Ash's skeptical look, clarified patiently, "Yes, my young Master. It provides me both emotional gratification and physical sexual arousal to attend to your every need."

Ash groaned. "You would put it that way."

"I speak in plain terms to avoid being misunderstood."

"I *don't* understand, though," Ash admitted. "I don't understand how I'm supposed to be self-sufficient in the office but also just…giving up any idea of self-sufficiency at all to let you be this way with me."

"Few people truly stand on their own, young Master." Brand's touch left shivers over Ash's skin as long, rough fingers wove into his hair, stroking slowly down to his scalp, a rhythm underscoring each word. "We all rely on those in our lives whom we care for, and who care for us. Even those who live independently draw comfort and strength from the relationships in their lives."

Ash leaned into him, eyes slipping closed; a lovely, boneless feeling went through him, languid and soft. "That…makes perfect sense and none at all."

"Which is typical for people, regardless of their station or any unique…*preferences*." The latter word came out on a soft growl. "You may draw comfort and strength from my care, allow me to shelter you and manage your life…and still stand on your own as you make the choices necessary to grow into the life you have inherited. The two are not mutually exclusive. And for some whose public lives revolve around controlling critical decisions, it can be very freeing, to the point of providing sexual release, to give up control in their private lives."

Ash bit back a grin. "So that's a complicated way of saying some people get off on being pampered and told what to do."

"Yes, you impertinent wretch." Brand let out an exasperated, but not unamused sigh. "In some small way, you are American royalty—while I appear to have taken on a role not only as your manservant, but your knight. I protect you…but you may still command my loyalty, young Master." Brand let out a thoughtful rumble. "Even if I may, at times, rebel at being commanded myself."

"You are a very hard man to boss around, Brand."

But that was what Ash liked, he realized. That every time he tried to command Brand, the man looked at him like he might take Ash over his knee at any moment—and even when he acquiesced, he did it in a way that somehow made him the one in control. The one calling the shots.

And there was something sweetly intimate in *trusting* him to do that.

"I do answer when you ask," Brand pointed out.

"Yeah…you do." Ash worried at the inside of his lower lip with his teeth…then told himself it was *all right* and tentatively settled to press into Brand, tucking up close even if it hurt to move. He was rewarded by a firm, rather possessive hand against the small of his back, curling in his hospital smock and holding him close and shooting liquid heat down to his stomach and up from his inner thighs. He shivered, resting his head against Brand's shoulder. "This…*thing*…with us…it's weird, isn't it?"

"It is what it is," rumbled against his ear.

"It's…kind of quick…"

"Serendipity happens." Brand's hand smoothed slowly up his back, as if mapping him, shaping him. "We each had an absence in our lives. That we happen to fill each other's absences can make things seem to fall together rather quickly."

It was such a clinical answer—and it left Ash rather disquieted, biting back a protest. "I guess that's what it is, isn't it." He stared at the wrinkles of suit coat and shirt just before the tip of his nose, and only held that much tighter to Brand. "We're easy for each other. Filling a need."

Even if that explanation left Ash feeling so very empty.

"Yes," Brand replied—only to let out that patient,

almost fondly exasperated sigh again, his voice softening. “I am telling you the answer you seem to want to hear, young Master Ashton.” He captured Ash’s hand against his chest, then lifted it to kiss his knuckles. “That does not mean that answer is the truth.”

“I want the truth. Don’t lie to me,” Ash demanded. “If you want me to trust you, don’t ever lie to me. Not even if you think it’s what I want to hear.”

Brand studied him gravely. A shadow hovered over him, unspoken and dark. “I don’t think you’re ready to hear what I have to say.”

“Tell me anyway,” Ash whispered, even if his own voice was almost lost to the half-frightened cry of his pulse.

For an instant, doubt flickered across those elegant, subtly lined features, sinking the faint marks of age deeper into Brand’s handsome face. He searched Ash’s face as though looking for some answer there, then murmured,

“I want you to depend on me.”

Ash frowned, shaking his head. “I don’t understand. I…I already depend on you. Isn’t that your job?”

“No, young Master Ashton,” Brand corrected gently. “I want you to be *dependent* on me. I want you to need me until you are helpless without me. I want you to want me to control you.”

Ash stared at Brand. Brand met his gaze in waiting,

expectant silence, as if waiting for it to sink in. For the pieces to come together into something that Ash could understand.

What he understood were the words *helpless* and *control.*

Even if he didn't understand why they sent a breathless tremor through him, something wild and hot in his chest, in the pit of his stomach, that he told himself could only be nervousness, fear.

"O-oh," he fumbled out. "Is this like…Dom stuff?"

"No. Not quite. Not in the conventional sense, at least. No whips, no cuffs, no collars, no chains."

Brand explained with the same quiet simplicity with which he explained everything else—Ash's responsibilities, the impact of market volatility on steel prices, how to tie a proper Windsor knot. Yet underscoring that low voice was something else—a roughness, a darkness, something Ash could only call *yearning.*

And it wrapped him in its velvet touch, drawing him in, leaving him straining toward Brand even as he listened.

"Simply willing dependency," Brand continued. "Putting yourself entirely in my hands, and trusting me to care for you to the point that we cannot survive without each other. I would dress you. Bathe you. Fetch and carry for you. You would do nothing on your own, not without asking permission first. And if you failed to ask permission…" A dark, hungry gleam in Brand's eyes; an edge of a growl in his voice. "I would punish you."

Ash's gut tightened, his pulse leaping sharply, heart turning over. He stared at Brand. "That…doesn't….sound normal or healthy."

"It's not," Brand admitted frankly. For a moment his hold on Ash tightened, before loosening as if already preparing to let him go. "Not unless both parties want it. Not unless you gain from it as much as I do. A mutual exchange for mutual pleasure."

Don't let go, Ash begged silently. It caught him off guard how desperately he didn't want Brand to let go, when he should be climbing out of bed to get away from him. He clutched his fingers tighter in Brand's clothing, begging without words: *Stay. I'm just trying to understand, please…please stay.*

"Wh-what…what do you get from this?" Ash whispered.

"The pleasure of being needed." Brand unwound one hand from Ash's hospital smock—if only so he could curl his knuckles underneath Ash's chin, his thumb brushing rough against Ash's lower lip, leaving it tingling. "Perhaps the satiation of an obsession."

Ash's mouth felt too hot, too soft. His blood was ringing in his ears, stirring in his veins, this strange frightened thrill making him ache deep down with a trembling and needy pleasure. He parted his lips against that caressing thumb.

"You…want to be obsessed with me?"

"And you with me," Brand whispered. Back and forth, back and forth his thumb traced, slow pressure just firm enough to remind Ash of his strength; of how much larger he was, how easily his touch could turn crushing. "Again…it must be mutual, or it asks for disaster. Even if I would not be materially dependent on you…emotionally, I would need you just as deeply to function at all."

"You don't even know me," Ash breathed.

"That is what time is for. That is what this is an invitation to, as well." Brand leaned in, pressing his mouth to Ash's—giving him a taste, once more, of that barely-restrained dominance, that complete and utter control as Brand's lips teased Ash's into softness, coaxed him into submission. He trembled, pressing into Brand with a whimper, his mouth aching for more—but Brand drew back, parting their lips with one last grazing touch of his thumb, half-lidded green eyes locked on Ash's. "I am asking you to let down your guard with me, young Master Ashton. To relax certain barriers and learn to know each other intimately on a level more personal than physical."

"What you're asking me to do…" It took everything in Ash to pull his thoughts together from the scattered rush of frightened heat Brand's kiss had roused. Everything in him not to just say *yes*, when he wanted to go belly up and let Brand take all his fears, all this pressure away from him. But… "It's way more than just…just…relying on you as a close advisor and someone who can be discreet if we sleep together sometimes. That's…" He inhaled shakily. "What you're asking me to do is *scary*, Brand."

Brand went stiff against Ash. Hurt flickered in his eyes for a moment, before closing away behind quiet acquiescence—neutral, glassed over, Brand the valet rather than Brand the man who refused to be chased from Ash's bed. "I'm sorry," he said, his hold loosening once more, that touch falling away from Ash's mouth. "I didn't mean to frighten you. You may consider my offer retracted."

Ash caught Brand's hand before it could retreat too far; before he lost his nerve. "But…"

"But…?"

Ash lowered his eyes—then lifted that broad, coarse hand to rub his cheek against curled knuckles, against the faint bristle of coarse hair against his skin, each touch, each texture, a frightening yet wonderful burst of sensitivity.

"I do like it…how it feels," he admitted, barely able to manage a shaking whisper. "When you take control away from me. And I'm just…small, next to you. Helpless. To everything. To you." He darted his tongue over his lips. "It…it makes me want…"

Brand watched him intently—a certain waiting stillness about him, a tension ready to snap. "What, young Master? What do you want?"

"You," Ash confessed simply. "I don't…get it. That when you make me feel that way, it makes me want you. And I don't get why you want me."

"Do you doubt that I find you attractive?"

"It's not about me being hot. Something like this…it's not about looks." Or maybe that was what that quiet, needy part of Ash wanted; to matter to someone as more than a pretty face. He ventured, "Would you want anyone you worked for to be dependent on you like this?"

"No. Not like this." No less dry and factual—yet no less sincere, either, honest in that raw way of Brand's that cut right into Ash's heart. "I am not sure I have the words for it. It is simply…an innate sense. A rightness. As if I can see the shape of an absence inside you, and where the edges are…they match the shape of an absence inside me. Your mother described it as the red string of fate."

Ash stiffened, gut lurching, horror drying that molten pool of desire to just crumbles. "You talked to my *mother* about this?"

Brand trailed into low, thunder-murmur laughter.

“No. Not in so many terms.” That laughter gentled into a smile; Brand’s fingers slipped down the line of Ash’s jaw, leaving trails of heat. “She only tried to advise me on whether or not I should let you run…” Then his fingers were against Ash’s throat—gentle, but encircling nonetheless, capturing him with his breaths hitching and his heart stuttering. “…or if I should hold you down and refuse to let you go.”

Ash took several frantic, shallow breaths; he didn’t know if he was frightened or painfully aroused or maybe *both*, when *both* seemed to be what made this work. “Y-you know codependency is really fucked up,” he whispered. “There’s like…DSM shit about what it does to people.”

“I know.” Yet Brand’s hand remained where it was, massive and making Ash feel so delicate, his neck so slender and easily crushed if that touch turned from gentle to cruel. Slowly, deliberately, Brand’s thumb traced down over his jugular, teasing a line of rough fire-touch over Ash’s skin. “But I also know that sometimes we choose for ourselves what feels right, what feels best, as long as it sates both our needs.”

Ash held completely and utterly still, yet his entire body was shaking, his heart slamming painfully against his ribs. What Brand was asking of him might seem simple…but it required trusting Brand the way Ash had never trusted anyone in his life.

It scared him.

Yet there was some quiet, hungry part of him that *liked* being scared; that liked the thrill of that hand against his throat, and the promise in that tall, hardened, weathered body that made him feel so small and vulnerable and young.

"It's…" His voice trailed off into a soft whimper as Brand's hand tightened subtly; a rush of need surged right to Ash's cock. "I-it's…just a roleplay thing with sex and private time anyway, right?"

"If that is what you wish it to be," Brand murmured, and yet something in those dark, hypnotic eyes said *no*.

No, it was so much more than that.

And it was so much more than a simple agreement, when Ash licked his lips and mustered his courage and whispered, "Yes."

Brand made a low, pleased sound. His hold slowly curled tighter against Ash's throat, fingertips against the back of his neck, drawing him in. "Then you will do as you are told?" Brand rumbled.

Ash peeked up through his lashes, meeting that deeply possessive gaze…then swept his lashes down once more, bowing his head obediently, his entire body taut and burning with the rush of anticipation. "…yes."

Clenching fingers. Just a touch of pressure, and his

body responded with such explosive heat he nearly whimpered, shifting restlessly, aching to rub his entire body against Brand's to ease this sudden hot, desperate *feeling*.

"Say 'yes, Brand,'" Brand commanded softly.

"Yes, Brand," Ash repeated, then licked his lips when he could almost feel the words caressing them, as if sealing this with a phantom kiss.

"Very good, my young Master."

And then that grasp was drawing him in, thumb catching under his jaw and tilting his face up, exposing his vulnerable throat…and pulling him in to the lips that descended on his, smiling with a promise and a hunger that said Ash would beg for Brand's particular brand of control very soon, teasing with a confidence that whispered of a darkness waiting to be explored. "Very good, indeed."

CHAPTER TWELVE

IT WAS ALMOST ANTICLIMACTIC, THE following morning, for Ash to get up and just…*leave* the hospital. Just like that. Especially after nearly dying in a hit and run.

And especially after a night spent trembling in Brand's arms, soft and submissive while the man simply *kissed* him in a way he'd never been kissed before in his life.

He was accustomed to quick, rushed, messy kisses. Aggressive and pushy kisses that tasted of Jaegermeister and hot young hormones, thoughtless and acting on sheer instinct and self-gratification.

The way Brand kissed…it was with slow, lingering deliberation, intimacy. Brand kissed with *purpose*—and that purpose was to leave Ash completely vulnerable, completely exposed, no part of his mouth left untouched, untasted, unexplored.

And Ash had been left with no control over what shivering height Brand might push him to next when the man held him so firmly, cradled his head in long fingers, dwarfed him against his bulk…and guided him where Brand would lead, leaving Ash gasping and trailing helplessly in his wake.

Brand had teased him for hours, until Ash was a melted, whimpering mess, boneless and desperate for anything—any touch, any kiss, anything Brand would give him to ease the molten feeling flowing through him and pooling down in that slow-burn, needy place that pulsed just below and behind his cock.

And Brand had given him nothing.

He had only kissed Ash's forehead, drawn the thin hospital blanket up over both of them, and quietly ordered Ash to go to sleep.

Then closed his eyes himself, a quiet statue where Ash couldn't tell if he was awake or asleep, only that he had every intention of leaving Ash writhing if he didn't do as he was told.

So that was his first taste of exactly what Brand wanted from him. This…*control*, this dependency that made fear twist up hot and delicious in the pit of his stomach, and only made that deep, sluggishly warm arousal even worse; this thing that he now realized Brand had been holding back from him, giving only just enough their first time together to let him glimpse, but never truly *know*.

His second taste came that morning; he'd finally managed to sleep, only to wake not long after dawn to Brand stirring and slipping out of bed. Ash had curled against the pillows, reaching across the bed to the wrinkled warm spot where Brand had been, yawning and looking up at him shyly, sleepily.

"Where are you going?" he'd mumbled, rubbing his cheek against the pillow.

"To the manor to fetch you proper clean clothing. Yours was ruined in the accident. I will return within the hour." Brand fixed him with a stern look. "Stay in bed."

Ash pouted, pushing himself up on one hand and rubbing at his eyes sleepily. "But I feel fine—"

His breaths knocked from him in surprise as Brand's hand firmly pressed to his chest, a skin-shivering, enticing flex of strength pushing Ash easily back to the bed and holding him there. Brand leaned over him, blocking out the light, taking up his world, making his heart beat faster with the way those dark green eyes cut into him.

"You will stay in bed until I return," Brand commanded softly, an edge of menace to his voice; his splayed fingers stroked slowly down Ash's chest. "If I have even an inkling that you have been out of this bed, I will *tie* you to it until the doctor arrives to take you for your MRI, or release you. Do I make myself understood?"

Breathing shallowly, heart rabbiting, Ash nodded, mouth too dry to even speak, thoughts circling too sharply to form words.

"Good."

Then Brand had dipped to kiss him, just the quickest moment of domineering, needy pressure, a taunting caress of a heated tongue…

Before he was gone with one last look of warning, leaving Ash curled up in bed and breathing in short, panting gasps and so fucking *hot* he thought he was going to spontaneously combust.

And so very tempted to find out if Brand would make good on that promise, if he got out of bed.

But he was good; this was still too new, too confusing for him to test it, and he was still sorting out his feelings about it. About *Brand*, when he felt like…he felt like…

Like he was seeing Brand as a whole person for the first time, without the careful barrier Brand kept between his feelings and those who might find them unacceptable. Brand had been intriguing from the start, but this new side to him was fascinating. Compelling. *Real.*

And Ash couldn't help flushing, as he curled against the pillows and lingered over the taste of his valet's lips, the firm and commanding touch of steady hands.

He was such a cliché, wasn't he?

Falling for the hired help.

He was still blushing, when Brand returned with a clean, freshly-pressed suit. And he was rewarded for his obedience with another of those kisses that left him melted, making it even harder to endure Brand's hands on his body, the slow deliberation of every touch, the skimming caress of Brand's fingertips tracing over every inch of him as the man dressed him.

When the doctor came for one last look at him and signed off on discharge, Ash managed to pull himself together enough to act like he was actually the one in charge here, while Brand retreated dutifully to his shoulder, silent and watchful.

Yet there was a charged portent around him, a wordless reminder.

Ash might be his employer, and perhaps they might keep up appearances…

But Ash was in no way the one in control.

He couldn't take his gaze away from Brand's profile, on the drive home. Now and then a warm, lingering glance caught him in the rear view mirror and he flushed again, glancing away with a faint smile.

That smile vanished, though, when they pulled in at the house. Brand had barely pulled the car door open for him and helped him out with a guiding hand before the front door of the house opened and his mother spilled out, pushing his father in a wheelchair—only to abandon the chair and tumble down the walk to pull Ash into a tight hug.

"*Ash,*" Amiko gasped. "When we got the call from

the hospital, I—just—you're all right?"

Ash stood still. He couldn't bring himself to hug her back, right now. This sudden concern, this…*presence*, he just…didn't know what to do with them. "Nothing broken," he said tightly. "Not even bleeding. I'm okay, Mom. Promise. The car's in worse shape than I am."

His father shifted in his chair as if he would try to stand, then slumped, this bag of brittle bones. "Son," he said gruffly.

"Really. I'm all right." Ash forced a smile. "You don't need to worry. I just need a day off to rest, and then it's back to work tomorrow." He caught Brand's eye almost desperately and tossed his head toward the door. "Forsythe."

"Young Master," Brand replied smoothly, gliding around him and pulling the door of the house open.

Ash flashed his parents another weak smile, then ducked inside, moving quickly toward his suite. Brand caught up with him in a few long strides, hovering at his shoulder.

"You were rather short with your parents."

With a shrug, Ash slowed, glancing back. "Mom and Dad both…" He sighed. "Suddenly they want to talk to me about…being parents. When before they were more like silhouettes on the other side of a screen." He grimaced. "I'm twenty-three. I don't need a mother and father now, but…I don't hate them for it, either? I just don't know what to do with it."

They paused so Brand could hold the door to Ash's suite for him, only to follow him inside. "Was there ever a time when you did need them?"

"Maybe when I was ten and wondering why my father sent me to boarding school in fucking Liverpool, and my mother was suddenly on the other side of the world."

Sighing, he flung himself down on the bed, reaching up to loosen his tie—only to freeze when Brand brushed his hands aside. Ash stared up at him, eyes wide, pulse ticking hard against his throat as Brand gently began to unknot his tie. Even the smallest things carried so much more *weight* now, knowing that when Brand did something so simple as tug his tie away, the hiss of silk on cotton so loud in the silence…

It meant more, to him.

Brand slowly wound Ash's tie around his fist, smoothing it meticulously. "Do carry on," he said softly.

Ash swallowed, searching for his train of thought again when his mind was intensely riveted on the hard play of Brand's knuckles against his gloves, the firm surety in each movement, almost menacing.

"Um," he managed. "I…no. I've…never really needed that. I know…I *know* what I must look like to you.

This helpless mess careening everywhere." He smiled faintly. "But all I've ever been dependent on anyone for was money. I guess because I was too busy avoiding responsibility, so I wouldn't have to be dependent on anyone for anything else. I've just…never needed anyone." He reached for the top button of his shirt—*just* so Brand would stop him; just so Brand would capture his hand, pulling it away. "Not the way I seem to need you," he admitted.

Brand laced their fingers together, one at a time—then pushed Ash's hand up over his head, gently pinning it to the bed; Ash's breaths hitched, everything inside him drawing tight as Brand leaned over him, gloved caress stroking his throat as he slipped that one button open…then trailed his fingers down, until he found the buckle of Ash's belt and meticulously slipped it free.

"You did hire me for a reason, young Master," Brand murmured.

"…yeah." Ash bit his lip, then reached up with his free hand to trace Brand's lips. "Can we talk about anything else, right now? Anything at all?"

Brand's eyes gleamed. His fingers tightened on Ash's. "We can talk about this erroneous idea that you are taking today off."

Heat vanished instantly. Ash groaned, thunking his head back against the bed. "…goddammit, Brand."

"You are working from home today, but you are still *working*."

"…can I at least work from bed?"

"My bed."

Ash grinned, sitting up, scooting toward the edge of the bed and dragging his grip on Brand's hand with him. "I can work with that. Now get me out of these fucking shoes. They *pinch*."

With a snort, Brand rolled his eyes, sinking to one knee. "As my young brat commands."

IF BRAND WASN'T CAREFUL, HE was going to crash the car.

He couldn't seem to stop watching Ashton in the rear view mirror of the sleek black Dodge Jeep that had taken the place of the wrecked Mercedes, for now. Then again, he'd hardly been able to take his eyes off the young Master since Monday night. First that fear that he had almost lost him, that limp and lifeless form spilling out of the smoking car, the terror that his breaths might stop at any moment…

…and then that quiet *yes*, that tremor of apprehension and sweet longing in Ashton's eyes, that moment when

Brand had been certain he'd destroyed everything with the honesty he couldn't help when he'd almost lost the chance to claim his young Master at all.

When Ash begged so softly, that aching need pleading to be fulfilled…how could Brand not tell him the truth of what he craved?

And when Ash blushed for him, when he pressed into Brand with that demure, submissive body language that said *take me, own me, control me, consume me…*

How could Brand not oblige, with everything in him?

Yesterday and last night had been sheer torment. Sprawled in bed next to Ashton, leaning shoulder to shoulder with him and murmuring over the numbers scrolling by on his laptop screen, now and then catching each other in sidelong glances and lingering gazes. Ashton had a way of catching his breath, when that happened. Catching his breath, parting pink and wanting lips as if waiting, begging, and if his young Master had not just left the hospital after a car crash then Brand would have tossed the laptop aside and pushed him back against the bed and answered that need again and again with his lips, his touch, his body, his cock.

But he was supposed to be the responsible one. The one with *control*.

And so he kept himself under control, and reminded himself that anticipation only made the promise in parted lips that much sweeter.

That promise would have to wait a touch longer. Ash had fallen asleep against him early last night, clearly wrung out and emotionally exhausted, barely stirring when Brand had undressed him and slipped him into his pajamas and tucked him in to rest. And this morning…

This morning it was back to the office, and slow, meaningful glances exchanged in the rear view mirror on the drive to the city.

He caught Ash watching him in the mirror again, before his young Master looked away with a subtle, sweet smile, fidgeting at the cuffs of his suit. "…I Googled this shit with me and you, you know," he murmured. "What we're doing."

"Ah. Did you learn anything informative?"

"We're supposed to have a safe word."

"Mine is 'Thatcher," Brand countered.

"Then I guess it's mine now, too. But I'm never calling you Daddy," Ash said, grinning.

Brand chuckled. "I would not want you to, young Master Ashton."

"*And* don't you ever call me a good boy."

Brand lofted his brows. "Would 'good lad' suffice?"

Ash tried to scowl, but only burst into delighted laughter. "*Brand.*"

"Apologies, young Master."

"Asshole."

Brand only smiled, and turned the car into the parking garage at Harrington Steel.

Ash felt almost like a prince, with the way Brand treated him.

Not that Brand hadn't always waited on him hand and foot…but it was *different*, now. Something almost reverent in the way Brand handed him down from the back of the SUV, first holding his hand to steady him and then catching his waist to keep his balance as he navigated the rather high drop from the runner to the ground. Something beyond deferential in how Brand held the lobby door for him. Something almost fixated in how Brand's gaze never left him, as they headed inside. Ash felt like everyone in the lobby who greeted him, that hasty little head-bob and murmur of "Mr. Harrington," could tell the difference, charged in the air between them.

And he couldn't seem to look away from Brand, so completely absorbed that he didn't even stop to think as they paused in front of the elevator and he reached out to press the Up button.

Making it there a second before Brand, who had already been reaching for the button himself.

Brand stilled, letting his hand fall. His gaze sharpened, but he said nothing. Ash parted his lips, a confused question on his tongue—but then the elevator doors opened. Brand stepped forward, his bulk crowding Ash back with every deliberated stride; Ash stared up at him, something in that stone-set expression making trepidation quiver in his stomach. Swallowing, he backed into the elevator; Brand followed. The doors closed behind them. Brand reached over without looking to press the button for the top floor. The elevator lurched upward with a jolt that made Ash's stomach drop out, falling in a mess of twisting knots.

"Brand…?" he whispered, looking up at that forbidding gaze.

Still Brand said nothing.

But with a pointed, precise motion, he pressed the emergency stop button on the elevator panel. The elevator ground to a jolting halt between floors. Brand stepped closer to Ash, backing him against the wall—only to reach over his head. Heart thumping, confusion swirling through him, Ash tilted his head back, watching as Brand caught the opaque black plastic dome covering the security camera, detached it neatly, then disengaged the cable for the camera. The blinking red light went dark. Brand propped the cover neatly on the hand rail.

Then caught the tip of one glove in his teeth, that bizarre little habit of his that nonetheless riveted Ash's gaze on the erotic cruelty of his stern mouth, on the sheer sensuality of working lips as the gloves slid away from those long, elegant hands.

"Now, young Master," Brand murmured, a husky and whispered growl, "I believe it is time that you learned a lesson."

BRAND FORSYTHE WAS APPARENTLY A very, very bad man.

He must be, to be so very *irritated* that Ashton had done something so simple as pushing an elevator button for himself. And he must truly be terrible, to savor so deeply the look of wide-eyed confusion on that lovely face, blue eyes glimmering with trepidation. For all that he was no virgin, for all that he had steeped himself in worldly ways, young Master Ashton was so *innocent*, and it showed in his shallow breaths, in the beat of his pulse against his throat, in the touch of fear with which he regarded Brand in the silence between them.

And it should not arouse Brand so much, but it did.

The young Master would learn his place.

And perhaps, now, he would truly understand what he had ensnared himself in.

Brand finished peeling his gloves off, and dropped them into his pocket. He wanted skin to skin, for this. Ash's gaze darted to his hands, then back to his face; he backed up another step, until his shoulders hit the wall.

"B-Brand…?"

"You did not wait," Brand said—and caught his young Master around his slim waist, jerking him away from the wall and close against him.

Ash let out a soft cry, his back arching, for a moment struggling before he went limp against Brand, clutching at his coat, lowering his eyes in that way he had that set Brand's blood on fire with the soft, demure downsweep of his lashes, the way his pale amber cheeks flushed against golden freckles, the glisten of his parted pink lips.

"I'm sorry," Ash whispered. "I…I didn't realize…"

"Exactly. You did not realize." Brand caught Ash's chin lightly, tracing that tempting lower lip with his thumb—then pushed Ashton away, curling his hand in the back of his suit coat to guide him, turning him swiftly around to push him face-first up against the elevator wall. "But you will learn."

"Wh-what are y—"

Brand didn't give Ash a chance to finish. He slipped his arms around him from behind, pulling that lithe, agile body against him, savoring the tremor that went through Ash and rolled into Brand like seismic waves. When Brand caught the tongue of the young Master's belt buckle and drew it open, Ash sucked in a sharp breath; when Brand teased the button and zipper of his slacks open, Ash went tense.

And when Brand slipped his hand inside layers of fabric to press skin to skin, grazing his fingertips to the base of Ash's cock…

Ash went boneless against him with a low, whimpering moan, as shocked as wide blue eyes before those eyes fluttered closed.

Brand wrapped his hand firmly around Ash's cock. The young Master shuddered against him with shallow, gasping breaths as Brand stroked him, explored him, coaxed him to hardness and savored the feeling of hot flesh thickening, swelling, firming against his palm. Ash sagged against the elevator wall, writhing between it and Brand, hands curling helplessly against the polished steel as he cried out in low, erotic, breathless sounds that whispered as much of fear as of pleasure, as much of protest as of plea. Those were the sounds of someone confused, violated, inundated in pleasure and yet entirely distressed by it.

And they were exactly what Brand craved to hear.

"B-brand," Ash keened softly, helpless and low. "Oh *God*, Brand…wh-what are you…"

"Did I not say you are to allow me to do for you?" Brand breathed against Ash's ear, and was rewarded by a sharp tremor, a sudden surging throb of Ash's cock against his palm, slickening with the warm liquid musk of dripping pre-come. "Did I not say you are to do as you are told?"

He tightened his grip just enough, then—just enough to make Ash rise up on his toes with a cry. "Y-yes!"

"And you did not."

"I…I…" Ash was nearly sobbing in his harsh, gasping breaths, rolling his hips into Brand's touch. "I'm…I'm *sorry*…"

"Not yet, my young Master."

Brand brushed the fingertips of his free hand to Ash's mouth…and Ash answered by parting his lips for him, opening for him as if blooming for him, that wet, hot mouth inviting. Brand slowly slipped his two middle fingers into Ash's mouth, delving into that slick heat, filling his mouth in intimate mimicry of what he craved to do to his young Master's body. Ash's tongue fluttered helplessly against his fingers—before those soft lips closed over his flesh, parting again and again on keening gasps only to glide and suckle at Brand's fingers, leaving them slick with the licking, caressing touch of his young Master's tongue. Brand's cock throbbed almost painfully, pressed against the young Master's back, begging for relief—but this was not for him.

This was so his young Master would learn a lesson.

He traced his mouth against Ash's ear, whispering. "I would suggest you hurry." Faster he stroked, tracing his thumb underneath the flared head of Ash's cock, finding every sweet spot, every vein, every ridge. "We do not have long before security comes to investigate."

"Brand—*Brand!*" Ash whimpered.

Only to arch back, his head falling against Brand's chest, lovely features slack with gasping, lost pleasure as his body tensed, trembled…and unraveled into sweet bliss for Brand, spilling wetly over his fingers.

He caught Ash's weight gently as the young Master sagged against him, and gingerly freed his hand from the confines of Ash's slacks—only to press his slicked, dirtied fingers to Ash's lips, replacing one hand with the other, painting his mouth in glistening streaks. Ash moaned softly, lashes fluttering—before his lips parted submissively and his tongue snaked out to lick Brand's fingers clean as they delved inside.

Perfect, Brand thought, watching with a slow and patient pleasure. Entirely perfect.

As Ash licked the last of his come away, Brand

gradually withdrew his fingers, then retrieved a handkerchief from his pocket. Still holding his young Master up with one arm, he dabbed his mouth clean, then wiped his own fingers before slipping back inside Ash's slacks to clean him gently. Nonetheless Ash cried out at the touch of the cloth, arching once more, hands falling to clutch at Brand's wrist.

"Shh," Brand soothed, and bent to kiss the corner of his mouth. "Almost done."

Once he finished, Ash went limp against him again, unresisting as Brand set his young Master's clothing to rights, then guided him to his feet, drawing him around to face him. Ash looked up at him with dazed, satiated, darkened eyes, his cheeks still flushed and his lips still parted. Brand cradled his face in both hands, leaning down to kiss him, stealing the taste of Ash's pleasure from his lips.

"Now do you understand what I expect from you?" he whispered.

Ash's lids fluttered downward, and he swayed into Brand. "Y-yes," he sighed.

"Say 'yes, Brand.'"

Ash bit his lip, plush mouth moving against Brand's, before he said those words that made pleasure curl so deep. "…y-yes…Brand."

"Good," Brand murmured.

Then pulled away, leaving his young Master standing there looking entirely lost and disarrayed, while Brand hid his satisfied smile and reconnected the security camera, before setting the elevator into motion again.

Chapter Thirteen

ASH WASN'T ENTIRELY SURE HE knew what just happened.

Only that his knees were weak, his cock was sore, and everything in him wanted to drop down to his knees and rub himself against Brand until Brand dragged him up and pinned him against the wall and did it all over again.

He watched the man sidelong as the elevator glided upward, but Brand had once again resumed his formal, proper posture, shoulders squared, hands folded.

But when the elevator stopped and the doors slid open, Ash hung back until Brand reached out to hold the automatic door.

And Ash caught a hint of a satisfied smile, as he ducked under Brand's arm and into the reception area.

Ms. Vernon was already at her post, and when she flashed a smile and trilled "Good morning, Ashton," Ash made a strangled sound, blushing up to his ears, and strained a smile of his own.

"Uh. Hi. Good morning."

"And Mr. Forsythe," she said, earning a brief, respectful nod before she turned her gaze back to Ash. "Are you all right? You look feverish."

"Fine!" Ash said, hurrying quickly toward the office door. "Cold out, you know? And so it's hot in here and I get all—um—I'm fine!"

She stared after him. He scurried across the floor, reaching for the door.

Then froze just short of the handle, gulping and glancing over his shoulder for Brand.

Brand caught up smoothly, pulling the double doors to the office open with a small and secret smirk.

"You are learning, young Master," he whispered.

"*Asshole,*" Ash hissed back, darting one last nervous glance toward Ms. Vernon before skittering inside.

He couldn't breathe, not until the doors closed. He exhaled heavily, pressing a hand to his chest over his rabbiting heart, then turned on Brand, just staring at him.

"Oh my God," he rasped out. "You're a dirty old man."

Utterly nonplussed, Brand shrugged, retrieving his white kid gloves and tugging them back on again. "You didn't use the safe word."

Ash ducked his head. "…I…I didn't want to." Clearing his throat, he pulled away, crossing to his desk. They were at work and they were supposed to work, damn it. But he couldn't help asking, "So I misbehave, and you punish me with sex?"

Brand cocked his head, considering with an arched

brow. “That does describe it rather succinctly.”

Ash let out a startled laugh. “That doesn’t exactly motivate me to behave.”

“You make it sound as if I do not enjoy punishing you.”

“That’s hardly punishment.”

“There’s punishment…” Brand’s eyes gleamed darkly. He adjusted his glasses. “…and then there’s punishment.”

Ash only snorted, started to pull his chair out—then stopped when Brand closed the distance between them in long strides and did it for him. Right. His stomach fluttered. Willing helplessness was strange…but not unpleasant.

But when he went to sit down he encountered not plush leather, but a hard, firm body in tailored wool. He jumped…and ended up falling right into Brand’s lap.

One powerful arm snared around his waist, when he tried to lean away—dragging him back, enfolding him in the heat of Brand’s tightly toned body. Ash flushed hotly.

Then sucked in a sharp, aching gasp as he felt the hardness pressing up against his ass.

“…Brand!” He squirmed in the man’s grip, darting a nervous glance over his shoulder, then at the door. “What if Ms. Vernon walks in?”

“She will not.” Hot breaths washed against Ash’s

neck as Brand nuzzled into him. Possessive hands spanned his stomach, then slid down, over his thighs. “You cannot work like this?”

Biting his lip, Ash shifted gingerly, shivering as that hard heat slid against him. “…you’re…you’re kind of distracting…”

“Am I?”

Roughly, Brand’s hands hooked underneath his thighs—then spread them wide, jerking taut until his inner thighs strained, opening him until his legs fell to either side of Brand’s with Brand’s own knees keeping his legs apart. He bit back a cry that might draw Ms. Vernon’s attention—but had to stifle his whimpers by pressing the edge of his palm to his mouth when Brand slowly began to spread his own legs, thickly muscled thighs tense and forcing Ash to spread wider and wider. He arched back against Brand, hips lifting, his body aching with a pulsing emptiness and heat pulling in straining lines at the base of his cock.

“And now?” Brand whispered, stroking one confident, firm hand down Ash’s trembling inner thigh, his cock a hard, insistent pressure against Ash’s ass and the small of his back. “Am I distracting now?”

“Brand…oh my God, I…I…” Ash writhed, but he was thoroughly trapped, spread vulnerable and helpless and feeling so *exposed* and tiny and weak, sitting in this massive man's lap and utterly at his mercy. Ash clutched at the arms of the chair, struggling to get himself under control, fighting back whimpers. "Y-you…you *asshole…*"

Brand's grip on him tightened, digging in just enough for the promise of sweet, bruising pain. "If you think I will not bend you over this desk for your impertinence, young Master, you are sorely mistaken."

"Don't you dare," Ash hissed, when what he really meant was *please*. When Brand was so hard against him he couldn't think of anything else, and he *wanted* it—wanted to find out what it would feel like when Brand let go of that shield he kept over his need to control Ash; wanted to find out what Brand would do to punish him if he was so brazen as to *demand*.

Brand nipped at his jaw, pain blooming. "Are you commanding me, young Master?"

The promise of menace in Brand's voice sent tremors rolling through Ash. He didn't understand why it thrilled him so deeply to feel that spark of fear, but it made him feel almost naked, stripped down to nothing in Brand's eyes. He closed his eyes, trying to calm his shaking, but those hard, gripping hands did nothing to calm the quaking in the pit of his stomach, the tightness clutching through him, the heat suffusing his already-sore cock.

"I'm…" He licked his lips nervously. "I'm…I'm begging you. *Don't.*"

Don't stop.

"I believe," Brand murmured, "I told you that I am the one in control here."

Ash knew it was coming. That didn't stop him from gasping as Brand pushed him forward with a hand pressed hard against his back, knocking him off balance until he fell against the desk, barely catching himself with his hands braced against the driftwood. He caught the clatter as Brand swept both their laptops out of the way—only for that hard hand to clamp to the back of his neck, shoving him down fully until his cheek pressed against the wood, rough and cool against his skin. His entire body prickled, exhilaration and terror and need and delicious anticipation and just that perfect breath of humiliation at being bent over like this, pinned and on display.

And half-naked from the waist down, as Brand deftly slipped the tongue of his belt buckle and dragged his slacks and boxer-briefs firmly around his thighs.

"Don't—" he gasped—only to strangle off as one firm hand came down sharply on his ass, a sudden stinging explosion of pain. He jerked his hips forward, moaning as that pain reverberated right to the base of his cock, pleasure shocking through from root to tip. The swelling sensation in his shaft *hurt*, after he'd just come not so long ago, sensitive and pulsing between his thighs.

Brand's fingers stroked against the back of his neck.

"I would not say that word again, young Master," he practically purred. Ash braced himself for another slap, squeezing his eyes shut.

Only to force his knuckles hard against his mouth to bite back a scream as Brand's naked, lube-slicked fingers suddenly drove into him.

Two at once, the lube doing almost nothing to stop the spearing, hot sensation flashing through him as if he'd been stabbed. He sank his teeth into the back of his hand, whimpering, sobbing against his fingers, struggling not to let Ms. Vernon hear him as he writhed and bucked his hips, played like a helpless little marionette on those demanding, thrusting fingers. Oh God---oh God, he was going to come right now like this—

Except Brand stopped.

He *stopped*, leaving Ash writhing against the desk, chest heaving, tears beading on his lashes in pure frustration and denial. Yet Brand didn't make him wait for long; the faint rustle of fabric, and then he felt that thick, dripping cock-head against him, that shaft as cruel as Brand himself, hardness sliding against the cleft of his ass and smearing both lube and hot-smelling pre-come against his skin. Ash whimpered, small in the back of his throat, tensing for pain. Tensing for that scouring sensation he'd known once and craved again, that *fullness* that only Brand could give him. He caught his breath, squeezing his eyes tighter shut, as those teasing strokes stopped, the tip of Brand's cock pressing between his flesh and kissing against his sore entrance.

Then screamed against the back of his hand, biting down until he tasted blood, as thickness forced into him, spreading him wide.

He was too small for this. Too small for Brand, but that was what made it delicious and perfect and *right*…that Brand could make him feel all wrong and all right and so deeply violated and sheltered and protected at the same time. There was a sick, dark intimacy in how young and fragile he felt beneath Brand's heavy bulk, unable to resist those hands that kept him so firmly pinned, one against his nape, the other against his hip, holding him still and giving him no choice but to suffer in sweet agony as that long, heated shaft slid slowly, slowly deeper. He felt like it was *licking* him from inside, hot against his inner walls, and he lifted his hips toward that burning cock and begged with his entire frail body to be broken.

Only to choke on a sharp cry as Brand's hand came down once more, and struck sharply enough across Ash's ass to *burn*.

His hips jerked forward, his body tightening—and a mewl startled from his throat as that sudden clutch made him squeeze against Brand's cock, imprinting his shape from inside. Ash gasped out a sobbing breath as Brand did it *again,* hand coming down in a punishing slap…but this time countered by a short, sharp thrust, cock moving inside Ash demandingly. Ash could barely muffle his cries against his fist, his other hand snapping up to grasp the edge of the desk, holding on for dear life, for something to anchor him when Brand was going to destroy him like this.

Again and again—that vicious hand, that cruel cock, abusing him in tandem rhythm until he was dizzy and screaming again and again against his hand, biting over and over and spreading his thighs until his disarrayed clothing bit into his flesh. Every thrust slammed him into the desk; every deep surge of Brand's cock pushed at him from inside until he could *feel* it, ridged against his belly where he pressed against the desk; every punishing crash of that hand against his ass made his cock jerk until he was *dripping,* painfully hard, nearly sobbing for release but his sensitive flesh refusing to let him come again so soon.

Yet he nearly fell over the edge, as Brand suddenly stiffened against him, ground deep, working inside him…and then a soft catch of breath, a sudden rush of wet warmth, a slick and spilling feeling pouring into Ash and making him feel perfectly dirty and sullied inside. He whimpered against his knuckles, struggling to catch his breath as Brand spent himself. There was a moment of silence, the feeling of something almost like a second heartbeat inside him, rushed breaths…and then Brand's fingers slipped around the edge of his hip, teased against his cock, slid down to cradle his sac in one broad and weathered palm.

"Are we not finished yet, young Master?" Brand mocked, his mouth hot and wet against Ash's ear, his voice an insidious thing slinking inside him. Ash could only answer with a hoarse, gasping keen as Brand toyed with him—rolling and cradling his sac until sensitive flesh drew up tight, fingertips grazing the underside of his cock, playing him as if tugging his strings to make him obey Brand's every command. And what Brand's touch commanded?

Was Ash's pleasure. His wholehearted undoing.

He barely lasted another minute—a minute of twisting, of helpless writhing, of quivering inner thighs and tight heat in the pit of his stomach—before that hot sharp sensation cut through him like a whip breaking skin, lashing him violently, leaving him shuddering in helpless convulsions against the desk as he wet Brand's fingers.

Then nearly collapsed to the floor, his legs sagging out from beneath him as Brand let him go and parted their bodies.

He let himself be handled dazedly as Brand set both

their clothing to rights—then gathered Ash up, lifting him to sit sideways across Brand's lap, cradled and sheltered warm and safe in his arms as he came down from that. Too fucking intense. And fuck, he hurt inside so bad, as if he'd been completely hollowed out and left empty…but he wouldn't change it for anything.

Nor would he change these quiet moments, when Brand extracted a tissue from the desk drawer and produced a bottle of witch hazel from his bottomless pockets and, watching Ash with fond warmth clear in that green gaze, began cleaning his bitten hand gently, tending to him with utmost care.

"Feel better now?" Brand murmured.

"Mm." With a tired sigh, Ash shifted to lean against Brand, resting his head to his shoulder and closing his eyes. Like this he could feel the chuckle that reverberated through Brand, sardonic yet affectionate.

"Do not think I don't know you entirely baited me into doing that."

Ash peeked one eye open, biting back a smile. "Did you mind?"

Brand's gaze softened, and he kissed Ash's temple. "No."

With a pleased sound, Ash tucked himself up and snuggled against Brand, holding himself dutifully still while Brand finished cleaning his hand, then taped a

Band-Aid over the stinging spot where he'd bitten himself.

"I liked that," Ash admitted. "I wish I could stay like that all the time. Like *this* all the time."

"Alas, real life must be attended to." Brand's arms settled around Ash, warm and comforting. "But we may indulge more tonight, at the manor."

"I'd like that." Ash sighed. "I have to work now, don't I?"

"You do."

"Nnngh don't make me."

"You know that only entices me to make you." Brand's arms tightened around him, a tacit reminder of what that strength could do. "Be good, young Master. I'll make it worth your while."

Ash peeked at him again, and this time couldn't restrain his smile. "Yeah?"

"Yes."

Biting his lip, Ash murmured, "…stay?"

"Of course."

And it was as simple as that. Even if they would have to work soon…Brand stayed, letting Ash be small and comfortable and tired and safe in his lap. Ash nearly drifted off, letting himself languish in the pleasant feeling of dozing against Brand, a faint scent he didn't quite recognize drifting between them, a scent he thought might be…

He opened one eye. "Brand?"

Brand let out a lazy rumble. "Hm?"

"…how do you always have lube?"

A faint smirk curved Brand's lips. "I have pockets, young Master."

"Yeah, but…" Ash laughed. "Don't say it. A proper valet is always prepared."

With a low chuckle, Brand caught Ash's chin in his fingertips. "Indeed," he murmured, and drew Ash up to kiss him.

UNFORTUNATELY, THEY HAD TO PART before noon—when Ms. Vernon ducked in to confirm a question about next week's schedule, and Brand had to very quickly dislodge his young Master, replace him in his chair, and reclaim his own seat.

He did, of course, have to preserve his young Master's reputation.

When they were no longer so entangled, it was easier to focus on work—and Brand fixed his attention on sorting through out-of-date accounting records rather than on Ash. Yet he couldn't help watching him from the corner of his eye; he didn't even think Ashton realized how well he was settling into his role. His hands were more capable on the keyboard, rattling through emails and stock projections, checking things without needing to be told, gaze sharp as he took in information, asking more informed questions instead of sounding so lost. When the phone rang he actually answered it himself instead of using Brand as a buffer—and in this, Brand stood back and let his young Master have the reins.

And kept his quiet smile of pride to himself, lest he get his bloody damned head bitten off.

By the time afternoon sank in, though, Ash had slowed—drifting off more often, taking longer to notice he'd been spoken to and respond, pulling out of a lost daze and glancing at Brand as if just remembering he was there, before losing himself staring out the window again. Brand tried to keep his own focus, but with that silent, pained need tugging on him he could no more resist than the moth could resist the flame.

"Young Master." He leaned against the arm of his chair, reaching across to cover Ash's pale hands, resting lifeless on the keyboard. "You are thinking about your father, are you not?"

As shook himself, eyes clearing, and glanced at Brand with a wan smile. "Is it that obvious?"

"It is one of a small few options that could cause that expression."

"It doesn't matter." Ash sighed, sagging back in his chair, rubbing at his temples. "Just wait, right? And hope. And grasp on to whatever little bits of happiness I can in between." A smile tried to cross his lips, but faded before it had a chance to bloom, his mouth a bitter line. "Did you know most people with bone cancer don't last longer than four years once it metastasizes? And he…" He thunked his head back against the back of the chair. "He's been hiding it from me for *three*."

Another thunk, head impacting against the leather—and then again and again, until Brand couldn't take it anymore and he reached across to gather Ash against him. Ash tumbled out of his chair, falling into Brand, clutching at him with a hitching breath and burying his face in his throat.

"I want to be mad at him," Ash whispered. "I want to be so *mad* at him, because if I'd known I wouldn't have…wouldn't have…"

"Wouldn't have what?" Brand prompted gently, stroking over Ash's back.

"Wasted so much," Ash breathed, trembling with the edges of tears. "Wasted so much time…on things that don't even matter."

Brand held Ashton until his tremors quieted. Until they were calm and quiet against each other, and the need to comfort simply became comfortable. The sky was gray outside, the rain a thing of small tiny mirrors making refractions all down the glass office walls, and its whispered sound was a soothing thing, cocooning them in gentle quiet.

And Brand was content to stay like this, so long as he had his young Master safe in his arms. He couldn't protect him from what was to come, or shield him from the pain it would cause.

But he could at least give him shelter and solace, if nothing else.

Yet his troubled thoughts lingered with him, as he breathed in Ash's quiet scent that made him think of rainfall on city streets, as if the day itself was shivering with Ash's silent grief, his essence permeated throughout the city and its towering concrete palaces. A decision weighed heavy inside him, waiting to be made if only he would look at it head on.

And he refused to be a coward about this.

He drew back to look down at Ash, curling his knuckles against his young Master's cheek. "I would ask something of you, young Master."

Ash looked up at him. Still so trusting, so innocent, looking at Brand with such utter faith. He didn't understand how a young man could grow to adulthood and still be so sweet in his own way, but Brand hoped…

He hoped he never broke that.

"Sure," Ash murmured. "Anything."

"My contract does allow for a set number of personal days, does it not?"

Ash's brows knitted quizzically. "I mean…yeah, everybody gets days off."

Brand smiled dryly. "Do you think you would fall apart in my absence tomorrow?"

"I'll find a way to manage," Ash retorted with an echo of his usual merry sarcasm, wan and tired. "Where are you going?"

"To attend to a personal matter," Brand deflected, and pressed his lips to Ash's brow. "I should return by noon, if you have need of me. But for now…" He stood, drawing Ash with him, diverting any questions with distractions. "…for today only, perhaps we could leave the office early. I'll make you a proper dinner instead of something cobbled together after midnight."

"Sure," Ash said, the unspoken question in his eyes.

But Brand only turned away, beginning to pack up his young Master's things, grateful when Ashton didn't ask.

Because Brand didn't know if he could answer, right now.

Not yet.

ASH HAD LIED. HE HADN'T meant to, but Ash had most definitely lied.

Because he was falling apart in the office without Brand, and cursing himself with every new thing he fucked up.

It had only been a few hours. Brand had woken him, dressed him, fed him, and dropped him off at the Tower with a promise to be back by noon. Ash had shut himself in his office to handle some paperwork, review a few contracts, sort out an issue with a supplier in Norway.

And promptly made a half-dozen mistakes within the first half hour.

He could *do* this. He was figuring his shit out and he didn't even need Brand to explain these things anymore, but he'd gotten so used to Brand being his heated, overwhelming shadow that his absence left a void that seemed to suck all of Ash's attention and capacity into it.

And he was just about ready to throw in the towel

and give up until he could get his fucking attention span under control—before he sank the company with a goddamned lawsuit over the use of the Harrington Steel trademark on third-party-crafted products in foreign countries—when a polite rap came at the door. His heart jumped, then sank an instant later. Brand wouldn't knock.

Ms. Vernon would, however, and she leaned in with a polite smile. "Ashton? Your friend Mr. Newcomb is here to see y—"

"No need for the fanfare, luvvie, I'll show myself in," Vic interrupted with an easygoing laugh, then slipped around Ms. Vernon and into the office.

Vic was as dapper as the last time he and Ash had met up for lunch before Ash's life had fallen apart—tall and rangy in a neat white shirt and deep red waistcoat and black slacks, his dark brown hair slicked back; even if he and Ash were the same age, he had that air of *presence* about him that Ash envied, that came from growing up knowing how to handle things Ash was only just beginning to take in hand. Vic looked like someone ready to step in and take over his father's company, far more than Ash ever could.

But he'd get there one day, he thought.

And he felt far more capable now than he ever had before.

Though all he felt right now, was mortified as Vic

waved Ms. Vernon off with an affable grin and crossed the office with his lazy swagger to drop a folded stack of newsprint on Ash's desk. Ash frowned, unfolding the tabloid—only to flush fire-hot all the way down to his collarbones as he saw the headline splashed in giant letters.

Harrington Heir Has Harrowing Night – But Who's His Handsome Hottie?

The photo taking up the entire front page of the gossip rag showed an intersection at night, the Mercedes, street lights shining down on its crumpled front end and smoke rising through the beams of golden illumination.

And Brand, on his knees, pulling Ash from the car with an expression of pure, raw terror and grief and hope on his face, transforming that handsome, stony visage into a minefield of chaotic emotions.

"Oh, *God*," Ash groaned, covering his mouth with both hands. Oh fuck, that wasn't good.

So why was he all lit up inside, fizzing like a corked bottle of champagne?

"Something you neglected to tell me?" Vic needled. "When were you going to call and tell your best friend you'd been in a near-fatal accident?"

"It wasn't that bad!" Ash protested. "I just got tossed

around a little. The bruises are fading already."

"And you're just like your old man." Vic snorted, flinging himself with devil-may-care grace down into the chair Brand usually occupied. "You'd never have told me if not for that tabloid sheet."

Ash winced. "I've worried people enough, don't you think?"

"Seem to worry Brand quite a bit," Vic said pointedly.

Cringing, Ash ducked his head. Oh fuck, if he could tell anyone he could tell Vic, but he didn't even know what there was to tell and—

"Oh my fucking bloody God, *Ash*," Vic said, sucking in a breath, staring at him. "You're fucking him."

Ash's head whipped up. "What? No! I mean yes, but no, but—how did you know?!"

"It's all over your face, you fucking lovelorn sod! And he's no better, moping over you all over the front page news!" Vic let out a half-incredulous, half-horrified laugh. "Bloody hell, I wasn't serious about him being your type!"

"I didn't think he was either!" Ash flung back, then shrugged uncomfortably, looking away. Fuck, his head was going to explode, so much blood was rushing to his face. "But then things just…happened."

"You do know how to get into some trouble." Vic

laughed again, then shook his head. “So it’s just…sex? Or are you all lovey-dovey, or…?”

“Or. Or is good.” *Or* was easier than trying to explain…any of this. Or the chaotic, conflicted feelings he had around Brand. “I…look, it’s new and complicated and I don’t get it myself. It’s sex, but it’s something else.”

“I’ll not pry. I’ve already heard enough about your sex life to tide me over for a lifetime,” Vic retorted dryly. “Bit long in the tooth, isn’t he?”

“*He’s not old,*” Ash shot back fiercely. “He’s just…Brand.”

Vic whistled, holding both hands up. “Sally withdrawn. I’m not going to war with you over your valet.”

“Nngh.” Ash fidgeted. “It’s not weird?”

“Oh it’s plenty bloody weird, but if it makes you happy, who cares?” Vic arched a pointed brow. “*Does* it make you happy?”

“I think so.” Biting at the inside of his lip, Ash leaned forward, folding his arms on the edge of the desk. “Everything’s just too much lately. With Dad, with figuring out how to run a company, with my mother suddenly being back in the country…everything’s just up in the air.” He shrugged. “Brand…nails things down. And makes all the noise quiet. It’s just not so hard to cope with things when he’s around. I don’t feel like I’m in freefall anymore. It's like he caught me right before I hit the ground."

"That's not such a bad way to feel around someone then, innit?" Vic said with unaccustomed gentleness. "How are things with your Dad, then?"

"I…" Ash stared down at his folded arms, throat tight. "Not good. He's out of hospice, but it's just…relocation. He's weak and not getting any better, and there's nothing to be done for it."

He was startled by Vic's hand on his shoulder, squeezing gently. They'd been friends since a food fight in the cafeteria at their boarding school had pitted them against a group of older boys at the tender age of ten, but they'd always been the kind of friends who showed affection through sarcasm and shoving. Yet Vic was reaching out to him, offering that warmth, that solidarity…and it nearly broke him.

Especially when Vic murmured, "Hey. You're gonna make it through this. I know it doesn't feel that way right now, but you will."

Ash tried to smile, but it came out watery, choked. "Thanks, Vic. I…I just…thanks."

Anything Vic might have said was cut off as the door opened, and Brand quietly let himself in—only to pause, arching a brow as he saw Vic in his chair.

"Young Master Newcomb," he said, bowing a touch

stiffly. “It’s been some time.”

“Good to see you, Brand.” Vic levered smoothly to his feet, clapping Ash’s shoulder. “I was just visiting with our darling little Ashton here, finding out how he’s getting on with you.” His smile was bland, but there was a touch of subtle mischief there. “I’ll get out of your hair.”

Brand fixed Vic with a pointed, dry look that said he wasn’t fooling anyone, but kept his mouth shut. Ash sighed, dragging a hand over his face.

Sometimes, his life felt like a circus.

“I’ll catch you soon, Vic,” he called, as Vic swaggered for the door. “We’ll do lunch next week.”

“You are completely booked with investor lunches next week, young Master,” Brand interrupted.

“Fuck. Next month?”

“That may be possible.”

Vic laughed. “Just call me when you get a free minute.” He paused at the door, though, shoulder to shoulder with Brand, his smile fading, leaving him sober, studying Brand thoughtfully. “Take care of him,” he murmured.

“It would never cross my mind to do otherwise,” Brand responded.

And with a nod, Vic slipped out, leaving them alone.

Brand closed the door, cocking his head. “That was

interesting."

"Vic wanted to yell at me for not telling him about the accident." Ash groaned, sank down in his seat, and weakly flicked his fingers at the newspaper. "We made the tabloids."

Brand crossed to the desk—and that was when Ash noticed something off. A stiffness to his gait, listing to one side. Worry curled its fingers around his heart.

"Brand…?" he asked. "You're limping."

"It's nothing," Brand murmured. "I slept poorly on my back. It will straighten out shortly." But he avoided Ash's eyes, as he settled in his chair and picked up the newspaper. "Now let's figure out how to do damage control about this."

ASH HAD TO BUILD UP more stamina.

He used to stay awake for over forty-eight hours for weekend-long parties. Now he couldn't even last until he made it home, passing out in the car every day while Brand drove. He was barely aware of Brand lifting him out of the SUV and carrying him inside; he only snuggled into him, and was out cold again within moments.

It was more mental and emotional than physical

exhaustion, he knew. The stress and pressure every day, trying to take on so many large decisions that could break everything to pieces—compounded by drama after drama, exploding over him.

But he'd like to have a life, he thought, that didn't involve spending every waking hour at the office and passing out before he even had a moment to cling to Brand for more than a single tired kiss. At least he usually woke to the comfort of Brand's body curled around him, a heavy bulwark of muscle that seemed to shelter him from even the worst of his dreams.

Which was probably why the absence in the bed woke him, when he rolled over to burrow into Brand and Brand just…wasn't there.

He blinked blearily, rubbing at his eyes and glancing at the clock. Oh. It was barely after ten PM; Brand was probably…doing Brand things. Tailoring more of Ash's suits. Terrorizing the chef. Plotting more ways to make Ash regret actually brushing his own teeth instead of waiting for Brand to do it for him.

…actually, Brand probably *would*.

Still a fucking demon.

Snorting to himself, Ash stretched and yawned his way out of bed, scratching at his hair. He was *hungry*; he kept passing out without dinner. Maybe he could catch Brand in the kitchen and help him make something. Spend some actual time with him that wasn't about work. He just…had this low and whispered need to *know* Brand, as more than just the packaged entirety of his kinks and a few little tidbits of his history.

He wanted to know the daily things that made him tick, and find out how it felt to just *be* in Brand's presence, in ordinary and normal ways many people took for granted.

The kitchen was probably the best place to start looking. He padded through the night-dimmed hallways, biting back another yawn…and almost missing the sound of voices coming from the living room, drowned under his own sleepy breaths. He frowned, pausing in the hall. That was his Dad's voice, and…Brand's? Curious, he switched paths and ducked toward the living room, leaning around the open arched door.

His father was bundled into a corner of the long, low white leather couch, tucked warmly in several afghans; his mother curled against his side, one hand on his arm as she looked between him and Brand gravely. Brand rested on one knee before him as if swearing fealty, but his expression was strained, solemn. All of them were, speaking as though at a funeral.

Ash frowned, drifting a step forward. Was something wrong? "Dad?" he asked. "Bra—Forsythe…? What's going on?"

Three heads came up toward him simultaneously. His mother smiled faintly; his father looked briefly guilty. Only Brand's expression remained the same, as he rose to his feet and offered a quick bow toward Ash. Even if Brand's eyes warmed subtly, it did nothing to ease the worry curdling in Ash's gut.

"It seems you've hired a very stalwart and dedicated valet, son," his father said, offering a wan smile.

Ash frowned. "Brand? What did you do?"

"It turns out I am a match," Brand said.

"…what?" It took a moment to sink in, what he meant.

Brand's bone marrow was a match for his father's.

Ash stared. His heart felt like it was ripping, torn between relief, dismay, worry, fear, *hope*. "I…y-you…that's where you went today? To get tested?"

"Yes," Brand said simply. "Considering your father's condition and the potential for further metastasis, Dr. Singh managed to expedite the lab results and called a short time ago. I am to begin donation procedures tomorrow, while your father begins high-intensity chemotherapy to prepare him for bone marrow replacement."

"Oh," Ash said numbly. "*Oh*."

Brand had…he'd…he was going to *hurt* himself, just so Ash's father would have a better chance to live…

"Why?" he whispered. "Why would you do that? You…you don't even know my Dad…"

"I know you," Brand replied softly—and there was no hiding the naked emotion in his voice, in the way he looked at Ash.

No. *No*, this…this felt wrong, it felt *all* wrong, and Ash wanted to be happy but he just…he just…

"Do what you want to do," he bit off, then turned on his heel and flung himself from the room—ignoring Brand's voice, rising after him, twin to his mother's call of,

"Ash!"

BRAND STOOD HELPLESSLY IN THE living room of the Harrington estate and watched, for the second time, as Ash ran away from him.

"I," he said, "am very confused as to what just happened."

Amiko let out a low laugh, while Calvin Harrington just snorted. "Boy's as contrary as I am, that's what just happened," Harrington said.

Brand frowned. "Does he not want you to find a transplant donor?"

"Oh, Mr. Forsythe." Amiko sighed with a touch of amusement. "I'm sure he does, but it gets rather complicated when that donor is you, don't you think?"

Brand glanced at Calvin Harrington uncertainly. He wasn't sure how much the man knew of what Amiko Arakawa seemed to have gleaned of Brand's relationship with their son, and he was hesitant to speak—until the elder Master Harrington made an amused, almost derisive sound.

"Don't look at me like that. I'm not oblivious. You think any man's going to offer to put himself in that kind of pain for me if he's not in love with my son?"

"I'm not—" Brand protested, then stopped and made himself say more honestly, "I don't know what I am."

"Confused isn't a bad way to be." Harrington glanced at Amiko, gaze softening. "Hell, our confusions gave us Ash."

"And years of trouble." Amiko returned his gaze fondly, patting his arm, before offering Brand a smile. "Why are you still here, dear?"

"Perhaps because I am once again not certain if pursuing the young Master is wise."

"Well you're never going to find out why he's so upset with you if you don't, are you?" Amiko clucked her tongue. "Don't be silly."

Brand had never been called *silly* in his life. It was

rather a new thing, but then so was standing here feeling as helpless as a boy half his age while he tried to sort out the conflicting mess of his feelings toward *a boy half his age*.

Somehow, Ashton Harrington had managed to turn his life halfway inside out and upside down while Brand was busy getting Ashton's life back together.

He sighed, pushing his glasses up and rubbing his fingers against his eyelids. "I will make haste to do so, then," he said, then bowed his head to Ash's parents. "Thank you."

"No," Calvin Harrington said. "Don't you ever thank me for anything again. I owe you more gratitude than I can say, for giving me a chance."

Brand...Brand had no idea what to say to that. He wasn't accustomed to being on the receiving end of such heartfelt sincerity.

And so he said nothing, and only turned from the room and set off in search of his confusing, frustrating, extremely indecipherable young lover.

HE FOUND ASH IN THE master suite, almost completely buried and invisible in the massive bed, if not for the silent jerk of his shoulders giving him away. He was crying, Brand realized as he stepped tentatively into the room—face buried in the pillows he clutched close and crying in silent, shaking gasps that wrenched at Brand's heart.

He closed the door gingerly behind him, then crossed to settle on the edge of the bed. He wasn't certain if his touch would be welcome, but after a moment he reached over and rested his hand lightly to Ash's back.

"Young Master," he murmured. "I didn't mean to upset you. I'm not certain how I did."

Ash pushed himself up, flinging a wet-eyed glare at Brand, his face flushed with crying, eyes and nose pink and swollen. "You went behind my back," he shot back. "You couldn't even tell me what you were going to do; you went behind my back! And now you're…you're sacrificing yourself when it might not even *work*…"

"But it might work, as well." Brand met that red-rimmed gaze in confusion; wasn't some chance better than none? "I'm sorry I did not tell you beforehand. I didn't want to raise your hopes, only to crush them if I hadn't been a match."

"But why are you *doing* this?" Ash demanded. "It's…it's like you're fucking furniture and you don't even care if you get shoved around to suit everyone else's needs!"

Brand shook his head. "Don't you understand that I need to? I am not furniture. I made a conscious choice. This…this is what I need. For you, not for him. If I can't…" Brand fought the urge to swear, struggling to articulate himself. These were things he had held inside him like close-kept secrets for so long he'd forgotten the words for them, like ancient stories lost to time. "If I can't *be* for you, then I'm not…I am not *anything*, young Master."

"Yes, you are!" Ash flared with such vehemence that he caught Brand off guard, striking his heart with an impact as sharp as a blow. "How can you not *see* that?"

While Brand stared at Ash, Ash pushed himself up to his knees, fumbling in pajamas several sizes too large for him and looking like nothing more than an upset little boy caught up in the fury and fire of such unchecked, raw, pure emotion. His lips trembled, as he glared up at Brand with his heart in his eyes and on his lips.

"You are the biggest asshole I've ever met," Ash bit off. "But if not for you I'd have fallen apart and ruined everything in less than a day. And not just because you keep sacrificing yourself and putting me first. Because underneath that fucking asshole exterior you're kind, you're smart, you're selfless, you're gentle, you're *good*. Fuck, you're even fucking funny sometimes." With a miserable little sound that trailed into a hiccup, Ash sniffled and scrubbed at his nose. "You're someone to look up to. Someone I want to be proud of me for the things I've done. *That* kept me moving more than anything you did to put my needs ahead of your own."

Brand felt as though he had swallowed his heart and lodged it in his throat. He could only *look* at Ashton—at this fierce, beautiful young man overflowing with so much emotion, and giving that emotion to *him*. Telling him he was worth that emotion, whether he chose to give up pieces of himself to Ashton or not. He tried to remember if anyone else had ever said such things to him.

And it ached inside, that he couldn't recall a single instance.

"I…young Master, I…" He bowed his head—then leaned in, unable to resist his young Master's magnetism, resting his brow to Ashton's. "…Ash."

Ash brought his hands up to curl against Brand's throat, leaning into him hard. "I don't want to lose my dad," he whispered. "But I don't want you to hurt yourself just to feel like you're worth something to me, either."

"What if I simply want to do it?" Brand asked—and after a moment of self-doubt, he enfolded Ash in his arms, pulling him in close. Where he *belonged*. "It…simply feels right. It feels like the right thing to do and since I am able, my conscience will allow little else. I can suffer some small few days of pain to give Mr. Harrington a longer lease on life."

Lashes trembling, wide eyes searched Brand's face. "If you're really sure that's what you want," Ash said, voice choking. "Only if you're really sure."

"I am."

Ash's lovely face crumpled, his eyes welling with fresh tears. "*Brand*," he breathed almost reverently—then drew him in and kissed him.

Brand almost didn't feel worthy of the reverence with which Ashton kissed him—and yet he would never deny that affection, that warmth, that unshielded emotion that he cherished so deeply. He sank into Ash, taking that lovely mouth and making it his until Ash yielded for him in that perfect way that made his lips so soft, that made him so *open*, this waiting vessel begging to take Brand inside him.

And Brand answered that unspoken plea—delving past his lips, tasting his sweetness, drugging himself on those delicate, gasping reactions when Ash trembled for him like an ingénue every time, shivered himself into fragile ecstasy as he surrendered himself over to Brand. Brand burned with the pleasure of his young Master's submission, ached with how small he felt beneath Brand's touch, that slender body nearly vanishing into the grasp of Brand's enfolding hands. When Ash kissed him this way, clutched at him this way, Brand wanted nothing more than to make his claim complete.

To mark Ashton in a way that would make him Brand's forever, forbidden and secret yet undeniably his.

And so he parted himself from those sweet lips, even when they sought his again, so needy, so damp, begging in little kittenish mewls that set his blood aflame. He pressed his fingers to plush lips, caressing them, as he kissed a trail made of the luscious taste of skin and boyish sweat and the heat of desire, following its path down Ash's jaw, his neck. His lovely boy rewarded him with a willingly bared throat, his pulse moving so hard against his skin—and fluttering against Brand's mouth. He sucked the first sheen of perspiration from Ash's skin, laved fragile flesh with licking tastes, drew that soft pulse into his mouth.

Then bit down, taking in the flavor of flesh until the flavor of flesh became the flavor of a bruise, of a mark, of complete and utter possession.

In their first meeting Ash had tried to hide a mark on his throat. A mark left by a dalliance, a meaningless fling, a nothing. Brand would leave his mark so that no other would eclipse it again, searing himself into his young Master's body. Ash clutched at him, fingers grasping up weak, helpless handfuls of Brand's sleeves, his very powerlessness only inflaming Brand more. As much as the way his young Master arched against him with his body shaking and his cock pressing hard between them; as much as the high, pleading, almost frightened cries of confused, vulnerable arousal that did terrible things to Brand. As much as the way those parted lips gasped out helpless sounds….

…but never once chose to say the word that would make that fear real, that would end this, that would tell Brand to stop.

No matter how he writhed, how he struggled, Ash held fast to him. No matter how deep Brand bit, how harsh his hands were as he stroked at his young Master's flesh, tore his clothing open, left bruising, claiming marks of his fingers against ribs and hips and slim sweet thighs, Ash never stopped him.

He only pressed himself willingly into Brand, panting those delectable cries into his ear on wet breaths, as locked in this moment of desire as Brand himself.

Only when he came just short of tasting blood did he let go of that darkly bruised mark on Ash's throat, standing out livid and promising against that pale skin, that racing and fluttering pulse. Almost hypnotized, Brand traced his fingers against that mark…then tumbled Ash back, spilling him to the bed in a tangle of disarrayed clothing and tousled, sweat-dampened hair.

Ash laid against the sheets, looking up at him with wet-sheened, wide eyes, their blue the darkness of the sea at night, swallowing Brand deep. How could his young

Master look up at him with such a trusting, needful gaze, and not understand how Brand would give anything for him? How could Ash lay beneath him so helplessly, so yieldingly, trusting that Brand would hurt him only as much as they both craved, and yet not see how Brand could devote himself to his service, to his needs, to his every trembling breath?

He pressed his fingertips to Ash's lips again—and shuddered as that wet pink tongue darted out, tasting him. He trailed wet streaks down that lovely golden skin, making him glisten—then followed them with his mouth. One suckling, savoring kiss at a time, he tasted Ash: the peak of his chin, the hollow of his throat, the dip between his pectorals. The rise of his nipples, the arch of his ribs, the smooth sleek slope of his stomach, sucking in on a soft and pleasured gasp. The crest of his hip, as Brand drew his pajama pants down and threw them aside. The delicate and fragile crease where his thigh blended into his hip. The soft flesh just inside his knee.

The salt and musk taste of his cock, as Brand ran his tongue over its full length, then drew it into his mouth.

Ash's fingers were soft and feverish in his hair, clutching, as his young Master moved beneath him—legs grasping at Brand's shoulders, toes arching and curling, head tossing back and forth with little protesting mewls as Brand tasted every inch of him, felt the throb of his heartbeat resting on his tongue, drank every bitter-salt drop spilling from the tip of his cock. He teased those places he had learned could make his young Master scream, and relished the choked sounds as Ash struggled not to be heard by the entire house. Deeper he took Ash, deeper, until the round warm tip of his cock hit the back of Brand's throat and he swallowed without thinking and Ash threw his head back and cried out Brand's name, filling the room with his gasping, throaty voice. Brand felt that swelling, that pulse against his lips, that said this would be over too soon—and pulled back, stopping just short of giving his Master mercy.

Ash collapsed against the bed, looking up at him with soft, pleading keens, reaching for him with slender hands. Brand caught both those hands, kissing either palm, lingering…then transferred them both to one of his own, capturing them in his fingers, pushing them up over Ash's head and pinning them to the bed. Ash looked a debauched and lovely mess, like this—his pajama shirt open and falling around him, his pants thrown away to leave him naked, his cock resting hard against his belly and dripping in clear, glistening streams, his hair a tangle and his eyes dilated and his nipples roused and hard and as pink as his flushed cheeks, his lips.

Brand had to close his eyes lest he do something he would regret, his cock surging painfully against his slacks.

He couldn't wait. Not this time, not now, not when Ash was twisting and whimpering and sliding his inner thighs against Brand's hips. Brand spared only half a moment to find the bottle of lube inside his coat, to free himself from his slacks, to coat himself in a glistening layer of slickness that made his skin feel too tight, too hot.

Then he hooked his free hand under his young Master's knee, lifting him up, spreading him, baring him. With sweet eagerness, Ash spread his thighs further, biting that beautifully lush lower lip. When Brand rolled his hips forward to press against that deliciously tight flesh, Ash's lashes fluttered downward, his head tossing back on a gasp. A gasp that trailed into a cry, as Brand gave his strength into sinking into him; a cry echoed by a growl, a shudder, a panting exhalation Brand couldn't hold back as he poured himself into his young Master's body.

He was so *tight*—and so soft inside, and Brand realized that softness, that plushness wrapping around him and swallowing him deep like a sucking mouth was the swollen soreness of his young Master's abused body, still tender inside from being taken before. Tension ripped through him, wild raw need demanding he *take*—but if he would control his young Master, he would control himself, and he drew in shallow, measured breaths as he made himself move slow. If only to torment himself; if only to torment his young Master, when each inch of heat and gripping tightness that joined them made Ash cry out in those soft, distressed sounds that were everything wrong and everything right about this.

He crushed down harder on Ash's wrists, just to feel those delicate bones beneath his palm; he dug his fingers into the yielding flesh of his thigh for the pleasure of that lean sinew giving under his touch. The entire time he could never take his gaze from the tortured bliss on that pretty face, the way Ash gave himself so wholeheartedly, pain and fear knitting his brow and yet pleasure and desire flushing his cheeks and parting his lips until he was the perfect juxtaposition of the willing victim, the captured innocent.

Marked by that brand on his throat, as possessed as Brand could make him.

As Brand sank in fully, as he buried himself in that body that was far too small to take him, Ash let out a low, pleading whine and tugged at his wrists; his eyes opened to glazed, wet-sheened slits, looking up at Brand in soft entreaty. Brand could deny him nothing. He released Ash's wrists. Soft fingers curled against his back, slipped into his hair. Ash drew him up to kiss him, as Brand enveloped him in his arms.

And together they moved, locked in a tangle of sparks made flesh and sweat-slicked skin and mating, melding mouths meeting in caressing tongues and bruise-tasting lips and the wet hot fire of joining bodies.

Brand couldn't stop *touching* him, the damp silk of Ash's skin under his palms, the way sleek sinew writhed and flexed each time Brand drew himself free only to sink deep again and again, chasing friction, chasing wildness, chasing the intimacy of seeking so far inside his young Master they might never be separated again. Ash was beautiful…and Brand worshipped him with his mouth, with his hands, with every inch of his body.

And when he lingered, toying his fingers over Ash's cock…he felt like a man at prayer, as he devoured the way Ash sank into pleasure. The way his entire body moved with their rhythm, completely lost. The way his lips parted, sighing Brand's name.

The way he went tight, so tight, as he gave in, fell apart, collapsed as Brand teased him to pieces.

The tight convulsions of his body were too much. That softness gripping around Brand, massaging and stroking his cock. His back arched. Fire bolted down his spine, and his blood became dark embers, his breaths cinders and ash.

And his young Master's name was on his lips, whispered again and again and again, as he gave in service once more…and spilled his every desire into his young Master's flesh.

THEY RESTED TOGETHER IN DROWSY silence, after Brand had tended to the marks of use and abuse on Ashton's body; after he'd soothed the pain he'd left his young lover in. Something hovered in the air between them, something that made a third presence in the room, soft-spoken and whispering in things unsaid, things that need never be spoken.

And Brand was content.

He had just started to drift off, Ash tucked against his body with one hand across his chest, their bodies cooling together, when Ash let out a sigh.

"Thank you," he murmured.

Brand opened his eyes, stirring drowsily to look down at him. "For what, young Master?"

Ash pressed a kiss to his shoulder. "For being everything you are."

Brand smiled, drawing him closer and sinking down the headboard. "I've told you there is never any need, Ashton."

"I know."

And that was that, letting the silence reclaim them once more.

Yet as the night sank deeper, as Brand relaxed into

the feeling of Ash's fingers playing over his skin, Ash lifted his head, looking toward the window.

"It's snowing," he whispered.

Brand glanced up, watching as faint soft drifts of white fell down against the deep blue of night, wisping like feathers, like an ash cloud, like a drift of small and quiet dreams. Like whispers, little words tumbling down, sighing those things that still stood between them, delicate and soft.

"So it is," he murmured, and pulled his young Master into a kiss.

Chapter Fourteen

There was something almost criminal, Ash thought, about seeing Brand looking anything other than perfectly put together and completely formidable, taking up so much space that he blocked out everything else.

He looked older, somehow, lying on a gurney in a hospital gown—the streaks of silver at his temples more prominent, the lines around his eyes settled deeper. Frailer, too, the smock seeming to shrink his bulk and turn him small and fragile.

Ash hated it.

He fucking *hated* it. One day wasn't enough to be ready for this, suddenly rushing headlong into this complex procedure—and yet he wouldn't reject the gift Brand meant to give to both him and his father, no matter how frightened he might be. After seeing his father wasting away in a hospice bed…

The parallels were a little too close for Ash to endure seeing Brand this way, surrounded by the horrible smell of the hospital and too pale beneath the light of the claustrophobic little room.

"You," Brand said quietly, "are fretting, young

Master. I can practically smell it."

"I'm worried," Ash said, and clasped the long, thick-knuckled hand resting against the gurney. "They're going to be taking out *pints* of your bone marrow. That's…that's a lot."

"And I am a perfectly healthy man of not particularly advanced age, and there will not likely be complications." Brand turned his hand to lace his fingers with Ash's, squeezing gently. "It will be fine."

Ash smiled weakly. "I feel like you're not supposed to be reassuring me here."

"But I'm not the one who's worried."

"Because you never worry about anything."

Brand lifted their twined hands to his mouth and brushed his lips across Ash's knuckles. "I worry about you."

"I keep trying to stop giving you reasons to."

Brand chuckled, then caught his glasses and tugged them off, deftly folding them one-handed and offering them to Ash. "Hold on to these for me, hm?"

"Yeah." Ash curled his hand gingerly around the glasses. "Yeah, okay."

"Try not to break them."

"I won't."

"…or smudge them."

Ash choked on a laugh that felt like he'd swallowed a spike into his throat. "*Asshole*."

Brand smiled faintly. "You are not worrying now."

"I'll worry until you're back on your feet and aggravating the fuck out of me."

"Not long, then," Brand promised softly, stroking his thumb over Ash's knuckles.

A polite rap at the door interrupted them. "Mr. Forsythe?" A tall, lean, capable-looking woman in pale green scrubs leaned around the door with a reassuring smile. "I'm Pamela, your anesthesiologist. I wanted to give you a quick overview before we go in."

Brand shifted to sit up a little more on the gurney. "Of course."

With brisk movements, Pamela crossed to the foot of the gurney and retrieved Brand's chart, flipping through it before murmuring, "Now, you understand you've consented to full anesthesia?"

"Yes," Brand responded.

"What does that mean?" Ash interrupted.

Pamela glanced at him with that particular guarded look so many people had—that look that said she knew who he was, but was trying for the sake of professionalism to treat him as she would anyone else. She considered him, then explained, "It's a long procedure to extract enough bone marrow for a transplant. Local anesthesia can wear off, not to mention it's not effective enough to fully prevent all pain. We've opted to put Mr. Forsythe into an induced state so he doesn't experience the pain of the extraction for hours at a time."

"You're knocking him out," Ash realized, and clutched at Brand's hand even harder. "Isn't that dangerous?"

"I promise you it's safe," Pamela assured. "Thousands of people undergo full anesthesia every day, and they're perfectly fine after it's done."

Brand squeezed his hand. "I'll just take a brief nap, young Master. Once I wake up, the worst of it will be over." He smiled faintly. "Don't worry."

"I'll…" Ash swallowed hard. His heart felt sick and heavy—this soggy thing saturated in fear, squeezing it out in oozing drips on every slow beat. "I'll try."

"We'll take good care of him," Pamela said with a quick smile, then checked her watch. "It's time."

She shifted to the head of the gurney, adjusting it a bit before beginning to push it toward the door. Ash scrambled to keep up, holding on to Brand's hand as long as he could.

"Brand," he whispered, clutching on tight. "I'll be waiting."

Brand met his eyes with that quiet certainty that seemed to pin the world in its place and hold the stars in their configurations in the heavens, so long as Brand believed them to be there.

"I shan't keep you waiting long."

Then Ash had no choice but to let go, when there was no room for him through the narrow doorway. The nurse pushed Brand through, out into the hall, wheeling him away until he was just a distant figure vanishing through one set of double doors after another.

And leaving Ash alone.

ASH SHUFFLED INTO THE WAITING area and found a spot out of the way, curled in a chair with Brand's glasses clutched in both hands, letting them go only to occasionally touch his fingertips to the throbbing mark on his throat, hidden beneath his collar. He watched people stream through the hospital, families clinging to each other anxiously, a few people alone like he was, with that pinched, drawn look on their faces that he understood far too well.

He didn't know how to handle this alone. His mother had volunteered to come with him to wait, but he couldn't pull her away from his father when he was so fragile and needed constant monitoring before he underwent intensive chemo. All of the people in Ash's past—Andrew, so many others he couldn't even name—were just cardboard cutouts of people pasted in his memories with no real permanence. They weren't the kind of people he could call when he needed to say *I'm afraid.*

I'm afraid, and I can't be alone right now.

After long, trembling minutes where every second screamed through him with agonizing awareness of the passing time, he pulled out his phone and tapped out a text to Vic.

you busy?

His phone buzzed back a few minutes later. ***just facilitating a hostile corporate takeover, bored off my bloody gourd really, what's up***

Ash bit his lip. ***brands in surgery***

what? why? is he ok?

i think so, Ash texted back quickly. ***he's donating bone marrow for my dad, its supposed to be routine, i'm just really scared for him***

Vic's answering text was just an emoji heart, at first, followed by, ***he's gonna be okay – he's got you, don't he?***

Ash smiled to himself. His heart shouldn't be aching like this. ***yeah, he does***

then everything's gonna be okay

Over and over again, Ash reread that message. A reminder. A mantra. A hope to hold on to, for interminable hours on end.

That everything would be okay, in the end.

He distracted himself reading work emails on his phone, curling up in his chair with his legs tucked up. He read until his eyes ached, dry and sore and tired; read until it felt like weeks had passed, instead of just—fuck his life, three hours? That was it? He groaned and thumbed the screen to the next email.

Only for his blood to ice over at a commotion from down the very same hall where they'd wheeled Brand.

He shot upright, watching as shouting people went running down the hall, doctors and nurses and orderlies, calling something about codes and throwing medical terminology back and forth that he didn't understand, but that sounded terrifying. He rocketed from the chair, calling after a nurse who went running past.

"What's happening? What's wrong?" he asked, then, "…Brand?"

But she barely glanced at him, not stopping, before she went thrusting past the swinging double doors and disappeared.

Leaving Ash standing there, trembling, Brand's glasses clutched to his chest and the walls of his heart crumbling to pieces.

It was over another hour before a bulky man in scrubs and a lab coat emerged from behind the double doors, tired-looking with deep lines sunken into his face; he flipped through a clipboard with several sheets of paper, then lifted his head, gaze searching.

"Ashton Harrington?"

Ash froze in his pacing tracks; he'd been back and forth so many times his feet hurt, and he'd practically worn a rut in the floor. Barely breathing, he whirled on the doctor, swallowing back the knot of tears in his throat.

"Is Brand all right?' he demanded breathlessly.

"He's fine. Resting," the doctor reassured, only to erase the rush of joy, relief, by adding carefully, "There was a brief…*incident*."

Ash stilled. "What kind of incident?"

"His heart stopped on the table." It came out so easily, so nonchalantly, Ash could have strangled the man. "It happens, sometimes, and it just means being a bit more careful with him during recovery. Sometimes people have an adverse reaction to the anesthetic—"

"Wait. Wait. Back up." Ash shook his head sharply. "What do you mean, his heart stopped?"

"It was only for a moment. We brought him back in

less than sixty seconds. His heart function is fine. *He's* fine."

It all sounded like useless platitudes, roaring in Ash's ears in mindless, meaningless noise. This was too much—after all the ups and downs and explosions and catastrophes of the last week, this was the last straw, too fucking *much.*

"Where is he?" he gasped. "I need to see him. Where is he?"

"He's being transferred to a recovery room. You can see him tomorr—"

"Now."

"But—"

"I said *now*."

The doctor stared at him uncertainly. Ash stared back, setting his jaw. He wasn't taking no for an answer. He'd been passive about so many things in his life, letting whim and happenstance push him wherever he'd happened to fall, washing up on so many shores like so much driftwood.

He couldn't be passive about this.

The doctor faltered, then nodded. "I'll make an exception just this once," he said, and stepped back toward the doors. "This way."

BRAND WOKE TO THE SOUND of soft, hitching breaths, the muffled noise of tears.

He didn't have to open his eyes to know that sound was Ash, when he'd know his young Master's voice anywhere.

His eyelids didn't want to open. He *hurt* everywhere, his entire body sore and his senses fuzzy, though the greatest pain was concentrated around his pelvis and the primary extraction point. If he hurt this much now, he'd rather made the right choice in choosing to go under anesthesia for the worst of it.

With a wince, he forced his eyelids open. The room was fuzzy around him, worse than it should be even without his glasses—but he could make out Ash, curled up in a chair and hugging his knees to his chest, Brand's glasses clutched in one hand and the other hand locked around Brand's wrist. At Brand's soft groan, though, Ash's head snapped up. His liquid-sheened eyes widened.

"Brand," he gasped, "*Brand*."

Then flung himself from the chair, nearly draping himself over Brand as he wrapped his arms around him and burst into a fresh spate of tears.

"…young Master," Brand managed to croak, his

throat dry, scratching. He swallowed, trying to wet it, and forced his arm to move enough to rest a hand to Ashton's back. "You are crying."

"Y-your…" Ash broke off into sniffles, choked inarticulate sounds, then managed, "Your heart stopped under anesthetic."

"Oh dear." That…was rather taking a moment to sink in, when Brand's mind hadn't quite caught up with the fact that he was even conscious yet. "It would appear my age was more of a hazard than I thought."

"Don't you…don't you…" Ash pushed himself up, glaring down at Brand—and Brand thought he'd never seen anything more lovely in his life. Such fragile emotion, shining through Ash with such intensity, giving himself so wholeheartedly to *feeling*. "All you have to say is 'oh dear'?" Ash demanded, vibrant in his anger, flushed, eyes bright. "You can't *do* that to me!" he choked. "You can't show up here and just make me need you overnight and then nearly die on me!" He buried his face in Brand's chest again, thumping a fist weakly against his shoulder. "I can't…I can't…"

Despite himself, Brand smiled. His young Master was a thing of wild and vivid feelings, when he wished to be—this bright thing emerging from behind the grieving, pallid boy who had retreated from everything before.

You are beautiful like this, Brand wanted to say, but

held his tongue.

"I am sorry, young Master," was all he said. "I did not mean to worry you."

"*Asshole*."

Brand chuckled—even though it hurt, his entire body protesting. "I should hope you will forgive me for forcing you to give the erroneous impression that you care for me."

"…*massive* asshole." With a sullen sound, sniffling, Ash pushed himself fully up onto the bed. He took a careful moment to unfold Brand's now slightly bent, *entirely* smudged glasses and ease them onto Brand's face—then tucked himself against Brand, making room in the cramped space and fitting against him until he felt just *right*, so close against Brand's body. "I feel like I spend all my time with you in hospital beds."

"I would not be remiss to going home," Brand murmured.

Ash flushed, ducking his head, hiding his face in Brand's shoulder. "…I like that."

"Like what?"

"Hearing you call it home," Ash said shyly. "It makes me feel like you're not going to quit and just leave."

"The thought had never crossed my mind."

Ash peeked with a sweet, hopeful smile. "Yeah?"

"Indeed." Brand turned his head, just enough to brush his lips to Ash's hair. Just enough to breathe in that sweet scent that reminded him that he was alive; that he was indeed home, when he didn't think his young Master understood…he, more than the Harrington estate, was what Brand called *home*. "Clearly not even death could keep me from your side, young Master. If that could not take me away…how could I ever leave?"

EVEN IF THERE WERE FEW things worse to Brand Forsythe than idle hands, he had to admit that after the last week…

It was good to just be *still* for a while.

It had been a rather remarkable thing, watching Ashton bully the hospital staff into releasing Brand to recuperate at home. Eyes flashing, voice firm, Ashton had spoken with the clear expectation that he would be obeyed, and the authority to back up his demands. For those few moments, while he'd marshaled everything from orderlies to help dress Brand to transportation to pick them up, he'd been every inch the CEO of Harrington Steel.

Only to collapse into a very worried, very tired young

man the moment Brand had managed to haul himself from a wheelchair and into the bed in Ashton's suite.

Brand lay against the sheets and just let himself *hurt* for a few tired moments; he had a prescription for painkillers, but he didn't want the haze of drugs just yet. Not when it would take him away from the sweet feeling of Ashton tucked up against him like a kitten, watching him as if afraid, if he blinked, Brand would disappear.

"I guess it's my turn to take care of you," Ash murmured.

"I fear for my recovery prognosis," Brand groaned dryly, and Ash grinned.

"Even I can't burn toast."

"The house would be a smoking ruin, but you would leave the toast intact."

Ash laughed. "Oh, fuck you."

"In a week, you will regret those words."

"So you can't do anything for a whole week?" Biting his pretty pink lower lip, Ash pushed himself up on one hand. His other hand slipped beneath the duvet, trailing down Brand's side in sweetly ticklish touches…only to ghost over his hips, tracing the line of his cock through his loose cotton sleep pants. "Not even this?"

Then that slim hand curled over him—kneading his cock in slow, massaging strokes, pleasure cutting through the pain with a knife's keen edge to leave Brand gasping, burning, as his cock swelled to hardness, that bold little monster teasing him with light swirling caresses only to firm his touch as if enveloping Brand in the tightness of a clutching, willing body.

"Ah—ah, *Ashton*—" Brand tried to lift his hips toward that touch instinctively—only to subside with a hiss when every muscle protested. Gasping, he rolled his head against the pillow, toward Ash, watching him with slitted eyes. "I did not give you license to be such a brat."

Ash's eyes glittered wickedly. "I'm still your boss. Sometimes I get to decide."

"Only if you want your arse smarting for it later," Brand growled.

"You just like having excuses to keep me in line."

"And you like giving me reasons to," Brand countered—only to break off in a sharp inhalation as that light touch stroked once more, teasing him to full hardness, the throb of it aching all the way to the pit of his stomach. He closed his eyes, curling his fingers tight against the bedsheets. "Mnnh…young Master…"

"Can I, Brand?" Ash pleaded softly. "Can I take care of you?"

That soft note of entreaty drew Brand to open his eyes, looking up at his wide-eyed young lover. In those eyes he saw what Ash was really pleading for: something to remind Ash that Brand was alive. That he was *here*. That they were together, and no single sideways twist of fate could pull them apart.

"Yes," he whispered, when there was no other answer he could give.

Not when he would give his young Master anything.

And he gave him his pleasure, as with a low, needy sound Ash drew the duvet down, bared Brand's flesh…and pressed that mouth that begged so sweetly to the head of his cock. Liquid warmth enveloped Brand, submerging his entire body in pleasure, until the pain was only a taste of something sharper to accent that heat. He curled his fingers in Ash's hair, parted his lips on broken gasps…

And this time, let himself give up control.

Ash snuggled against Brand's side, nearly burrowing into the bed. Brand was asleep again, after eating a rather messy sandwich Ash had made and at least managed not to poison him with. He'd spent nearly half an hour making a medication chart on his laptop so he'd know when Brand needed what pills.

Then promptly glued himself to Brand's side, content

to count his breaths and remind himself that Brand was *okay* with every rise and fall of his chest.

Brand was okay. His father was going to be okay, once he came out on the rougher side of chemo and the transplant. The company was going to be okay, now that Ash had half an idea of what he was doing.

And Ash was going to be okay, as long as he had Brand to hold his world together.

It probably wasn't right. Wasn't safe. Wasn't smart, to hinge his well-being on someone else this way. But he was in too deep now, and didn't know if he wanted to pull back. Not when it was what they had both said they wanted.

Not when it made him feel so right.

"You know," Brand grit out drowsily, "it's very hard to sleep when you're fretting."

Ash winced with a sheepish smile. "Sorry…just thinking a lot."

"It makes you tense." Brand shifted against him, yawning like a great lazy lion, his mussed hair spilled across the pillow. He looked so much *better* now, shirtless and sprawled in languid glory against the sheets, his eyes half-closed and smoky with sleep. He moved to fold one powerful arm underneath his head, corded muscle bunching and flexing, while the other arm gathering Ash close. "What are you brooding about now?"

"I don't brood!" Ash laughed. "…I brood a little."

"You're avoiding."

"God I hate you for that sometimes." Ash sighed, reaching out to drape his hand over Brand's chest, tracing his fingertips to the base of that old, long-faded scar. "I was just wondering why you stayed."

"Pardon?"

"The day I hired you. Interviewed you."

Brand snorted. "I would not call that an interview."

"You know what I mean." Ash propped his chin on Brand's shoulder, watching him thoughtfully. "You kept looking at me like I was trash. And then it was like you just…decided. And I don't know why. Was it just a favor to Vic?"

A faint, almost sweet smile touched Brand's lips, unlike any Ash had ever seen from the rather stoic, sardonic man. "If I had not wanted to work for you, not even loyalty to a former employer would have compelled me to."

"Then why?" Ash asked—but Brand fell silent, gaze darting away. "Brand. I need to know."

Still Brand said nothing, until he exhaled heavily, words thoughtful, deep, soft as if coming from some quiet and heartfelt place. "I saw more in you than you saw in yourself," he said. "I simply hoped to be here to see the day when you understood that."

Ash's heart fluttered as if Brand had taken it into his hand and caressed it with those knowing, capable fingers. "I…what if that day had taken years? Decades?"

"Then I would have waited," Brand promised.

"I…I don't understand you."

Those dark green eyes fixed on him—capturing him, holding him, drawing him down into the plain, stark honesty of the emotion swimming in their depths. "Do you need to understand me to care for me in at least some way?"

"Is that what you do?" Ash whispered. "You meet someone and you just…*decide*, right then and there, that you'll just…just…*be* there for them, no matter what, even if you don't quite understand them?"

"Is that not what loyalty means?"

Ash couldn't stand it. The weight of that gaze, the warmth in it, the *promise*. He lowered his eyes, his chest hitching tight. "I…I don't deserve that kind of loyalty."

"I think you do."

"Because I sign your paychecks."

"Stop paying me, then." Brand caught his chin gently, tipping his face up until he couldn't escape. Not the depth of Brand's quiet emotions, not the raw, hungry truth in his words. "I will not leave."

"Why?" Ash pleaded, even as he feared the answer.

"Because," Brand answered with that simplicity that could only make it real, "I could easily see myself falling in love with you, young Master Ashton."

That one word, *love*, struck Ashton like a blow. He didn't understand it—but he didn't need to, to know he craved it. Craved it the way he'd never craved anything before in his life. Not even Brand's kiss, his touch. They were nothing to that word, that promise, that potential inherent in this moment and every moment that would come tomorrow, and the next tomorrow, and a thousand tomorrows after that.

Ash wet dry lips, struggling to breathe. "You say that when you won't even use my name," he said, only for Brand to counter with,

"*…Ash*." Fervent, worshipful, spoken with the same soft certainty as that single damning word.

Love.

And Ash collapsed.

He curled forward, resting his brow to Brand's shoulder. "Fuck. *Fuck*, Brand. You're…" He clutched so hard at Brand, only remembering to gentle his touch when the man was injured, hurting, he'd put himself through *so much pain* for Ash, he'd nearly *died* and just…and just… "You're everything," Ash breathed. "You're the only thing keeping me together. It's selfish. It's so selfish of me to need you."

"Even if I want to be needed?"

"I shouldn't…I shouldn't even want you." Yet Ash closed his eyes, savoring the feeling of Brand's fingers threading into his hair, the warmth and surety in that touch, the silent reassurance: that Brand would be his wall, his shelter, his everything if Ash would only ask. "You're a cocky asshole. You piss me off so much. And yet…and yet…"

Brand chuckled low. "I am rather beginning to think you enjoy having reasons to shout at me."

"Feel like giving me a few more?"

Brand's silence stretched so long that Ash wondered if he'd fallen asleep again. But when he peeked one eye open, he found Brand watching him—intently, consumingly, drawing Ash deep and capturing him once more.

As he captured Ash's face in his palms, cradling him as if he were the most precious thing in the world, as if nothing—no hardship, no pain, no loss—could shatter Ash so long as he was safe in Brand's hands.

"Young Master," Brand said, as he drew him up and into the touch of claiming lips, "Ask, and I shall give you everything you desire."

EPILOGUE

ASH WAS GOING TO THROW that fucking alarm clock across the room.

Why was it even going *off?* He groaned and buried his face deeper into the pillow, fumbling for the nightstand to hit the snooze.

Only for a firm hand to catch his wrist, stopping him—then silencing the alarm.

"If you are alert enough to turn off the alarm," Brand said sternly, "you are alert enough to get up."

Ash swore under his breath, lifting his face from the pillow and giving Brand a foul look. Of course he was already up. Already up, perfectly dressed, and looking down at Ash like he hadn't just fucked him raw up against the headboard less than six hours ago and left him boneless and too tired to even *move*.

Six months. Six months of this, and he still didn't know where Brand even got the *energy*.

He flopped his face back into the pillow. "…it's Saturday. You can fuck right off."

"And you still have months of work to catch up on. Stocks are finally holding stable at an average five points of daily growth, but one day of inattention could undo that." Brand sighed, deep and long-suffering—and then whipped the covers off Ash, ripping them away in a single smooth motion. "We can eat breakfast at the office. Get up."

Ash yelped, grabbing for the covers. When he failed, he flopped on his back, groaning and looking up into Brand's implacably calm face. "No."

"Yes," Brand insisted, and Ash pouted.

"…I don't wanna."

Eyes glinting, Brand pushed his glasses up his nose. "If you are going to be a child about it—"

"I'm probably going to end up on my back with my legs spread, because you're a dirty goddamned pervert."

Brand lifted his chin with a haughty, prideful sniff. "I am no such thing."

Ash pushed himself up enough to sit up, then leaned back on his hands, watching Brand from beneath his lashes. He knew exactly what he looked like right now—considering he was wearing nothing but one of Brand's pajama tops, a good five sizes too big for him, falling loosely off his shoulder and clinging to his body and just barely falling to skim his thighs to keep him decent. Not only did he know exactly what he looked like right now…

But he knew *exactly* how it got under Brand's territorial, possessive, domineering skin to see Ash bundled up small and half-naked in Brand’s clothing.

He toyed at his lower lip with his teeth. “How bad do you want to fuck me right now?”

“You say that as if the desire ever ebbs.” A touch of heat sparked in Brand’s eyes. “At the moment, however, I am not above bloody well spanking you.”

“That’s just foreplay. And proof that you *are* a dirty goddamned pervert.” Sighing, Ash flopped back again, letting himself sprawl. “No. I’m the boss, and I say we’re taking the day off.”

“I am your valet, and I say we most certainly are not.”

“You’re fired, then.”

Brand made an amused sound. “As your valet, or as your lover?”

“Both.”

“Neither.”

“Braaaaaaaand.” Ash kicked his bare feet against the sheets, then rolled over and propped his chin on his folded forearms. “*No*. One day. Come on. I want to go do something fun. With you.”

“We do fun things,” Brand pointed out. “You enjoy your father’s physical therapy sessions in the park. We are going to tend to your horses tomorrow.”

“A different *kind* of fun thing. A date.”

"A *date?*" Brand repeated incredulously, as if he'd never heard of such a thing.

"You have been fucking me for six goddamned months, and we've never even been on one date."

Brand sighed, sinking down to settle on the edge of the bed, leaning over Ash on one hand. "You make it sound like our relationship is nothing but sex."

"...it's more than sex." Ash scooted over until he could pillow his head on Brand's thigh. He just...liked to be *touching* him, feeling that warmth and breathing in that earthy scent. "Maybe that's why I want to spend time with you outside either the office or the bedroom."

Brand exhaled a slow, patient sigh. "As my young Master wishes."

"Really?" Ash perked—then scowled. "You don't have to sound like it's going to be a chore."

"I fear whatever ordeal you are about to drag me through," Brand retorted flatly.

"An amusement park is not an ordeal."

"An amusement park for a man in his forties is the ninth circle of hell, and you are too old for such things."

"I am never too old, and neither are you." Ash pushed himself up onto his knees—then slid across Brand's lap, straddling him and draping his arms around his neck. "Come on. I've never gotten the chance to do stuff like this. Coney Island, that kind of thing. You own a pair of jeans, right?"

Brand settled his hands on Ash's hips with a borderline offended look. "No."

"…shorts?"

No borderline about it, this time. Offended, horrified, absolutely incensed. "*No*."

Ash laughed and leaned in, pressing his nose to Brand's. "You can't go to an amusement park in a suit."

"I most certainly can," Brand grumbled, "and I most certainly will."

"…oh my God." Ash couldn't help stealing a quick kiss, nipping at Brand's upper lip. "You are the cutest, stuffiest thing."

"There is nothing cute about me."

"There is everything cute about you." God, Ash almost couldn't stand how…*everything* Brand was. He didn't have words for it, for the way Brand made his every emotion turn up to such intensity he could nearly drown in them. Including in the fond warmth that swelled inside him, as he touched his nose-tip to Brand's. "You're almost lovable," he admitted shyly.

Brand stilled, his scowl easing. Darkened green eyes locked on Ash, the curl of his hands turning possessive. "Almost?" he repeated softly.

"Entirely," Ash corrected, heart in his throat.

Brand's sharply inhaled breath was like a gunshot cracking across the room, leaving trembling silence in its wake. He leaned in closer—such strength, such heat, the way his bulk enfolded Ash, turning the man into the entirety of Ashton's self-contained world.

"So you love me," Brand whispered.

Ash bit his lip, his pulse a thing of wildfire, his heart a vessel of fragile glass so full he thought it would break its seams and shatter. "You said it, not me."

"I want to hear you say it."

"You first."

A slow, warm smile spread across Brand's lips, softening the stern lines of his face. "I should think I show it in everything I do." His mouth ghosted across Ash's. "And the fact that I have not *quit* yet."

That smile cradled Ash's heart in delicate fingers and stroked it until it trembled; he couldn't help smiling back, feeling like he would burst with it. "Say it and I'll let you get out of the amusement park."

"Yet suffering through the amusement park is how I intended to show it."

Ash burst into delighted laughter. "*Brand,*" he chided, and Brand echoed with a husky, rolling chuckle.

"You are a petulant, pouting child," Brand said, "and I love you, young Master Ashton."

He barely got the words out before Ash kissed him—

needing to taste those words, needing to feel how Brand's mouth softened when he said them. That kiss tasted like a promise made months ago, whispered in words he hadn't known how to understand, then.

He understood, now.

And understood the pull on his heart, every time Brand touched him, spoke to him, whispered his name. Fate or no fate, every pull on his heart was the tug of the red string tying him to Brand, a contract deeper than any employment document. He was tangled in Brand, and Brand was tangled in him, the knots so inextricably twined they'd never come free.

And he never wanted them to.

He couldn't breathe for the brightness inside him, and he broke back, leaning his brow to Brand's with a giddy little smile. "And I love when you indulge me," he teased. "I also kinda love you."

Brand arched a brow. "Kind of?"

"Oh, come on. You've got to let me deflect a little."

"I will allow it this time." Brand's splayed fingers slid over Ash's back, molding them together, jerking him in roughly until his thighs ached to span Brand's bulk, until he couldn't escape the shivering reminder that he was naked beneath the oversized pajama top. "Kiss me again, you unrepentant brat."

Ash chuckled, eyes lidding as he slid his fingers into

Brand's perfectly slicked hair, mussing it into a tangle and drawing him in to trace his tongue along Brand's upper lip. "You are the bossiest, cockiest, biggest asshole of a valet on the planet."

"And that, young Master," Brand said, already tumbling Ash back to the bed, hands sure and steady and knowing on his body, "is why you love me."

THE END

Get HIS COCKY VALET: AFTER STORY Free

Want more of Ash and Brand? Reunite with your favorite billionaire brat and his ever-faithful valet in Undue Arrogance #1.5, HIS COCKY VALET: AFTER STORY. This **free** novelette catches up with Ash and Brand three years into their relationship, when Ash's father meddles a little too much…and stirs up trouble in paradise. Get:

- A 65-page, multi-chapter novelette following Ash and Brand years into their relationship
- Two entirely new sex scenes
- More angst
- More sarcasm
- A sneak preview of HIS COCKY CELLIST (Undue Arrogance #2)
- Look I'm not saying there's wedding talk but I'm not saying there's not, and there's a ring on that cover for a reason
- ...and it's all **free to subscribers**

http://blackmagicblues.com/hcv-signup/

Get A Little Bit Cockier

The Undue Arrogance Series continues with Vic discovering he's not as straight as he thought when he meets Amani Idrissi in HIS COCKY CELLIST (Undue Arrogance #2). But Vic's going to learn about far more than just his sexuality when Amani teaches him about a new brand of power, control…and utmost submission.

See the Series on Cole McCade's Amazon Author Page

https://www.amazon.com/Cole-McCade/e/B00RYHHVLI/

DISCOVER CRIMINAL INTENTIONS

Are you a criminal?

DISCOVER THE THRILLING M/M ROMANTIC suspense serial everyone's talking about. Follow Baltimore homicide detectives Malcolm Khalaji and Seong-Jae Yoon as they trail a string of bizarre murders ever deeper down a rabbit hole—that, if they can't learn to work together, may cost them both their lives. **Full-length novels released once per month!**

Browse on Amazon and Amazon KindleUnlimited

https://www.amazon.com/gp/product/B07D4MF9MH?ref=series_rw_dp_labf

See the series on Goodreads

https://www.goodreads.com/series/230782-criminal-intentions

Afterword

With how long this book's been out, it's pretty well-known that I wrote this half as a joke, 100% out of spite against She Who Shall Not Be Named—who, in her overwhelming hubris, thought she could trademark a single extremely common English word and then use that trademark to pursue and bully self-published authors with legal threats.

You can imagine how well that went over.

So I wrote this book to prove you can't own a word. To provide grounds to either weaken her claim in court or give her more balls to chase, in the hopes of helping to exhaust her time. Others wrote their own cocky books, produced anthologies, challenged the validity of her trademark with legal action. Since then she's been dragged, read for filth, and defeated in court, with the trademark claim dismissed. If you want a full rundown of everything that happened and why this matters to both authors and readers, Google #cockygate or check out the hashtag on Twitter; it'll point you to some fairly informative blog posts and threads that break down why this was a victory for the indie publishing community—and make it very clear why you don't fuck with romance authors.

Because we fuck back hard, and with *feeling*.

Now that the trademark on "cocky" has been dismissed, the original reason for starting this series doesn't exist anymore…but something new was born. Somehow, someway, this book took on a life of its own. More than just the general community enthusiasm around following along aboard the Good Ship Petty while I wrote this in a frenetic burst, the book became something that some people loved, some people hated, but it's become more than just a middle finger at an unduly arrogant author.

It's become a series I adore, and working on the next books in the trilogy has been just as enjoyable as those rage-fueled seven days in which this story came to life.

It's also changed my career as an author, and in a lot of ways completely changed my life for the better. It's part of why, for so many years, I was happy to be part of the romance community. Because even when we're spite-filled hellions…

We take the ugly you give us, and we turn it into something wonderful.

And that's no small thing.

Shine on, you crazy diamonds. Because even if we have our stumbles, and our falls…

The romance community always has and always will

make me proud.

-C

Additional Author's Note

HIS COCKY VALET IS PRETTY obviously fluff fantasy, not meant to be taken as a depiction of the real world. Still, as many of you who read my work know, I often take elements of my real life and history and integrate them into even the most fantastical elements of my stories. This book is no different.

A couple of years before publication of this book, my Dad died in hospice. Alone. Complications of Alzheimer's, and lung cancer from a lifetime of smoking. No one was there for him; not my mother, not my stepmother, not my siblings, not me. I hadn't even known his condition had deteriorated so far, because my stepmother kept him isolated from anyone to do with his prior relationships, from exes to children.

Fuck, I didn't even know he was *dead* until he was weeks buried, when my mother called and goaded me into Googling his obituary (don't...ask about that situation, you don't even want to know). Just like that, he was gone. A ghost, when at the very least before that he'd been a sort of distant something, a presence at one remove, one of the quiet but constant pillars of my reality even if we rarely spoke and lived half a country away from each other. At least I knew he was *there*.

Until suddenly, he wasn't.

I didn't get to see him one last time. I didn't get to be there for him, hold his hand in the last hours, watch him slip away, beg him not to go. I didn't get to say goodbye. It's been...I think, a little over two years now and I still haven't been able to cry properly because there's this awful, hurting part of me that won't accept that it's real, to the point of receding that terrible phone call into a clouded memory I can't even place concretely in time.

So this story is part of how I cope with grief. When I can't deal with my feelings, I put them into my books. This is a comfort fantasy where I got to be there for my Dad. Where somehow he magically recovered, magically lived, magically got just the right treatment he needed at just the right time. Where I had someone with me who could do anything, be anything, handle any situation, because most of the time that's the person *I* have to be. I was raised to be self-reliant and to handle everything on my own, even when it's completely humanly impossible for me to do so and I'm breaking inside from the pressure. So it's as much wish fulfillment that my Dad lived as it is wish fulfillment regarding someone uber-capable standing there to shelter me and take the fear and pain out of my hands.

The thing is, people cope with grief and pain and loss

differently. What's a comfort fantasy for me and for others with similar perspectives may be painful and difficult for others with different perspectives to read. Sometimes there's no black and white, where one experience is valid and one isn't, and only one experience can ever be allowable and acceptable. Life doesn't work that way. We're all different people. Expecting us to have the same feelings on grief coping methods is like expecting BIPOC to be a monolith—basically, we can't all speak for each other and there is no One True Experience that serves as a reference and standard for what's right and what isn't, and what may accurately reflect my experience may not accurately reflect someone else's.

That doesn't make those different perspectives or their pain less valid. I'm not sorry I wrote the story, but I am sorry if it was difficult for anyone to read. Your experiences are as valid as mine. Your feelings are your feelings and you have every right to them, as do I. You also have every right to dislike this book, return it, express your thoughts and feelings about it, etc. That's how this works.

I don't really have a concrete ending to this, other than to acknowledge that. So I guess I'm just going to end by saying love your people while you have them.

Because losing them really sucks.

-C

Unlock VIP Access

WANT STORIES AVAILABLE NOWHERE ELSE? Subscribe to the Xen x Cole McCade newsletter:

www.blackmagicblues.com/newsletter/

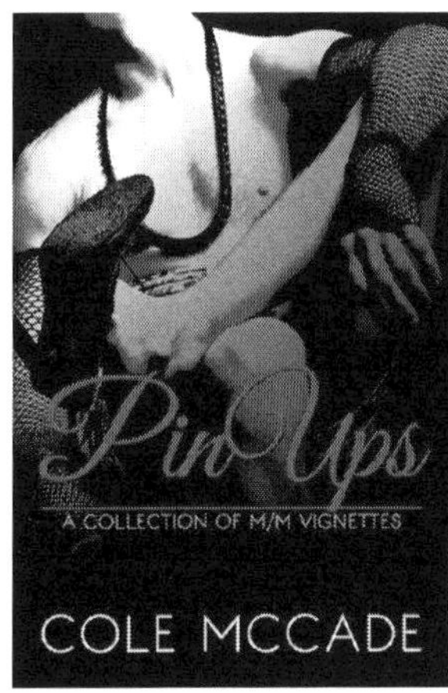

Get SOMETIMES IT STORMS (previously featured in IPPY Award-winning charity anthology WINTER RAIN), Red's story in PINUPS, as well as deleted scenes from A SECOND CHANCE AT PARIS and FROM THE ASHES – and deleted scenes, bonus content, episode soundtracks, and artwork from CRIMINAL INTENTIONS.

For Reviewers

Interested in advance review copies (ARCs) of upcoming releases? Apply to join Xen x Cole McCade's ARC reviewer team, A MURDER OF CROWS:

Acknowledgments

TWITTER, YOU KEEP MY PETTY game strong. I love you all, seriously.

Fight Club, y'all keep my creative edge sharp. You're everything to me.

And to my chosen family?

More love than I even know how to express.

I wouldn't be here without you.

…'cause y'all motherfuckers just as petty as me.

About the Author

Cole McCade is a New Orleans-born Southern boy without the Southern accent, currently residing somewhere in Seattle. He spends his days as a suit-and-tie corporate consultant and business writer, and his nights writing contemporary romance and erotica that flirts with the edge of taboo—when he's not being tackled by two hyperactive cats.

He also writes genre-bending science fiction and fantasy tinged with a touch of horror and flavored by the influences of his multiethnic, multicultural, multilingual background as Xen. He wavers between calling himself bisexual, calling himself queer, and trying to figure out where "demi" fits into the whole mess—but no matter what word he uses he's a staunch advocate of LGBTQIA and POC representation and visibility in genre fiction. And while he spends more time than is healthy hiding in his writing cave instead of hanging around social media, you can generally find him in these usual haunts:

- Email: blackmagic@blackmagicblues.com
- Twitter: @thisblackmagic

- Facebook: https://www.facebook.com/xen.cole
- Tumblr: thisblackmagic.tumblr.com
- Instagram: www.instagram.com/thisblackmagic
- BookBub: https://www.bookbub.com/authors/cole-mccade
- Facebook Fan Page: http://www.facebook.com/ColeMcCadeBooks
- Website & Blog: http://www.blackmagicblues.com

Find More Contemporary Romance & Erotica as Cole McCade

http://blackmagicblues.com/books-by-xen-x-cole-mccade/

Discover Science Fiction, Fantasy & Horror as Xen

http://blackmagicblues.com/books-by-xen-x-cole-mccade/

Made in the USA
Monee, IL
18 March 2021

63228522R00203